Praise for Catherine Fisher

'One of today's best fantasy writers.' *Independent*

'Catherine Fisher is an artist with words.' *Carousel*

'A writer of rare talent.' *Sunday Times*

'Catherine Fisher writes with consummate skill and depth of feeling.' *The Bookseller*

'An extraordinary imagination, always coming up with some new twist that is both weird yet utterly convincing.' Nicholas Tucker, *Rough Guide to Children's Books*

'. . . one of the most skilled and original writers currently working in young adult fantasy.' *New Welsh Review*

'One novel stands out above all others – Catherine Fisher's *Incarceron*. One of the best fantasy novels written for a long time.' *The Times*

Also by Catherine Fisher

THE OBSIDIAN MIRROR

CATHERINE FISHER

Hodder
Children's
Books

A division of Hachette Children's Books

The section heading quotes are from *Hamlet* by William Shakespeare

Copyright © 2012 Catherine Fisher

First published in Great Britain in 2012
by Hodder Children's Books

A Catalogue record for this book is available from the British Library

ISBN 978 0 340 97008 9

Typeset in Berkeley Book by Avon DataSet Ltd,
Bidford on Avon, Warwickshire

Printed and bound by CPI Group (UK) Ltd, Croydon, CR0 4YY

The paper and board used in this paperback by Hodder Children's Books
are natural recyclable products made from wood grown in
sustainable forests. The manufacturing processes conform to the
environmental regulations of the country of origin.

Hodder Children's Books
a division of Hachette Children's Books
338 Euston Road, London NW1 3BH
An Hachette UK company
www.hachette.co.uk

To Rachel Elinor Davies
the best niece in the world

The son of a dear father murder'd

CHAPTER ONE

I have discovered something totally impossible. I will be rich. Celebrated. A hero of science.

And yet in truth I am so bewildered that I can only sit for hours in this room and gaze out at the rain.

What can I do with such terrifying knowledge? How can I ever dare use it?

Journal of John Harcourt Symmes, December 1846

The boy put on the mask outside the door. It was a heavy black fencing mask and inside its mesh he felt different.

It made him dark, supple, dangerous.

An actor.

An assassin.

He was wearing the costume for *Hamlet*, Act 5, the duel with Laertes, and he had the fencing sword ready in his hand. He had to be very careful. This could all go badly wrong, and not just in the way he wanted. He took a deep breath, and peered in through the glass panel. The rehearsal seemed to have paused; people were sitting around and Mr Wharton was explaining something, waving an arm expressively to Mark Patten who was playing Laertes.

He opened the door and went in. At once, as if someone had switched it on, he burst into a world of chattering voices and music and loud hammering behind the scenery. Mr Wharton turned round and glared at him. 'Seb! Where have you been?' Without waiting for an answer he swung back. 'Well maybe now we can get on. Are you sure you've got the blunt sword? And you remember the jump over the table?'

The boy nodded, and climbed up on the stage. It was shadowy there; the lights weren't set up properly, and the cardboard scenery leaned at awkward angles. A mirror reflected him, slanting. He saw he was too tall, that the costume was a little tight. His eyes were dark and steely.

'Ready?'

He just nodded again.

'Please yourself,' Wharton muttered. The Head of Humanities – a big man, ex-army – looked hot and harassed, his collar undone, hair sticking up where he'd run a sweaty hand through it. 'Right, boys. All set to run through the duel?'

Run through. That was apt. The boy put the foil tip to the floor and carefully flexed the supple steel blade. He watched Laertes come up on stage. Patten, the one with the big-shot father. The one with the mouth.

'OK.' Wharton glanced at the script. 'So. Let's go from "*I'll be your foil . . .*" And let's have it sad, Seb, really sad and noble. You're confused, you're angry – your father has been killed and all you want is revenge, but instead of the real killer you have to fight this guy you hardly know. You're sick to the soul. Got it?'

He nodded, silent. They had no idea how much he got it.

The others took their places. He waited, inside the mesh of his hatred, his heart thumping like a machine out of control, the leather grip of the foil already sweaty in his hand.

Wharton scrambled down and sat in the front row. The lights flickered, a shudder of scarlet in the shadowy hall. His hand on the sword-hilt was suddenly blood-red.

'Sorry,' someone shouted from the back.

'OK. Laertes and Hamlet duel. Do the moves exactly as we practised yesterday.' Mr Wharton tipped his glasses to the end of his nose. 'In your own time.'

Patten faced his opponent. 'Get it right this time, prat,' he whispered.

'Oh I will.' The answer was a bare breath, intent.

Patten stared. '*What . . . ?*'

But the boy dressed as Hamlet had already lifted his sword, and was speaking, his voice hoarse with the built-up tension of weeks. '*I'll be your foil, Laertes; in mine ignorance, your skill shall, like a star in the darkest night, stick fiery off indeed.*'

'*You mock me, sir,*' Laertes snarled.

'*No. By this hand.*'

He moved forward. Their hands gripped, but he squeezed too hard, crushing Patten's fingers.

'What the hell?' Patten stepped back. 'You're not Seb!'

The boy smiled. And instantly he attacked, slashing with the foil. Patten's sword came up in alarmed defence. 'Hey! Idiot! . . . Wait!'

He didn't wait. He shoved against Patten's chest, sending him flailing back into crashing scenery.

Wharton jumped to his feet. 'That's all wrong. Boys! *Seb!*'

Thrust. Parry. Attack and keep on attacking. Fight the anger. Fight the pain and the loss. And then his head seemed suddenly to clear, and he was free and laughing, breathing easier, knocking away Patten's wild blade, ignoring the shouts, the people jumping up on to the stage, Wharton's roar of 'Stop this at once!' He chose his moment and aimed coldly above the guard, at the bare white flesh between sleeve and glove. Then, as if it wasn't even him doing this, he struck.

Patten howled. A great howl of pain and fury. He leaped back, flung down his foil and grabbed his wrist. Blood was already dripping through his fingers. 'He's sodding mad! It's a sharp sword! *I've been stabbed!*'

Clatter. Shouts. The cardboard balcony rippling backwards into a dusty, oddly muffled collapse. Hands grabbing him, tight round his neck, hauling him back, snatching the weapon from his fingers. He let them. He stood calm, breathing hard, in a circle of staring boys. He'd done it. They couldn't ignore him any more.

Abruptly, as if a spotlight had come on, brilliant glare blinded him. He realized Wharton had snatched the mask off him and was standing there, staring in astonishment and fury at his white face.

'Jake. *Jake Wilde!* What the *hell* do you think you're doing . . . ?'

He tried not to smile. 'I think you know the answer to that. *Sir.*'

'Where's Seb? What have you—'

'Locked in his room. I haven't hurt him.' He made

himself sound cold. Icy. That's what they should see, these staring, brainless kids, even though he wanted to scream and shout in their faces.

Behind the teacher, Mark Patten had crumpled on to the stage; someone had a first-aid kit and was wrapping his wrist in a tight white bandage that immediately went red. Patten looked up, his eyes panicky and furious. 'You're finished in this school, Wilde, finished. You've really flipped this time. My father's one of the governors, and if they don't expel you there'll be hell to pay. What are you, some sort of sodding nutcase?'

'That's enough.' Wharton turned. 'Get him down to the med room. The rest of you, out of here. Now! Rehearsals are cancelled.'

It took a while for everyone to go, an explosion of gossip and rumour roaring out into the corridors of the college, the last boys lingering curiously. Wharton kept a resolute silence until there was no one left but Jake and himself in the hall, and the echoes from outside were fading away. Then he took his glasses off, put them in his jacket pocket, and said, 'Well. You've really made your point this time.'

'I hope so.'

'They'll expel you.'

'That's what I want.'

8

Eye to eye, they faced each other. Mr Wharton said, 'You can trust me, Jake. I've told you that before. Whatever it is, whatever's wrong, tell me and . . .'

'Nothing's wrong. I hate the school. I'm out of here. That's all.'

It wasn't all. Both of them knew it. But standing in the ruins of his stage, Wharton realized that was all he was going to get. Coldly he said, 'Get out of that costume and be at the Head's office in five minutes.'

Jake turned. He went without a word.

For a moment Wharton stared at the wreckage. Then he snatched up the foil and marched. He slammed through the fire doors of the corridors, raced up the stairs and flung open the office with HEADMASTER printed in the frosted glass.

'Is he in?' he said, breathless.

The secretary looked up. 'Yes, but . . .'

He stalked past her desk and into the inner room.

The Head was eating pastries. A tray of them lay on the desk, next to a china mug of coffee that was releasing such a rich aroma that it made Wharton instantly nostalgic for his favourite coffee shop back home in Shepton Mallet where he'd liked to read the papers every morning. Before he'd come to this hell-hole of a college.

'George!' The Head had his elbows on the desk. 'I was expecting you.'

'You've heard?'

'I've heard.' Behind him, outside the huge window, the Swiss Alps rose in their glorious beauty against a pure blue sky. 'Patten's gone to the hospital. God knows what his father will do.'

Wharton sat heavily. They were silent a moment. Then he said, 'You realize what this means? Wilde's got us now, exactly where he wants us. That was criminal assault and there were plenty of witnesses. It's a police matter. He knows if we don't get him out of the country, the publicity for the school will be dire.'

The Head groaned. 'And Patten, of all boys! Are they enemies?'

'No love lost. But the choice was deliberate. And clever. Wilde knows Patten will make more fuss than anyone else.'

There was deep snow on the alpine valleys, gleaming and brilliant in the sunlight. For a moment Wharton longed to be skiing down it. Far from here.

'Well, we expel him. End of problem. For us, at any rate.' The Head was a thin streak of a man, his hair always shinily greased. He poured some coffee. 'Have a pastry.'

'Thanks. But I'm dieting.' How did the man stay so

skinny? Wharton dumped sugar in the coffee gloomily. Then he said, 'Clever is one word for him. Sadistic is another. He's wrecked my play.'

The Head watched the spoon make angry circles in the mug. 'Calm down, George, or you'll have a heart attack. What you need is a holiday, back in dear old Britain.'

'Can't afford it. Not on what you pay.'

'Ha!' The Head stood up and strolled to the window. 'Jake Wilde. Bit of a problem.'

Wharton sipped his coffee. The Head was a master of understatement. Wilde was the absolute rebel of the school and the torment of everyone's life, especially his. The boy was intelligent, a good athlete, a fine musician. But he was also an arrogant schemer who made no secret of his loathing of Compton's College and everyone in it.

'Remind me,' the Head said grimly.

Wharton shrugged. 'Where to start? There was the monkey. He's still got that stashed somewhere, I think. The fire alarms. The school concert. The Mayor's car. And who could forget the Hallowe'en party fiasco . . .'

The Head groaned.

'Not to mention writing his entire exam paper on *Hamlet* in mirror-writing.'

'Hardly in the same league.'

'Bloody annoying though.' Wharton was silent, thinking of Jake's hard, brittle stare. *You did say you wanted something totally original, sir.* 'If it was me I'd expel him just for the way he says sir.'

'I've bent over backwards to ignore all of it,' the Head said. 'Because his guardian pays top whack to keep him here, and we need the money.'

'I don't blame the man. But we can't ignore this.' Wharton touched the foil; it rolled a little on the table and the Head picked it up and examined the sharp point.

'Unbelievable! He could have killed someone. I suppose he thinks as he's the school's fencing champion he could handle it. Well, if he wants to be expelled I'm happy to oblige.' Dropping the sword the Head came back and touched the intercom button. 'Madame. Would you please send for . . .'

'He's here, Headmaster.'

'I'm sorry?'

'Jake Wilde. He's waiting.'

The Head made a face as if he'd eaten a wasp. 'Send him in.'

Jake came in and stood stiffly by the desk. The room smelled of coffee, and he could see by the gloom of the two men that he'd defeated them at last.

'Mr Wilde.' The Head pushed the pastries aside. 'You

understand that your actions today have finally finished you at Compton's College?'

'Yes. Sir.' Now he could afford to sound polite.

'Never in my career have I come across anyone so totally irresponsible. So utterly dangerous. Have you any idea of what the consequences could have been . . .'

Jake stared stonily in front of him. The Head's tirade went on for at least five minutes, but all of them knew it was just an act that had to be played. He managed to tune out most of it, thinking about Horatio, and how tricky it would be to get him on the plane. A few phrases came to him distantly. 'Incredible folly . . . honour of the college . . . returning home in disgrace . . .'

Then the room was quiet. Jake looked up. The Head was looking at him with a calm curiosity, and when he spoke again his voice was different, as if he meant it now.

'Have we failed you so badly, Jake? Is it so absolutely terrible to be here?'

Jake preferred the riot act. He shrugged. 'It's nothing personal. Any school – it would have been the same.'

'I suppose that should make me happier. It doesn't. And what will your guardian have to say?'

Jake's face hardened. 'No idea. I've never spoken to him.'

The men were silent. Wharton said, 'Surely . . . in the

holidays you go home . . .'

'Mr Venn is very generous.' Jake's contempt was icy. 'He pays for a very nice hotel in Cannes where I spend the holidays. Every holiday. Alone.'

Wharton frowned. Surely the boy's mother was alive? This seemed an odd situation. Was it behind this bizarre behaviour? He caught Jake's eye. Jake stared icily back. The old *Don't ask me any more questions* stare.

'Well, it's about time we informed Mr Venn all that's about to change.' The Head turned to his computer.

'Headmaster?' Wharton edged in his chair. 'Maybe . . . even now, if Jake . . .'

Jake's gaze didn't waver. 'No. I want to go. If you make me stay I'll end up killing someone.'

Wharton shut his mouth. The boy was mad.

'Let's hope he's on-line.' The Head typed a rapid e-mail. 'Though I suppose your guardian has a big staff to run his estate while he's off exploring the Antarctic or whatever?'

'He doesn't do expeditions any more. He's a recluse.'

The Head was busy, so Wharton said, 'Recluse?'

'He doesn't leave home. Wintercombe Abbey.'

'I know what recluse means.' Wharton felt hot. The boy was such an annoying little . . . But he kept his temper. 'Since when?'

'Since his wife died.' The words were hard and cold

and Wharton was chilled by Jake's lack of the least sympathy. Something was very wrong here. He'd read about the famous Oberon Venn – polar explorer, mountaineer, archaeologist, the only man to have come back alive from the terrible ascent of the west face of Katra Simba. A heroic figure. Someone young men should look up to. But maybe not the best person to be suddenly landed with someone else's child.

'Your father knew him?'

Jake was silent, as if he resented the question. 'My father was his best friend.'

Far off, a bell rang. Footsteps clattered down the corridor outside. The Head said, 'He seems a man of few words. Here's his answer.'

He turned the screen so that Wharton and Jake could read it. It said:

SEND HIM HERE. I'LL DEAL WITH THIS.

Wharton felt as if an arctic wind had blown out of the screen. He almost stepped back.

Jake didn't flinch. 'I'll leave tomorrow. Thank you for all—'

'You'll leave when I say.' The Head clicked off the screen and looked at him over it. 'Can't you tell us what this is all about, Jake? You're a promising student . . .

15

maybe even the brightest boy in the place. Do you really want to rot in some English comp?'

Jake set his face with the icy glitter Wharton loathed. 'I told you. It's not about the college. It's about me.' He glared at the screen. 'Me and him.'

The Head leaned back in his chair. As if he could see it was hopeless he shrugged slightly. 'Have it your way. I'll arrange a flight. Go and pack your things.'

'They've been packed for days.'

The Head glanced at Wharton. 'And you can pack yours, George.'

'Me? But . . .'

'Someone has to take him home. Have a few days off for Christmas while you're there.'

'I can take myself,' Jake snapped.

'And I have a ton of work to do, Headmaster. The play . . .'

'Can wait. *In loco parentis*, I'm afraid.'

They both stared at him, and the Head grinned his dark grin. 'I don't know which of you looks the most horrified. Bon voyage, gentlemen. And good luck, Mr Wilde.'

Outside in the corridor, Wharton blew out his cheeks and gazed desperately up towards the staffroom. Then he looked at Jake and Jake looked at him.

'Better do as he says,' he said, gruff.

'I'm sorry.' The boy's voice was still arrogant, but there was something new in it. 'Sorry you're dragged into this. But I have to go and get the truth out of Venn. To confront him with what I know.'

'And what *do* you know?' Wharton was baffled now.

The lunch bell rang. Jake Wilde turned and was jostled down the corridor as the boys poured along to the dining-room in a noisy, hungry wave. In all the uproar Wharton almost missed his reply. The words were so quiet. So venomous. But for a moment, he was sure Jake had said, '*I know he murdered my father.*'

CHAPTER TWO

For this Abbey lies in deep countrie, a place of fey and wicked spirits, and the traveller there should be ware of the woods of that land, and the crossroads where the dead are buried . . .

The Chronicle of Wintercombe

Sarah screamed.

She was halfway out of the world; her hand and arm through in some other cold, empty place, when the darkness leaped on her and bit her with a sudden savage pain.

She kicked and yelled. Not darkness. A lithe shape, a snow-white wolf with sapphire eyes; its teeth in her shoe, her heel, the agony unbearable. She fought, jerked the shoe off, tore away, and suddenly came free; the wolf snarled but she was already falling, falling out of the dark, arms wide, crashlanding abrupt and breathless on her back under a brilliant scarlet sky.

Sore, she lay still.

The ground was boggy. A black bramble spread its briars above her; she sat up and saw wide moorland, windblown and sparse, the dying sun sinking into heavy cloud.

It was bitterly cold.

Elation made her shout; she'd done it. But where were the others?

She stood, turned a complete circle. 'Max? Carla?'

Over her head a great flock of small dark birds streamed croaking to a distant wood.

She drew a cloudy breath. Face it. No one else had made it.

The wolf's muzzle and teeth exploded out of nowhere; before she knew it it had her sleeve, tugging powerfully. Only its head existed here, materializing out of the air as if through a slant of glass. If they got her back it was over – there was no way they would let her live.

Her feet slid in mud. She yelled, a wordless cry, but only the birds heard. Icy saliva soaked her arm.

Sliding, she hit a broken branch. She snatched it up, swung it.

'Let me go!'

The wolf flinched under the blow, eyes burning with fury. For a second it wasn't even there, and then she was free, running and stumbling over the tussocky, squelching bog.

Soaked, hair plastered to her face, she snatched a look back. The moorland seemed empty. But the sun had set; long shadows leaned from rock and tree.

Furious with herself she limped faster. She had to get away. Because it would come after her and smell out her trail. And they'd send a Replicant with it.

The moor was so cold! Ice cracked on the surface, and her shoeless foot was wet through. Her dress clung to her body and arms. And there was a ringing in her ears, as if after some huge, silent explosion.

She was shaking with shock, but she was here, she knew this place, and she knew there was a lane. It should be ahead somewhere – no more than a track. But when she crawled through a hedge and slithered down into its shelter she was surprised at the dark smooth tarmac surface, hardly broken by weeds.

Ahead was a cottage. From one of the chimneys a circular white dish sprouted like a mushroom. The door opened.

Sarah dived sideways, into plants that stung her.

A young woman came out. She had a basket of laundry;

quickly she pegged a row of clothes to the line. Trousers, vests, a shirt.

A baby cried, indoors.

'All right,' the woman muttered. 'Mummy's coming!' She went in, slamming the door.

Sarah moved. Keeping low she ran across the lane and crouched outside the garden. Through the gate she could see toys, a yellow swing.

And a vehicle.

It was black. It stood, all glass and metals, on the drive of the house. Fascinated, she inched through the gate, closer to it, and touched the icy metal. In its curved surfaces saw herself, warped and strange. Had she been altered? Become aged, unrecognizable? A thread of terror chilled her spine. But then the wing-mirror showed the same cropped blonde hair. The same sharp blue eyes.

Her relief was stupid.

The door opened. She leaped back round the corner of the house as the woman came out again, this time with a baby in her arms. Over the mother's shoulder the baby saw her, and screeched.

'Don't be naughty now. In you go.'

The vehicle flashed and clunked. Its door was open; the woman strapped the child into a small seat, then climbed in after it.

Sarah watched. The vehicle exploded into a roar of sound so terrible she flattened herself back against the wall, because how could anyone bear that? And then with a slur of gravel and a choking stink the car rolled down the lane and was gone.

It seemed to leave a hole in the air behind it.

Quickly she ran to the line and felt the clothes. The driest were a green woollen top and a pair of the same blue trousers the woman had been wearing; she snatched them down and changed into them behind the hedge, clumsy with cold, her hands fumbling over zips and buttons, desperately watching the bend in the lane.

The clothes felt soft and well-worn. They smelled of lemons, but she really needed shoes . . . She threw her own soaked dress in the green plastic bin, and as she slammed down the lid, she heard the Replicant arrive.

A footstep cracking a frozen puddle. A yelp in the lane.

Immediately she turned and fled through the winter garden, flinging open a gate, racing through a paddock where blanketed horses whinnied and scattered. She slipped, picked herself up, twisted to look back.

Shadows. One near the house, another round the bin, snuffling, long and lean. She stifled a hiss of dismay and slammed against a wooden fence, then leaped it, agile with terror.

Crossroads.

A weathered fingerpost leaned in a triangle of frosted grass.

EXETER 12 OKEHAMPTON 11

and in smaller letters underneath, pointing up a narrow lane

Wintercombe 2

The wolf howled; it had her scent. She turned and saw it streaking towards her, unleashed, a low shape hurtling through the twilight, eager to pin her down. She was running and it was behind her and she couldn't stop the terror now, it rose up within her like a red, snatched pain, the frozen lane quaked with it, the hedges roared.

And then it slid alongside her – a vast scarlet machine, stinking of diesel.

She flung her hand up, grabbed a metal pole, and leaped on board.

'Hold tight, love,' the driver said.

The bus roared away. Bent double, she dragged in air. The driver, his eyes on the road, said, 'Where to then?'

'Sorry?'

'Where to? Where are you going?'

The lane dwindled behind her, the wolf snarling in the

dark. She whispered, 'Wintercombe.'

'One forty.'

Baffled, she turned. 'I don't have any . . . currency.'

His eyes flicked to her in the mirror. 'I should put you straight off.'

'Oh give her a lift, Dave,' a woman said. 'You were young once.'

People laughed. There were five on the bus, all elderly, all watching her.

'OK. This once. And I still am young, compared to you lot.'

She said, 'Thanks,' and went and crumpled on to a seat behind the pensioners. A man glanced at her, disapproving.

The moor was the same. But nothing else. She'd never seen a bus before, was alarmed at how it scratched down the lane, its windows clotted with dried mud. The rattling motion and the smell made her feel sick; she held tight to the metal rail in front of her, her bleeding foot braced on the floor. On the next seat was a discarded newspaper. The page was upside-down; she turned it quickly. It showed a picture of a blonde girl in a grey dress. The headline was *Patient still missing from Secure Unit*.

She read the article carefully, feeling her heart rate thud to slowness. This was just what she needed. She folded it and dropped it under the seat.

The bus ran over a small hump-backed bridge and stopped in a street. The driver peered round his screen. 'Wintercombe.'

It was far sooner than she'd thought. She scrambled to the door, looked out cautiously and jumped down. 'Thanks.'

'My pleasure.' His voice was dry. Doors swished shut in her face. The bus roared away.

It was the village, but intact. People lived here. Over the huddled houses the sky was already darkening. Shouts made her turn, fast, but only a few men came laughing out of the pub. The Replicant and his wolf could be here in half an hour. She had to hurry.

Avoiding the houses she slipped down a footpath marked *Wintercombe Abbey*; it led into woodland. Great trees creaked overhead. She felt tiny under them, and uneasy because the wolf wasn't the only danger. Getting into the estate would be difficult. Through the Wood.

It was so silent the rustle of her own footsteps scared her.

The path descended into a deep hollow, banked on each side. Broken winter umbels lay snapped and trampled in the mud. After about a mile she stopped, holding her side, and listened. Everything seemed quiet. Then, as she turned to go on, she heard the sudden, excited howl.

Too close.

She ran, the momentum of the descent pulling her so fast that she almost tumbled out of the end of the path, and there were the gates, high black wrought-iron gates, streaked with rust, each of their pillars crowned with a sitting lion, one paw resting on a shield. She threw herself against them, but to her despair they were securely locked, and only a battered letterbox with WINTERCOMBE ABBEY. STRICTLY NO VISITORS leaned in the hedge.

She'd climb. As she put her hands to the metal a click alarmed her and she stared up. A small white camera, mounted on one of the lions, had shifted. It swivelled down. The round blank lens scrutinized her.

'Let me in. Please! I need to speak to you. It's urgent!'

A low growl. She spun round, back against the wet metal. Something was creeping through the dim undergrowth of the wood.

The gates moved.

A bolt slid. They shuddered apart, just a fraction, but it was enough, she'd squeezed through and was limping up the dark, overgrown drive, leaping logs, ducking under the untrimmed boughs of trees. The path twisted, all gravel and mud; over her head a mass of branches tangled against the twilight. She looked back once, saw the fleet snarling head, stumbled and crashed headlong over a fallen trunk.

The wolf's belly was low to the ground. Its eyes gleamed ice-cold, as if they caught the arctic sun.

'Go back,' she whispered. She groped in the leaf litter; clutched a brittle branch.

The wolf slavered, its spittle hanging. Then, quick as a flicker of moonlight, its eyes darted to the left. She turned her head. And held her breath.

In the eaves of the Wood a shadow stood. A boy in a green coat, barely visible in the gloom. He leaned on a spear tipped with a flake of sharp flint. He wasn't even looking at her, as if she didn't matter at all, but he had fixed his gaze on the dog and his lips were curled in scorn.

One-handed, he swung the spear and pointed it. 'Puppy,' he whispered. 'Little scared puppy.'

The wolf whined. It cowered, hunkering down as if it wanted to sink into the earth. It scrabbled, panicky, at the mud.

Sarah said, 'What are you doing? How are you doing that?'

The boy glanced at her. She scrambled up, watching the terrified beast abase itself in the dead leaves, watching it scrape itself backwards. Then it turned and fled.

Amazed, she turned. 'I don't know who you are but . . .'

'But I know you,' he said. 'Don't I?'

'No. You can't. I . . .' Her eyes widened. There was no boy. Just tree shadows. Gnarled and twisted.

For a moment she stood there. Then, slowly, she turned and limped on down the path, to the house that waited for her in the moonlight.

Wintercombe Abbey was no burned ruin. It stood tall, a rambling manor-house of gables and twisted chimneys, its darker, medieval stonework jutting out – the silhouette of a tower, a row of arcaded windows, all unlit. From gutters and gables waterspouts leaned, the long-necked gryphons and heraldic yawning dragons she had imagined for years in her dreams. The house crouched in its wooded hollow; its murky wings ran back into gloom, and with a deep roar somewhere beyond, the river crashed through its hidden gorge.

She moved carefully from tree to tree, as if the house watched her coming.

There was a lawn of waist-high grass; she would have to cross that, and she would prefer it if no one saw her from the high dark windows.

It was time to become invisible.

Sore and muddy, she summoned up the small itchy *switch* in her mind, just as they had taught her in the Lab.

Done.

Now no one could see her.

She stepped out and limped painfully through the dead grasses until the house loomed above, the moon balanced on its highest gable, then slipped round the side of the building, over frost-blackened flower-beds, through a small wrought-iron gate.

She came to a window, ground floor, but higher than her head. It was ajar. A fragment of curtain gusted through it in the cold breeze. She waited, secret and shadowless, listening. Nothing. The room must be empty.

She stretched up and grabbed at the sill. Barely reaching, she gripped it, then had to scramble on to a narrow rib of stone and climb the brickwork, hanging by toes and fingers, until she could haul herself up and peer over into the room.

It was shadowy. A fire burned low in the hearth, flickering red on dark panelling and shelves of old books.

She edged the casement wider. It creaked. Carefully she pulled herself up, getting one knee on the crumbling stone. She squeezed her head and shoulders in through the wide bars.

Then she saw him.

He was reflected in a glass clock face. A man in a high armchair with its back to her, legs stretched out, feet propped on a low table that was piled with documents, papers, books. In his hand was a glass of what might be whisky, but he wasn't drinking it or reading.

He was listening.

She kept completely still, not even breathing. To see him was astonishing. As if a character from a book had come to life, there, right before her.

With a sudden lean unfolding, the man stood. He turned and his face was a sharp silhouette in the gloomy room. She caught the puzzled, wary tilt of his head. He put the drink down on the table, and said, 'Who's there?'

The curtain gusted between them. She was invisible but all her weight was on one hand and it was already trembling.

'Answer me. Is it you, Summer? Do you really think you can get in here?'

His voice was scornful. He came straight towards her; she had to move. She slid through the casement on to the broad wooden sill, and he stopped instantly.

His eyes, ice-blue, stared right at her. He was so close she could see the shocked recognition come into his face, a spasm of stricken stillness. He reached out, till his hand was touching her cheek. He whispered, '*Leah?*'

She shook her head, devastated, her eyes blurry with tears. 'How can you see me? It's not possible.'

His hand jerked back, as if she'd slapped him. The

shock went from him; replaced with a vicious anger that took all the life from his eyes. 'Who the hell are you?' he snarled.

She jumped down and stood in the room in front of him, defiant, cold hands at her sides. 'Sarah. And you must be Oberon Venn.'

He didn't answer. All he said was, 'Your foot is bleeding all over my floor.'

CHAPTER THREE

I first met him on a remote glacier in the high Andes.
A friend and I were climbing and had got into trouble;
we had frostbite and the weather had closed in. We
curled in a snow-hole, freezing. Late in the night I
heard a sound outside, so I crawled out. The wind was
an icy rattle against my goggles.

Through the mist I saw a man walking. At first I
thought he was some creature of the snow, a phantom
of the tundra.

I must have been in a state of delirium because
I called out that he was an angel.

His laugh was harsher than the wind. 'My name's
Venn,' he said. 'And I'm no angel.'

Jean Lamartine, *The Strange Life of Oberon Venn*

Jake gazed out of the plane window at the blue sky.

Far below, the snowfields of the Alps glittered a brilliant white; the plane's tiny shadow moved over glaciers and secret valleys where only explorers would ever venture.

Explorers like Venn.

He focused on his own blurred image in the glass. The plan had worked, he was out of the school for ever. He felt strangely tired, though he should be elated. After all, there was no one at Compton's he cared about. He had said goodbye to them all with cool politeness, and then been driven away. Davies and Alec and even Patten had watched him go, standing in a silent group on the steps. He hadn't looked back.

They were probably at games by now. They'd probably forgotten all about him.

Fine. But there was still a problem, and it was a big one.

Wharton was sitting next to him, reading a book. Jake watched the man's reflection. Big for a teacher. Ex-rugby international. Having him along was not an option. He'd have to get rid of him as soon as possible.

As if it was Jake's mind he was reading Wharton turned a page and muttered, 'Whatever you're planning, forget it. I'm coming with you to the very door of the Abbey.'

'I can look after myself. I'm sure you want to get back to glamorous Shepton Mallet.'

'I do.' Wharton looked up. 'But the Head's instructions were crystal. "*Hand the scheming little brat over personally.*"'

Jake almost smiled.

Wharton watched him. Then he put a marker in the book and laid it on the fold-down table. 'So are you going to tell me what this is all about? This ridiculous . . .'

'It's not ridiculous.'

'Murder? A man like Venn? Come on! You'll have to convince me.'

Jake held himself still, but the old cold anger crept over him. 'What do you know about him? Only what you see in the news. Venn the *Boy's Own* hero. Don't you think someone like that – out there in the wilds, on the edge of survival – don't you think he could kill if he had to?'

'I suppose it's possible.' Wharton watched the boy's reflection. 'Tell me about him.'

Jake was silent a moment. Then he said, 'I've read everything on him I can find. He was the best. Explorer, mountaineer. Doctorate in plate tectonics. Virtuoso violinist. Collector of Cycladic pottery. You name it, he's done it.'

Wharton nodded. 'I've seen him in a few things on TV.

A series on volcanoes.' Venn's rugged face, his ice-blue eyes and dragged-back tangle of blond hair were familiar from documentaries and interviews. 'A very intense man, I remember. Driven.'

Jake laughed, but it was a mirthless laugh. 'Good word. But his life crashed. Four years ago he was driving a hired car along a narrow coast road in Italy. His wife was in the car with him. There was some sort of accident – an oncoming lorry. The car went down the cliff. Venn survived. His wife, Leah, didn't.'

The cold, cruel way he said it made Wharton very uneasy. 'That's a terrible thing for a man to have to live with.'

Jake shrugged. 'He was in hospital for weeks. When he came out he seems to have been like a different person. No photos, no interviews. He sold his London flat and went and holed up at Wintercombe Abbey, an old place deep in Devon that's belonged to his family for centuries. He set up some sort of secret project and works on it obsessively. He never leaves the estate or speaks to anyone outside. Except my father, David Wilde.'

Now we're coming to it, Wharton thought. But he kept his voice neutral. 'His best friend.'

Jake nodded. He kept his eyes on the sky. 'They'd been friends since they were kids. Been in some bad situations together. Dad used to say he was the only one Venn trusted.'

'And where were you at this time?'

'Home. We lived in London. Dad and Mum had just split . . . well, at least they were still talking at that stage.'

Wharton waited for more. When it didn't come he said gently, 'I wondered why you didn't live with your mother, after . . .'

'She's too busy in the US.' Jake's answer was curt. 'She doesn't want me messing up her new life.'

'Would you like something to drink, sir?' The air hostess was bending over him, the trolley blocking the narrow aisle. Wharton was glad of the interruption; he took his time choosing a glass of wine and a Coke for Jake. All this explained a lot, he thought, cracking the lid and pouring. The boy's cool unconcern was just front. He must be bitterly wounded underneath.

When the trolley had rattled away Jake pulled out earphones so Wharton said hastily, 'You were saying . . . about murder.'

Jake had one earphone in. He pulled it out and stared ahead. Then he said, 'In the July of the year following the accident Dad went to stay at the Abbey for some important phase of the project. I asked about it, but Dad wouldn't talk. "Top secret," he used to say, but he was really excited, I could tell. I got the feeling that it might be dangerous. I wanted to go with him but he said, Venn says no kids. So I ended up staying with my cousins in St Ives. It was OK – the beach and all that – but I missed him. He was away two weeks, then three, then four. At first there were phone calls, e-mails. He was careful not to give anything away. I remember him saying something once about a mirror, and then stopping himself. As if he shouldn't have mentioned it.'

'A mirror?'

'Yes. "*Of course, the mirror's giving any number of weird results.*" When I asked him what he meant, he changed the subject. I got the feeling someone had come into the room, or was there with him. He laughed. I remember that clearly because it was the last time I ever spoke to him.'

Wharton kept silent. Jake took a breath. Then he said, 'There were no more calls. When we rang the Abbey all we got was the answerphone. After three weeks of that my aunt got worried. She called the police. They went there and spoke to Venn. He said my father had left the Sunday before to catch the nine-thirty train to London. But he wasn't on the Plymouth Station CCTV, and he never arrived in London. And since that day, no

37

one has set eyes on him. My father just vanished from the face of the earth.'

Wharton had no idea what to say. He sipped the wine, barely noticing the sharp taste, and put the glass down. The plane veered, and the glass slid gently towards the edge of the table. He caught it. 'So . . . you were left all alone.'

Jake drank some Coke. 'I stayed on at my aunt's for a while, but it was awkward. Then she had a call from Venn. He said as he was my godfather he'd take responsibility for me. He arranged for the school in Switzerland. Expensive. And as far away from him as possible.' He turned, suddenly urgent. 'You see what he was doing? Paying a fortune to keep me away. Because he killed Dad.'

'Keep your voice down.' Wharton looked round anxiously. A dark-haired man across the aisle had glanced at them from behind his newspaper. 'You can't just go around making wild accusations . . .'

'Why not?'

'What on earth would be his motive?'

'This thing they were working on! My father knew too much.'

'Highly unlikely. And you have no evidence of . . .'

'Yes I have.' The words were very quiet, but they were

bitter as acid. Wharton felt a small shiver travel down his spine.

'What do you mean?'

Jake looked at him. 'Swear you'll never tell anyone.'

'Oh for heaven's sake . . .'

'Swear.'

'What is this? *Hamlet*? All right, I swear.'

Jake kept his eyes on him. Then he pulled out a small wallet from his pocket. Wharton stared at it. It was made of some dark leather, very worn and stained.

'Was that your father's?'

'Yes. He always kept it with him. He used to say it was crocodile skin, and that he and Venn had killed the croc one time in Africa, when it was terrorizing some village. It meant a lot to him.' Jake opened it; he took out a photo and a sheet of paper. 'Last term a parcel came for me through the post. I don't know who sent it. The postmark was British. These were inside.' Reluctant, he handed Wharton the paper. 'It's definitely my father's writing.'

Fascinated, Wharton took out his glasses and put them on. The letter was very short and had obviously been written in a hurry. The writing was scrawled; in places the Biro had broken through the paper.

Wintercombe Abbey
Sunday 14th August

Dear Jake,

*   Not sure if I'll get this to the post; it's a bit of a walk to the village so I may leave it till tomorrow. Sorry not to have called — we've been incredibly busy with the Chronoptika. I can't tell you how fascinating it is, and what success we've already had! If all goes well tonight we should go public, whatever O says. It will blow the scientific world wide open! Here's a little present for you. O wouldn't approve, but I can't resist sending it. See you in a few days, promise.*

*   Love always*
*   Dad.*

He folded it slowly and cleared his throat. 'I'm sorry, Jake. Really sorry.'

Jake took the note back, silent.

'O is short for Oberon, I suppose?'

'Dad always called him that. But you see the important thing?'

Wharton shook his head.

'*The date.*' Jake laid the note on the table and tapped it with his forefinger. 'The fourteenth is the day Venn says my father took the train to London. But this is headed Wintercombe – he was still there when he wrote it, and it's clear he wasn't going anywhere.'

Wharton read the central sentence again. *If all goes well tonight we should go public* . . . 'They were planning some sort of event that night.'

'Experiment. With this thing he calls the Chronoptika.'

'What *is* that?'

'No idea.' Jake stared ahead, brooding. 'I think things did go well, and Venn wanted the discovery for himself. Maybe they argued. Maybe he killed my father to keep him quiet.'

It was bizarre. Wharton shook his head. 'You're just looking for someone to blame . . .'

Jake snatched the letter up and folded it, his fingers shaking with anger. 'Right. Forget it.' He jammed the earphones in and turned away, hunched up in the seat.

'Jake. Jake, listen . . .'

No answer. The man opposite was watching again, a handsome dark-haired man, who turned his face quickly aside. Tugging out one of Jake's earphones Wharton said quietly, 'Show me the photograph.'

Jake didn't move. *I've lost him*, Wharton thought. But then Jake took the photo out and pushed it across the table.

41

Wharton turned it. It was a small grainy image, black and white, snapped with some ancient camera. A tall man in a camel coat smiled out. He looked enough like Jake for Wharton to be sure this was David Wilde. He was standing in a street. Old-fashioned London buses and a taxi were visible behind him. He was holding up a newspaper.

'I wish I had a magnifying glass. I can't make out the headline.'

'It says BEATLES STORM AMERICA. The date is 1965.'

Wharton frowned. 'Sixty-five? Even I was only a kid then. Your father . . .'

'Wasn't even born.' Jake picked the photo up. 'I don't get it. It must be some mock-up, but why? And why send it to me?'

'He didn't post it, clearly. Someone else did. Someone who waited two years after his . . . disappearance.'

'Death.'

'You don't know that.'

Jake's stare was bleak, and Wharton saw the fear behind it. 'He's my father. Something terrible has happened to him, because otherwise he would have called. He wouldn't just have abandoned me. I *know*.'

Warning lights pinged. 'Ladies and gentlemen, please fasten your seat belts,' a voice said smoothly. 'We are about to begin our descent.'

Wharton was glad of the chance to think. He wasn't sure what to do about any of this. And why in God's name hadn't the Head told him about the boy's father? At least he would have been prepared.

As the plane banked steeply and dropped through a long bumpy glide to Heathrow, he watched the clouds fleeting past and felt the deceleration build like an ache in his muscles. There was no question – he'd have to stay with Jake as far as Wintercombe Abbey. Someone needed to be there when the boy and his godfather met. Anything might happen, with this crazy stupid idea Jake had stuck in his mind.

Because, of course, it was crazy.

The plane touched, lifted, then bumped down hard. Wharton clutched the arms of his seat in rigid terror. He didn't mind flying but he loathed landing.

And there was one thing he couldn't explain, that was an oddity in the whole mess. The photograph. What was the point of the photograph?

In the baggage hall they hauled the suitcases off the carousel and piled them on a trolley. Wharton reached for Jake's rucksack.

'No, I'll take that.' Jake snatched the bag up quickly on to his back. But as he adjusted it, it made a strange, sleepy squeak. Wharton's eyes widened.

'Oh no. Don't tell me . . . You couldn't have.'

Jake shrugged. The rucksack squeaked again. Wharton pulled the top open and looked in. A small furry heap of limbs disentangled itself and peered up at him. The monkey's eyes were black-pupilled. It yawned.

He shut the bag instantly and glanced around.

'Don't panic.' Jake pushed the trolley away calmly.

'Panic! What about quarantine? Rabies! Have you any idea of the absolute hoo-ha if you'd been caught . . .'

'Well I wasn't, was I? The vet gave me something to keep him asleep. He was fine.'

'But a monkey?'

'He's not just a monkey. He's a marmoset.'

The casual arrogance was back, and it left Wharton furious.

'I don't care if it's a bloody aardvark. And we've got to go through Customs!'

Jake shrugged. 'It'll be easy this end.' He eyed the teacher with dark amusement. 'Venn can pay the fee, if they catch us.'

Trailing behind, Wharton sweated through the long corridors and moving walkways, and when they were waved through by a bored official he felt as much relief as if he'd been smuggling diamonds.

Outside the airport Jake opened the bag and the marmoset crept sleepily out and wound its arms lovingly round his neck. Its fur was a lustrous brown. It stared at Wharton like a baby stares, with total indifference.

'I wasn't leaving him at that pit of a school,' Jake muttered. They stood in the taxi rank, everyone staring at the animal.

'Put it away,' Wharton hissed.

'Him. His name is Horatio.'

By the time they got to their taxi the thing was wide awake and eating grapes. The driver looked at it doubtfully. 'If that beast makes a mess . . .'

'Just get us to Paddington Station.' Wharton tossed the cases in, climbed after them and sat on the warm squeaky seat, breathing in the smells and fumes of London. After Switzerland it felt like breathing fog. Glancing back, he saw the man who had been sitting opposite them in the plane was just behind in the queue; for a second their eyes met, and he was shocked at the deep scar that disfigured the man's left cheek.

Their car edged out into the raging traffic.

'I can manage on my own after Paddington,' Jake said, without hope.

Wharton shook his head. 'No chance.'

'I could bribe you.'

'I'm incorruptible. Just keep that thing out of my pocket.'

Under the garish Christmas lights they crept through gridlocked London. Far behind, deep in the traffic, a taxi slowly followed them.

CHAPTER FOUR

Fear not, fear not, my lord, said she,
The dead are dead and ever will be.
Dear is the ransom you must pay,
  If her lost face you wish to see.

Fear not, fear not, my lord, she said.
For who can render to the dead?
Dark is the journey you must take
  Her lost beauty to remake.
          Ballad of Lord Winter and Lady Summer

What startled them both was a knock at the door.

Venn's gaze flickered; in that instant Sarah turned and was halfway out through the window before he lunged and grabbed her, hauling her towards him. 'Piers!' he yelled. 'Get in here!'

She kicked him but he held on; he had her arms now and his grip was bruising and tight. He dragged her back and she fell hard to the floor, the breath knocked out of her.

'Get up,' Venn said.

She was too stunned to move. After a moment he held out his hand. She took it.

He pulled her to her feet and stepped away. 'I didn't mean to hurt you.'

She shrugged. 'Maybe I shouldn't have kicked you either.'

He was silent. Aware of a draught behind her, she saw that a very small man in a white lab coat had opened the door and was staring at them both. He had a tiny goatee beard and a sharp, inquisitive face. 'What's going on?' he said.

Venn straightened. He was tense and pale. 'Ask the most inept burglar in the world.'

'I'm not a burglar.' Keeping calm, Sarah faced him.

'So what are you doing breaking into my house? How did you get here anyway?' He turned on Piers. 'So much for your security.'

'I had her on camera all the way from the gate.' The small man looked at her thoughtfully. His eyes were bright as coins, missing nothing.

Sarah said, 'It was you who opened the gate?'

'*And*,' Piers said, 'the police are close behind her.' He turned to Venn. 'One man, at the door. Calls himself Janus.'

Venn's cold eyes moved back to Sarah. 'That's convenient. He can take her with him.'

'No!' She couldn't stop the gasp of dismay. 'Please! Don't tell him about me. Don't tell anyone.'

Venn stared at her, a long moment, then sat on the edge of the cluttered desk and said to Piers, 'Let him in.'

'Can I just suggest . . . ?'

'Do what I tell you!'

The small man shrugged at Sarah and went silently out of the room.

She pushed back her hair and walked over to the fire, her bare feet leaving a trail of mud and leaves. The warmth of the glowing coals was such a wonder that she crouched by it, trying to stop shivering.

'You're not dressed for house-breaking,' Venn muttered.

'You won't tell him. Will you?'

'Why not?' He was colder than she'd thought. Something had frozen hard inside him. She kept her voice low and calm. She said, 'Because, for a minute there, you thought I was someone else. You said, "*Leah*."'

She thought he wouldn't answer. Then he said, 'My mistake.'

'Don't betray me for her sake. And because I'm invisible.'

His eyes were as ice-blue as the wolf's. 'But I can see you.'

'You shouldn't be able to. I can make myself disappear. I have this special power. Only this time it hasn't worked. Perhaps it's you. Perhaps you're different from everyone else.'

She had his attention now. A faint change came into his tight, controlled face; he stood up and walked towards her and she saw how thin he was, how gaunt and restless. 'Are you insane?' he said.

'That's what they call it. But what if I'm not?'

'Why did you break in?'

'I'm running away. And I didn't break in. The window was open.'

'Don't get smart with me. Who are you?' An anxious look flashed in his eyes. 'Which one of them sent you? The scarred man? Or the Queen of the Wood?'

She had no idea who either was but she kept her face calm. 'Hand me over and you'll never find out.'

Footsteps and voices came down the corridor; she heard the creak of old floorboards. Venn didn't move for so long she thought she'd failed. Then he said, 'I used to think I could control what fate threw at me. I really used to believe that.' He stepped forward. 'You're on your own? No one knows where you are? What about your parents?'

'I don't have any.' With a pang of fear she realized that now, in this place, it was true.

He stared at her as if a sudden burning idea had come to him, an idea so brilliant it eased some deep inconsolable torment. Hastily, he pushed her towards a door in the panelling. 'In there.' He tugged it clumsily open with his left hand and she saw the top joints of two fingers were missing. 'Stay still. Silent!'

Before she could answer the door had slammed, and footsteps were loud in the study. Piers's high voice said, 'Detective Inspector . . . er, Janus.'

She spared a quick look round. This was some tiny storeroom, also heaped with papers and books. One small barred window showed sleet falling in the dusk on the neglected lawns. No way out. She pressed her ear against the door.

Venn was saying, 'I don't think we've met.'

'I'm new to Devon.'

At the sound of the voice Sarah clenched her hands into fists and breathed in, frozen with dismay. They must be desperate to get her back. They'd sent a Replicant of Janus himself.

'What's the problem?' Venn was nearest, his back to the door. The oak panels were thick, the voices muffled unless she pressed close.

'A missing persons enquiry. I'm sorry to disturb you – I understand you don't like visitors.'

'I don't like anyone. Aren't you a bit young for a Detective Inspector?'

'Maybe I work hard.' The voice sounded amused, ignoring Venn's rudeness. When it spoke again it was sharper. 'A patient is missing from the High Security Psychiatric Unit at the Linley Institute, about twelve miles from here. A young woman, seventeen, short blonde hair, blue eyes, wearing a grey dress and indoor shoes. You'll have seen the local news . . .'

'I don't watch TV.'

'Why doesn't that surprise me?' The Replicant's voice was smooth. 'A girl answering her description was seen today boarding a bus to Wintercombe. Enquiries are proceeding in the village, but . . .'

'Why would she come here?' Venn sounded bored. Floorboards creaked as if he had walked over to the desk. 'What's wrong with her? What was her crime? To lock up a seventeen-year-old girl in a place like that, it must have been something horrific.'

The Replicant said calmly, 'I gather she's very disturbed. They don't go into details, but some of the patients they have up there are a bit extreme. I understand your security is red-hot, but . . .'

'Piers can see a beetle climbing the gate. No one gets in here.'

Sarah scowled. He was taunting her? His answers were aimed at her, as much as the Replicant.

Suddenly she saw that a small knot of wood was missing near the handle. She knelt and put her eye to the gap.

'What's her name?' Venn asked.

'Sarah Stuart.' The Replicant was a shadow near the window, hard to see clearly. 'If she turns up we advise you to inform us at once, and not to approach her.'

'You make her sound like a wild animal.'

A pause. Then Janus stepped forward and Sarah's hands went tight on the door frame. *It was a young one*. He was wearing a dark almost military uniform and his hair was lank, and he was so slim and young! Twenty at most, she thought. But already he had the familiar grin, the small pair of round, bluish lenses that hid his eyes. He said, 'Mr Venn, this girl is seriously ill. She has delusions about secret powers, fits of violence. I'd like permission to search your estate . . . there are so many barns and outbuildings.' He stepped closer, smiling mildly. 'And then there's the Wood.'

Venn had seemed half hypnotized, but that word broke the spell. 'If she's in the Wood she's beyond your help.'

Sarah saw him glance at the door, as if he could see through it, see her pinned sideways like a moth on a board. She spread her hands on the varnished panel.

'So I'll just get our men in tomorrow.' Janus had seen. He did not look towards her, did not even flicker, but she knew.

'No.' Venn stood. 'No one's coming on to my land. If there's any searching to be done, we'll do it. If we find any mad girls, I'll certainly let you know. Piers will show you out.'

A bell clanked.

In the dark, Sarah allowed herself a tiny whistle of relief. Venn was as arrogant as Janus. Then, in the doorway, she saw the Replicant turn. 'I hope you don't regret this.'

Venn stood straight in the firelight. 'So do I.'

The door to the corridor closed.

Silence.

Very gently, Sarah turned the handle and tugged. It

was still locked. Then Venn's voice spoke near her ear, cool and close. 'I think you'll be staying in there for a while, Sarah Stuart. As you're such a dangerous axe-murderer . . .'

'Let me out. You can't keep me here!'

'I can do anything I like.'

She slammed a fist against the panelling.

'Besides,' he said, 'what if you managed to make yourself invisible after all? I'd never be able to find you.' The icy humour left his voice. 'I have a few things to see to. If Piers brings you some food, please don't murder him. He gets everything wrong, but he's useful.'

Footsteps.

She tried the door again and it opened, and she came out into the warm dark study and stood there, listening to the silence of the Abbey, a silence that had its own deep, velvety texture like the heavy brown curtains that hung to the floor, looped back at every window. Beyond, fractured in small glass panes, she saw her own reflections, multiplied as if in some dark kaleidoscope. Only the slow, oily swing of a pendulum in the clock disturbed the stillness.

To be in this house again filled her with wonder, and with a terrible piercing sadness.

It looked so crammed and dusty. So neglected.

She crossed the room and tugged the curtains shut. They were heavy with dust; it drifted down on her lips and face. Then she crouched again by the hearth, comforted by heat. It was something familiar in this winter world.

All at once she felt incredibly tired. She wanted to lie on the rug and sleep away the heaviness in her limbs and eyelids. But the Replicant was out there in the dark, and it knew she was here. Making a huge effort she scrambled up and began to walk about, forcing herself to stay alert and look at things. Now, while she had the chance.

There were so many books and papers. They were stacked in untidy piles; she turned a few over but they meant nothing, were just columns of calculations, pages of algebraic formulae. The books were in many languages; some were old leather-bound volumes, their spines eaten away, but there were towers of softer, paper-covered books too, on mountain ranges and icecaps, with great curling maps that had tea stains and ink marks and scribble all over them.

He obviously didn't use them any more.

Quick and deft, she tried the drawers of the desk. Each was crammed full of junk – pens, keys, receipts, staples. In one a whole collection of fossils lay tumbled and disorganized. She picked up an ammonite, feeling the coiled ridges of the ancient creature. It had been dead for millennia, and yet here it was. Under it was a small grey notebook, the pages empty. Just what she needed. She slipped the notebook into her pocket.

A coal slid in the fire. She glanced at it, shutting the drawer. As she did, her eyes caught a glint among the papers on a side table; the ruby-red reflection of flame in metal.

She inched the litter aside.

A battered tin box lay beneath. It was dented, as if it had been dropped more than once, and the initials *J. H. S.* were painted on it in faded white letters. She stared at it in astonishment, then dragged it out. Papers slid. A few books crashed to the floor.

The box was not locked. Hurriedly, her fingers slid across the lid.

A rattle of the doorknob. She shoved the box back, threw herself down by the fire, grabbed a book and just got it open as Venn came in with a tray.

'Glad to see you're not wasting your time.'

She looked up. 'Even lunatics can read.'

'Upside-down, too. Incredibly clever.'

She threw the book down, annoyed.

'I've brought you some sandwiches. Cheese and ham.'

She snatched the plate quickly. They were big and clumsy but the bread was freshly baked. She had never smelled bread so good. She ate with ravenous concentration.

Venn watched her, leaning against the desk. 'How long have you been on the run?'

'A few days,' she lied, through a mouthful.

He paced, turned abruptly. 'Why were you in the Linley?'

'My parents died. I couldn't cope. Had a sort of . . . episode. I'm fine now.'

She was afraid he'd ask again about her parents but he didn't. Instead he came closer and said, 'It's a criminal institute, Sarah.'

'Maybe I went a bit crazy. Smashed up the place I was living.'

'What place?'

'What is this? An inquisition?'

He didn't move. Then he said, 'It's an interview. For a job.'

She realized then that he'd already been on-line checking her story. She said, 'What job?'

'When are you eighteen?'

'Next month.'

He began to pace again, long strides around the room,

restless, moving papers. Seeing the box, he picked it up and put it into the lowest drawer of the desk, turning the key, preoccupied. As if it wasn't anything special.

'You can see the state of this place. Piers does what he can but he could do with some help . . .'

She couldn't hide her disappointment. 'You want me to be a cleaner?'

'To help out. With other things too.'

She waited. He pulled the curtain back, gazing out into the dark. 'I'm working on a project here. A very secret, very important piece of research. That's what the gates are for, and the cameras. You won't understand it, but it's reached a critical stage, and I need another . . . subject. Another volunteer.'

It was as if he was talking to himself, a low, rapid, passionate mutter. It scared her. 'Another? What happened to the first one?'

'He left.' He came and stood looking down at her. She got up and brushed the breadcrumbs off, because he was tall and there was a bleak, threatening urgency in him. He said, 'I need you to work with me on the Chronoptika.'

Her heart leaped.

'It's a device for . . . manipulating light. It's faulty, but I know I can get it to work. I just need someone with no ties, someone who won't be missed, won't go out there and blab. Someone like you.'

She shrugged. 'I don't know anything about . . .'

'You don't need to know. You're just the subject.'

'In some experiment? With drugs?'

'No drugs.'

She shook her head. 'No way. You're not wiring me up with electrodes like some lab rat.'

'No electrodes.' His voice had gone hard and cold. He stepped back. 'Maybe I'm not making myself clear here, Sarah. You have two choices. Work with me, or I phone the police. Right now.' He took a phone from his pocket, thumbed a number in and held it up. The faint square of light edged his face.

'Wait . . .' She wanted to say, *That man* wasn't *the police*. Instead she said, 'Turn it off.'

'You agree?'

'I don't have any choice.'

A gleam of relief was gone from his face before she could be sure of it. 'There's no danger. I promise you. And when it's over I'll give you a thousand in cash and a plane ticket to wherever in the world you want to go. You can do what you like with your life.'

She knew he was lying about the danger. And that he didn't care. 'How long will it take?'

He looked away. 'A few weeks.'

The house seemed to wait around her. Outside its windows the vast Wood bent under the slant of sleet. She remembered the shadowy green-eyed boy who had commanded the wolf.

'All right. I'll do it. But I'm not a prisoner. I get my own room, and the run of the house. I'll need some clothes, too. And shoes.'

'Tell Piers what you need. He'll see to your foot.' He went to the door, then turned. 'You can go anywhere except the Monks' Walk. And don't go in the Wood alone. It's a strange, scary place.' He seemed to want to say something else, and for a moment she wondered if he might be grateful, show some welcome that she realized she longed for. But all he said was, 'Come on. I'll show you the attic rooms. You can choose one.'

Later, in dry clothes and with her stinging foot tightly bandaged, she sat on the small white bed in the attic and leaned back against the lukewarm radiator. Here they were, the wardrobe, the chest of drawers, the window safely shuttered against the night. The room wasn't so different. Barer, colder. The blue chintz curtains were gone. Sliding down, she crossed to the floorboard near the window seat and touched it gently with her foot.

It creaked.

She knelt, and felt for the tiny slot where her fingers had always fitted exactly.

They still did.

She smiled, and carefully levered up the board. The cavity beneath was dark, full of dust. She put her hand inside and groped around but nothing was there. None of her secret writings, her private paintings.

Leaving it open, she sat back on the bed and curled her knees up. Then she placed the stolen grey notebook on the flowered quilt.

Next to it, carefully, from her pockets, she brought out the three treasures she had snatched from the Labyrinth.

Half an old coin, hanging on a gold chain.

A small black battered pen.

And, like a shimmering starburst, the diamond brooch. She stared at them, because it was hard to believe they had survived. That like her, they were really here. For a moment the memories of that terrible fight, the explosion of darkness, seemed to close back in on her.

She looked up at the familiar room, the warm fire. Then, suddenly urgent, she uncapped the pen and and wrote three letters in ink on the first page of the notebook.

J. H. S.

*20th December. I've arrived. I'm inside the Abbey,
and have even seen a box with these initials on its lid.*

Then.

Is anyone else here?
Is anyone left to read this?

As she watched them the letters faded slowly to invisibility.

CHAPTER FIVE

No one could have guessed what Janus would become. As a young man in the Militia he was quiet and watchful. Never one of those in charge, though if asked he always had a clever plan, a considered comment. His sight was poor, he was was slight and scrawny, considered a weakling by stronger, louder men.

Which only goes to show how wrong they were.

Illegal ZEUS transmission: *Biography of Janus*

The train from London took hours, travelling deep into the West Country. The land was bleak with frost, the trees black, the distant rim of Dartmoor grim under a hanging curtain of dark rain.

Wharton had to ask for them to stop at Wintercombe

– a request stop, because hardly anyone used it. As he stepped down, Jake could see why.

There was a concrete platform among trees and a rain shelter. Through a white gate a path led to a car park where one empty blue car waited.

Wharton climbed from the train after him, followed by a girl with a small bag. A few carriages up, a man walked hastily through the gate, his back towards them, not looking round.

No one else. The train pulled creakily away.

Wharton sighed. He was tired; he'd tried to sleep on the journey but the endless jolting had kept him awake. Irritated he said, 'No taxis.'

'Are you going far?' The girl had walked to the car and unlocked it. She was not much older than Jake, very tall, her long red hair heavy with a glossy fringe that almost hid her eyes. 'Can I give you a lift?'

'Er . . . well that would be kind.' Wharton looked at Jake, who shrugged. 'We're actually going to a place called Wintercombe Abbey. I gather it's not far . . .'

Her eyes widened. 'The Abbey! Really?'

'Is that a problem?' Jake muttered.

'No. Honestly, I'd love to take you! Jump in.'

But it had surprised her, he thought. More than that – startled her. He climbed into the front seat and Horatio put his head out of the bag and stared curiously around. The girl said, 'Wow. Is he yours?'

Jake held up a finger and Horatio bit it thoughtfully. 'Maybe I'm his.'

She started up the car. 'You'll fit in at the Abbey. They say it's a place for eccentrics.'

Wharton had time to say, 'Really?' before he was flung back in his seat. She drove awkwardly, scraping the car round in a three-point turn before jerking out of the car park. They were through the village before Jake got much of a look at it – old thatched houses, a post office, the pub, then narrow lanes, high-banked with thorny hedges.

'I'm Jake Wilde,' he said.

'Rebecca Donahue.' Her eyes met Wharton's in the mirror.

He said, 'George Wharton. One of Jake's . . .'

'Uncles,' Jake said firmly.

'. . . uncles. Right.'

Rebecca's eyes flicked between the mirror and the road. Jake knew she was puzzled at the obvious lie. He said, 'You live here?'

'I'm at uni. In Exeter. I'm home for Christmas.' She took a corner at a crunching angle that made Wharton breathe a brief swear-word.

'Do you know Venn?'

'Oberon Venn?' She looked surprised. 'No. Of course not. No one knows him. Well, maybe some of the older villagers used to, but not these days. No one goes to the Abbey any more. I'm desperate to know why you are.'

If they told her it would be all over the village – that was how these places worked. Jake said, 'Venn's my godfather. I'm staying for a while.'

The car squealed round a bend. 'Is he really? That must be so exciting.'

'Must it?'

'Well . . . yes. Wow, he was so amazing in that series he did. Volcanoes and stuff . . . And he's so hot!' She raised her eyebrows. Jake looked out of the window, disgusted.

They had entered a steep valley; the lane down it was narrow, branches scraping both sides of the car. As they descended Jake heard the crunch of frosted gravel under the tyres; starlings flew in the twilight, squawking from the trees above. At the bottom, surrounded by what seemed a thick wood, were two locked iron gates in a pillared wall. Rebecca slammed the brake on just before the car hit them.

'Sorry. I've never been down this way before.'

'As a matter of interest,' Wharton said mildly, 'have

you actually passed any sort of driving test?'

She glared at him. 'Last week.'

'I'm amazed.'

'Well, so am I actually. It was my third go.' She hit the horn; a long noisy hoot. 'Is he expecting you?'

Before Jake could answer, the gates shuddered jerkily open, as far as the massed overgrown holly on one side would allow. Tense with nerves, he said, 'We can walk from here, thanks.'

'No way.' Rebecca changed gear with a crunching effort. 'I want to see the famous Venn. Anyway, the drive is probably miles long.'

He looked back at Wharton, who said, 'In that case, please carry on.'

The girl smiled. Jake had the feeling she was laughing at him; he felt annoyed at her stupid adoration of Venn. Moodily he stared out at the overgrown driveway. Every moment brought him closer to the house . . . It made him shiver; he fingered the wallet in his pocket, picturing his father's cheery smile in the black and white photograph. Whatever secrets lurked here, he wouldn't rest till he'd clawed them out into daylight.

For a mile the car jolted along, Rebecca taking it carefully now, because the Wood this deep was a black and white kingdom of frost, the track pitted with potholes.

They came to the splintered trunk of a great dead tree lying right across the way.

'Good heavens.' Wharton opened the window and leaned out. 'Is that deliberate?'

'They say he doesn't like visitors. But someone must come because there's a sort of way round the side . . .' Rebecca manoeuvred the car clumsily round the obstacle, jolting Wharton and the suitcases violently in the process. The monkey gave a shriek of protest.

'Oh shut up. I'm doing my best.'

Suddenly space opened up; in the white landscape of winter frost they saw the Abbey, pale in the moonlight, its lawns rectangles of silver. It seemed to Wharton that it crouched down in the Wood, that the trees surrounded it like a threat, as if one day they would devour it, grow over it completely.

Rebecca stopped the car on the weedy gravel and turned the engine off. 'Wow,' she said, into the silence.

Jake gazed up at the ancient windows, the gargoyled gables. The place chilled him. He got out and stood facing it, like an enemy. Wharton hauled the suitcases after him. 'Thank you so much, Ms Donahue. It would have been tiring to have walked all this way.'

She wasn't listening; her eyes were on the house. He turned, and saw that a man had come out, a tall, fair-haired man who stood on the frosty steps with an upright, arrogant assurance.

'It's him,' Rebecca muttered. 'Oh double wow.'

Venn said, 'I don't know how you got in here but you can leave now.'

Jake turned and faced his father's killer. He felt only a coldness. As deep and numbing as if he could never be warm again.

Wharton stepped between them hastily. 'Mr Venn. Perhaps I should . . .'

'Who the hell are you?'

'Wharton. George Wharton. Head of Humanities, Compton's College.'

Venn's stare was blank. 'Compton's . . . ?'

'In Geneva. Switzerland.'

It was enough. The anger in Venn's blue eyes transformed to a swift wariness. He looked at Jake, who hadn't moved. Nervous now, Wharton said, 'This is Jake Wilde. Your godson.'

Venn was staring at Jake. 'You're David's boy?'

'Yes. He is.' Jake's silence made Wharton stammer anything to fill it. 'You remember, I'm sure . . . The e-mail . . .'

Venn said, 'I don't send e-mails.'

'You did, I assure you. We . . . the school, that is,

explained that Jake had . . . exceeded a few limits. Your reply was for us to send him home.'

Venn seemed to drag his gaze from Jake to Wharton. Then he turned and snarled, '*Piers!*' in a voice of utter fury.

A tiny man in a white lab coat came leaping down the steps and ran hurriedly towards them. Wharton caught the glint of a gold earring in his ear. Venn rounded on him. 'Tell me you didn't do this.'

Piers's voice was shaky. 'I did. I replied to their message. I told them to send the boy.'

Venn was breathless with disbelief. 'Are you mad? Am I living in a house of maniacs? What possible . . .'

'I felt it was the best thing to do.' Piers shot a curious glance at Jake.

'You *felt!*' Venn exploded. 'What gives you the right to *feel* anything! Don't you think I might feel something too? About him? About David?'

Piers held his ground, folding his arms. 'Yes, of course, but Excellency, you were off in the Summerland. I had to make a decision.'

'And you didn't think to tell me?'

'I was . . . er . . . I felt it was best to let them arrive. After all, it was too late to stop them.'

Wharton glanced at Jake. The boy's silence, the

intensity of his stare, was terrifying. 'Look . . . I'm sure we . . .' he started, but Jake's voice startled them all.

'*Don't think you can send me away.*' The words were low, hoarse, almost unrecognizable. 'I'm not going anywhere.'

Venn was still. Then he stepped closer, and they stood face to face. 'Your father was my greatest friend . . .'

'Was he? So where is he now?'

'I don't . . .'

'Don't care?'

'Of course I care.'

'Then where is he? What happened to him?'

'I don't know.'

'Liar.' Jake stood cold and tall. His hands were shaking. He felt as if something was burning and heavy in his chest. 'You do know. You're responsible. He never left this house. He never got on any train.'

Venn was white-faced. Even Wharton noticed his flicker of surprise.

Jake stepped close. 'He was all I had. You took him away.'

'Jake . . .'

He pulled fiercely from Wharton's grip. 'Did you think you could buy me off with some smart school? You must have known I'd turn up here one day, looking for you. You must have known I'd never let you get away with it.'

Venn stood rigid. Softly he said, 'What exactly do you think I did?'

'He knew too much about your secrets. You made sure he'd never talk.'

'Secrets? What secrets?'

'The Chronoptika.'

For a moment Venn's eyes were sherds of ice. 'What do you know about that?' he breathed.

Jake grinned, sour. 'I'm sure you'd like to find that out. That's what you killed him for.'

Wharton, appalled, held his breath. The force of the boy's accusation was raw, like the aftermath of lightning in charged air. The evening hushed to listen, the crows cawed over the Wood, a faint warm smell of oil drifted from the engine of the car.

Venn's response surprised them all. He seemed almost relieved; he shook his head and thrust his hands into the pockets of his dark jacket and stood there, gazing at Jake. When he spoke his voice was almost weary. 'You're so much like him.'

Jake didn't move.

'Listen to me, boy, I loved your father. He was my only friend. You don't seem to believe that, but it's true. I would give anything to find out where he is . . .'

'You admit you're responsible.'

'No . . . not in the way you mean.' Venn took a sudden step forward, his voice urgent. 'David's not dead. He's alive, somewhere. And I'll find him.'

Jake snorted, but he seemed shaken. 'I'm not going from here until I know what happened.'

'I see.' Venn flicked a glance at Piers. 'You! I suppose you've already got rooms ready.'

'South wing.' Piers scratched his thin scrap of beard. 'But I didn't expect an entourage.'

They all looked at Rebecca, who was standing by the car, staring at Jake. She seemed fascinated. Startled, she lifted her hands. 'Oh, I'm just the lift.'

'Good.' Venn turned away. Then he swung back. 'But you, Jack . . .'

'Jake. My name's Jake.'

'I don't care what your name is. Keep out of my way. Keep out of my business. Don't go prying into things you don't understand. You're only staying because it's what David would have wanted.' There was a sting of scorn there, a whiplash of pain. With a glare at Piers, Venn turned and stalked away from the house, ducking down a path into the darkening Wood.

Piers blew out his cheeks in relief, and began gathering

up luggage. 'Well I think that went quite well in the circumstances. Welcome to Wintercombe Abbey, gentlemen.'

'No, wait!' Wharton turned quickly. 'I'm not staying. At least . . .'

'Thanks for everything, and I'm sorry about messing up the play.' Jake held out his hand. 'Have a great time in Shepton Mallet.'

Wharton stared at the outstretched hand and then beyond it, at the shadowy gloom of the house. 'Will you be all right?'

'Fine. Maybe Rebecca will give you a lift back.'

'Oh . . . right,' she said. 'Why not use up all my petrol?'

Wharton hesitated. Then, over Jake's shoulder, high in a tiny attic window, he saw a face, watching him. A small, white face, young, like a girl's. It ducked away, and he saw that the window was barred.

He stared up. Had he imagined that? What sort of place was this dark house buried in wildwood? After all, the father had vanished here. What if the son did too? Around him the twilight had become night; there were stars in the frosty sky, and the acrid smell of woodsmoke. He cleared his throat.

'Well now . . . It's rather late. Perhaps I should stay . . . just till Christmas. See you settled in.'

Jake dropped his hand. He managed a wry smile. '*Loco parentis.*'

'Sort of.'

How could he leave the boy in this godforsaken place with a man as hostile as Venn? Besides, the Head would be avid to know all about it . . .

Piers was already crunching over the gravel with their cases under his arms and clutched in long, spidery fingers. Jake let the monkey out of the bag; it leaped wildly on to the car, shrieking with delight.

'Hey! Watch my windscreen wipers.' Rebecca put her hands in her pockets. 'Did you mean all that . . . about murder? That is so . . . weird.'

'My father went missing here. That's all I know.'

She gazed at him a moment. Then she leaned into the car and came out with a torn envelope; she scrawled on it hastily. 'Look. Here's my phone number and e-mail. I live nearby. If you ever want a drink or a chat or anything.' She held it out. 'I mean this place is pretty isolated. Give me a call.'

He took it, feeling awkward. She meant well, and so did Wharton, but he just wanted them to leave him alone. Though as he watched her drive off he felt a strange ebb of confidence, especially when the purr of the engine had faded and he and Wharton stood alone in the silent evening.

They looked at each other. The marmoset jumped down and ran to the lighted porch. 'He knows where supper is,' Wharton said, too heartily cheerful.

Piers was waiting for them on the porch. Next to him, seven black cats, all identical, sat in a silent row. Their green eyes watched Jake gravely. Climbing the steps Wharton said, 'Does anyone else live here, Mr Piers, apart from you and Mr Venn?'

The small man gave him a mischievous, sidelong look. 'My niece helps out. Otherwise, quite the bachelor establishment.'

Wharton nodded, stepping into the cedar-panelled hall.

Jake paused on the step. The faintest breeze touched him. He turned, and looked out at the Wood. For a moment he had felt as if someone out there in the tangled greenery had called him, had silently spoken his name. But there was no one, and he was cold, so he went in and closed the door.

Standing high in the oak branches, leaning back against the trunk, Gideon watched the human enter the Dwelling. Green as moss, his eyes narrowed, and he practised a laugh, as he often did, just to hear the sound, to be sure he could still do it. Because one day he might forget how, and the Shee would truly own him. That fear tormented him.

First the girl, now these two.

Things were getting crowded in the Winter world.

He swung himself down and landed light among the leaf litter. His clothes were a patchwork of velvets and denim tagged with scraps of lace; his face and long hair streaked with wood dyes. The starlings saw him but didn't rise in alarm, their beady eyes watching carefully.

Summer would need to know about this.

He turned. The birds blinked and squawked as he vanished into the Wood.

A forged process of my death

CHAPTER SIX

Christmas at Wintercombe – how wonderful! The great Christmas tree in the Great Hall, the masses of presents, the vast arrangements of holly and ivy and mistletoe all down the stairs and decking every windowsill. The whole house warm with the smells of baking and sweetmeats. I am living in a dream, my dear!

Letter of Lady Mary Venn to her sister, 1834

Sarah was eating toast in the kitchen next morning when Piers came in. He had some cartons of milk and a newspaper, so he must have been to the village. How had he got there and back so quickly? She glanced anxiously at the paper. Then she said, 'So who are they?'

'Who are whom, exactly?'

'The man and the boy. They arrived last night. They're

81

still here. And Venn – he didn't come back. He's been gone all night.'

Piers arranged some breakfast things fussily on a tray. 'You're an observer, Sarah. That's very good. His Excellency will need that. But don't get ahead of yourself. He does what he wants, and I assure you, no one is safer in the Wood than Venn.'

She frowned. He was avoiding answers. 'What about the others? If they find out about me . . .'

He was already working at the ancient range, pouring milk on to porridge. 'They won't. The boy is the son of an old friend of Venn's who's turned up out of the blue.' He looked over, a quizzical glance. 'They're not local. They don't know anything about you. You're quite safe.'

Unsatisfied, she sat at the empty table. It looked as if it had been made for a staff of forty. She pictured the room crowded with servants, bustling round the vast chimney, so big you could sit on a bench inside it. Down from its blackened stones hung a collection of spits and pans and copper pots, all too heavy to lift and coated with a frosty soot. Spiders had constructed elaborate cities of web among them. Three identical black cats snoozed on a chair in a heap.

She pushed the toast crust round the plate. 'Can I explore?'

'Please do. It's an ancient, rambling house. But don't go . . .'

'To the Monk's Walk. I know.' She looked up. 'Is that where it is?'

He smiled. 'It?'

'This Chronoptika.'

Piers did not pause in his rapid stirring, but maybe the spoon circled a little faster. 'You'll find out about that soon enough. Patience, Sarah.'

She got up and clattered her dish into the scullery sink. 'So what about you? Are you the last of the staff or something? There were dozens here once – butlers, footmen. Maids.'

'You sound as if you'd seen them.'

She shrugged. 'Even crazy girls read books.'

The small man gave an odd chortle of laughter and picked a scrap of soot out of the porridge. 'Do they really? Well, as for me, I'm His Excellency's slave. He rubs a lamp and I come out of it. He whistles and I appear. He bought me in a market in the wastes of the Kalahari for thirty camels and a bottle of whisky. He freed me from the eternal spells of an island sorceress.'

Was it a joke? If so it was a bitter one. She said, 'You work for him?'

'He owns me.' Piers's voice was acid.

She didn't know what to make of that. 'You've been exploring with him?'

'Many times. In the Andes. In Antarctica. He always loved to travel. You might say we put a girdle round the earth together.'

She decided to try her luck. 'But that all changed when his wife died?'

Piers stopped stirring. He turned and she saw all his quirky humour had gone. 'A word to the wise, Sarah. *Never* speak to Venn about Leah. Do you understand?'

For a moment she stared at him. 'This is such a house of secrets. Is he so scary?'

'His anger is never pleasant. But the truth is, he's eaten up with grief and shame. I don't want you adding to that.'

In the corridor, a bell rang. To break the moment, she got up and looked out. There were two rows of bells in the corridor, old spiral coils, each with the name of a room above it in faded gilt letters, almost worn away. But she knew them. The one that was trembling said *South Breakfast Room*. She came back, disgusted. 'Do they think this is some sort of hotel?'

'Maybe they do.' Piers had the porridge, toast and tea on a tray. 'And maybe we'll indulge them for the first morning. Why don't you take it up?' He held the door

84

open. 'You can see the fierce boy and the shrewd teacher for yourself.'

Jake watched Wharton pull the bell again. 'You're wasting your time. He's not going to treat us like guests.'

Wharton sighed and came to the table. He leaned his arms on it and gazed out through the window. The bitter night had left the lawns coated with a stiff, frozen rime. If you walked on it, he thought, it would wheeze and crack underfoot. He said, 'Sleep well?'

Jake shrugged. In fact he had tossed and turned until well past midnight, twice sitting up wide awake and alert, listening to soft creaks and movements somewhere deep in the unknown house. He said, 'Being under the same roof as my father's killer makes it hard to relax.'

'Jake, you have to rid yourself of this obsession.' Wharton turned to him anxiously. 'You really can't . . .'

'No?' He took out the folded letter. 'This is my proof. Don't tell me to forget, *sir*, because I never will. If you want to leave, leave. I can look after myself.' He laughed, bitter. 'After all, I'm safely home now.'

Wharton sighed, and scratched his rough chin. He hadn't slept well either. The house was uncomfortably damp and cold, the water had been too icy to shave with, and, oddly, neither his room nor the bathroom had a mirror.

'I'm going to find some food.' Jake jumped up and crossed the room, flinging the door open. He walked straight into a girl with a tray, who gasped and almost dropped it. They both grabbed at it. Cups and saucers slid. Porridge slopped hot on Jake's hand.

The girl snatched it from him. 'That was so stupid! I could have dropped the lot!'

He stood back. 'But you didn't.'

She pushed past him and dumped the tray on the table. Jake watched her. She was small and agile, her white-blonde hair cropped short as a boy's. She wore jeans and an old purple top that was too big for her, the sleeves rolled up. She had a pair of stripy woollen gloves on, and a scarf, as if the house was perpetually cold. And someone else's shoes.

'Porridge!' Wharton was delighted. 'Fantastic. Toast! And honey!' He began to unload the tray. 'I hope we haven't put you to much trouble, miss, er . . .'

'Piers made it.'

Jake came over and sat. 'Your uncle.'

'. . . Yes.'

He didn't miss the hesitation. He said, 'Horatio. Come down.'

The marmoset swung itself from the filthy chandelier, dust and spiders raining after it, and landed on the table. The girl gave a sharp cry, almost of wonder. Horry screeched at her, took a piece of toast in a dainty paw and began to nibble.

'Is that a monkey?'

Her utter disbelief astonished him. 'Haven't you seen one before?'

'Yes, of course. Only . . . Is he yours? Can I touch him?' Sarah stretched out her fingers with a wary joy and the monkey sniffed at them.

'Give it some toast.' Wharton held some out, and as she took it and offered it to the monkey he flashed a glance at Jake, who looked as if he was thinking the same thing. She had obviously never seen such a creature before. Indeed, it was as if she had never even imagined one could exist.

'That's enough. He eats too much rubbish as it is.' Jake came and took Horatio on to his shoulder.

Sarah dragged her gaze away from the wonder of the animal and looked at the boy. He clearly thought a lot of himself. He was tall and dark-haired, and his clothes, as far as she could tell, were expensive and carelessly worn. He was also rude and sullen. Her first instinct was to dislike him.

The teacher was another matter. A big, powerful man, he was tucking into the breakfast with a hearty joy and talking all at once. 'This honey is so good. You should try some, Jake. And the bread! Freshly baked. Mr Piers is an excellent cook.'

'I'm not hungry.' Jake turned to Sarah. 'Why don't you show me around.'

He seemed consumed with restlessness. She shrugged. 'If you like.'

He was already disentangling the monkey's grip from his neck. She had a panicky second of worry – she hadn't had time yet to see how different the house would be. But she could bluff. And it would be a chance to find out more about them.

'Have fun,' Wharton said. 'Sorry . . . I didn't get your name.'

'Sarah.' She opened the door and went out, quickly.

'This is the Great Hall.' She led him under its pale rafters. 'It's Elizabethan. I think the panelling is all original.'

Jake said, 'I don't want the official tour. Where's the furniture?'

She was wondering about that too. The tiled floor was almost bare. 'I suppose Venn's sold it. Must be expensive, keeping this place going.'

Jake snorted. 'My heart bleeds. He's got enough money to keep me at a Swiss college.'

'Maybe you're the reason he had to sell the furniture.'

She glanced sideways, but if he felt anything, he wasn't showing it.

The hall was an icebox. Tiny icicles hung inside the mullions of the windows, as if the damp had dripped and solidified in the long night. Someone – probably Piers – had made a loose arrangement of red-berried holly and trailing ivy on the wide sill. A black cat sat next to it, watching them.

'You're limping,' Jake said.

'Oh, that's nothing. A blister.' He was observant too, she thought.

They explored the ground floor. The rooms were small and nearly all panelled with intricately carved woodwork, hanging with swags and carved faces. The corridors were long and dim, the floorboards creaking noisily underfoot. Nothing in the house was straight; everything leaned or tilted; even the floors sloped, and Jake had the unsettling feeling that the Abbey was warping almost as he walked through it. Great sideboards carried pewter cups and bowls; the lighting was weak; from the small casement windows he glimpsed the green gloom of the Wood through tangled tendrils of ivy.

Sarah walked in front, amazed. She had expected the Abbey to be neglected, and uncomfortable, but not like this. It was filthy. Curtains rotted where they hung, some so threadbare they would dissolve at a touch. Ceilings dripped into buckets, plaster was damp and in places sprouted whole gargoyles of green mould. The smell of mildew clung in the air.

Below the stairs Jake looked at the bare spaces where portraits had hung. 'Has it always been like this, or is this since . . . his wife?'

She shrugged. 'It would have been splendid once. House parties, people, servants, warm fires. Especially at Christmas . . .'

They came out into a stone passage that led to the cloisters. This was familiar; Sarah opened the doors confidently. 'The oldest part – it's medieval. The real Abbey, where monks once lived.'

Jake saw pointed arches and pillared columns, a vaulted arcade leading round in a great square, open to the sky. It was littered with chopped wood, a wheelbarrow, a rusting bicycle.

'Other people have garages. Venn has a cloister. Am I supposed to be impressed?'

'I don't think that's possible, is it?' She just wanted to get rid of him now. 'This,' she said, 'is the watermill,' and flung the door in the wall open, knowing the spray from the great whirling wheel would soak him to the skin.

'Really?' he muttered.

The wheel was a ruined shell. It rotted under years of algae.

She stared at it. Jake watched her. 'Are you OK?'

'I'm fine.' She slammed the door and hurried on.

He strode after her. 'How long have you been staying here?'

'Weeks. I'm working to get some money, and help Piers out. What about you?'

'Like I said, a college in Switzerland. Now I'm back.'

'Seems like Venn wasted his money.'

'Sorry?'

'Well, you're hardly grateful, are you? Do you mean back for good?'

He stared at her, hostile. 'What's it to you?'

'Nothing.'

They went frostily together up the back stairs. He wasn't easy to shake off, she thought; even silence didn't dent his self-absorption. Then he said, 'Where's Venn's room?'

She had no idea. 'Probably off the Gallery.'

'Show me.'

She led him to a turn in the corridor and they went round it and stopped.

Jake stood still. 'Wow. As Rebecca would say.'

She smiled, secret. Everyone was impressed by the Long Gallery. Wider than a corridor, it was a room that ran the whole length of the building, maybe a hundred metres long. Old hessian matting covered its oak boards. The white ceiling was pargeted with scrolls and cherubs, and there were the familiar statues she had almost forgotten, in a comforting row on their pedestals of wood. It was dim this morning, as if frost had crept in and fogged the air.

'You all right?'

He was looking at her. She realized her eyes had pricked with tears. She shrugged. 'Cold,' she snapped.

They walked down. Jake looked closely at the glass cases of books, the sculptured busts. She caught him glancing at his own reflection, slanted in the sunlight, and hers, behind.

He said, 'Were you here, when my father disappeared?'

'No. I . . .' A cold shiver chilled her, as if a draught passed through the room. She said, 'What was that?'

They both turned, as one.

The room had whispered.

The sound had come from the far end of the Gallery,

a faint, distant sibilance. Damp air drifted in the dark spaces.

'Who spoke?' Jake stared, intent.

'I don't know.'

He listened a moment, then walked quickly down; she caught up with him. 'I don't think . . .'

He didn't stop. 'Scared?'

'No.' Her eyes glanced back, along the row of locked doors.

The oak boards creaked. There was a different smell down here, a musty stench of decay. She saw that the white ceiling was ringed with watermarks.

Jake stopped.

In a narrow embrasure a wooden panel leaned. At first he thought it was a painting, so with both hands he lifted it and turned it round.

Light flashed and slid.

He saw himself, angled.

It was a wooden framed mirror, its surface so mottled with age that it was patchy and blurred, dark nebulae obscuring his face and eyes.

He leaned the frame against the wall. 'Just a mirror. Which is odd because there aren't any other mirrors. I haven't seen one in the house. Why is that?'

The answer was not hers. It was a whisper so close

both their hearts jolted. A choked throaty gasp. And the fog in the air seemed thicker, and Sarah knew with sudden fear that it was oozing from the glass. She said quickly, 'Turn it back . . .'

Jake ignored her. He touched the glass, fingers to fingers. And then he gave a cry of terror, because the hand he had thought a reflection of his own caught hold of him and jerked him close . . .

'*Jake*,' his own face hissed. '*It's me. Dad.*'

CHAPTER SEVEN

Long ago, they say, a baby was born in a cottage at the edge of the Wood. The boy was healthy, and his mother protected him with charms and prayers and amulets of iron, hanging from his cradle. But he cried and gurgled so loudly the sound echoed under the trees.

Soon, she began to see the faces of the Shee at the window, and hear, every night, their soft tapping at the door.

She grew afraid in her heart.

The Chronicle of Wintercombe

Jake couldn't move.

The hand in the mirror was a grey fragility, but it gripped him tight.

He stared into the glass, so close his breath misted it.

'Dad?' he whispered.

The face blurred beyond the mottled surface. It was his own, and yet its edges were worn, its eyes terrified, its skin ashen.

'*Jake*,' it said.

'How can it be you?' He grabbed the mirror with the other hand, flattening himself against it. His legs went weak; only the frame held him up. His father's voice was as fogged as the mirror between them.

'*Venn . . . need to . . . trapped . . .*'

He couldn't understand. He pressed closer. 'Are you dead? Are you a ghost?'

Was he saying it, shouting it? There was movement in the mirror; a swirl of snow. The plane of glass was flat and smooth and yet it was deep; if he moved a millimetre he might fall into it and never stop falling.

The hand dragged him close. In his ear the lips whispered, '*Venn . . .*'

'I can't hear you.' His cheek was against the glass. It was ice on his skin. 'I can't hear you. Say it again. Tell me what I have to do!'

'*Venn . . .*'

'Did he do this? *Are you really dead?*' The words came out in a wild cry he barely recognized. Then Sarah had hold of him; she was pulling him away, but he clung on

96

and his own reflection was yelling, 'Dad!' to himself and the mirror toppled and wobbled and he let go and staggered back.

It fell with a terrible crash. A black star of cracks fractured it. He felt the sting of flying glass, tasted blood.

Sarah scrambled over and grabbed the mirror and turned it to the wall. Then she spun and stared at him.

Jake knelt, huddled. He had a stunned, bruised look, as if someone had punched him. His face was flecked with tiny cuts. 'Are you OK?' She squatted next to him.

'It was him.' He looked at her. 'You saw, didn't you? He spoke to me. My father!'

His own disbelief was raw. He couldn't take his eyes off the scatter of broken glass. She moved in front, so he had to look at her. 'Your father? He's dead?'

'Yes. He's gone. Do you think that was his ghost?'

'I don't believe in ghosts.' She sat back, thinking of her own father, rotting in one Janus's prisons.

'But you saw him.' He had hold of her arm. His need for reassurance was suddenly embarrassing to them both. Jake let go, quickly. She shrugged. 'I thought . . .'

A door closed softly somewhere close in the house. They both stared up the Long Gallery. As if the sound had broken the terror Jake pulled himself to his feet. 'My father is missing and Venn's responsible. This proves it.'

'A face in a mirror doesn't prove anything.' She scrambled up and went and sat on a window seat.

'It had hold of me!'

'Don't be stupid. You imagined that. You panicked.'

He glared at her. 'I don't panic! You don't even know me! Or anything about me.'

'Then tell me,' she said.

For a moment she thought he wouldn't. But he paced up and down restlessly, obsessively, and the words came out as if the shock had triggered them.

He told her the story of David Wilde's disappearance. She saw the anger and bewilderment that burned in him, the terrible betrayal he squirmed away from. He turned quickly and pulled out a small leather wallet. From it he took a piece of paper and gave it to her. 'Look. Read it for yourself!'

She read his father's scrawled words.

Sorry not to have called – we've been incredibly busy with the Chronoptika . . .

Her fingers went tight on the paper. She looked up and interrupted him in mid-sentence. 'What do you know about this Chronoptika?'

He stared, annoyed. 'Nothing.'

'He never said anything else about it? About their work here?'

'Obviously Venn swore him to secrecy.' He came closer. 'Have you heard of it?'

She shook her head, rereading. He was silent, so she looked up and saw he was staring down at her.

'Because if you had,' he said softly, 'we could work together. You could help me.'

She gave the note back and stood up. 'I'm sorry about your father, Jake, but I don't think Venn killed him.'

As she turned away he said, 'But you saw him in the mirror. You heard him speak.'

She didn't stop or look back. 'I just saw your reflection. I just heard you.'

Then, afraid he would come after her, she had to walk all the way up the Long Gallery with his angry stare at her back.

Wharton put his head round the door and looked in. It was a small side hall, as cold as every other room here. He was wearing a coat and scarf, because he made a point of taking a walk every morning, and the grounds would probably be warmer than inside. Now all he had to do was find a way out.

The Abbey was a confusing building, but he

remembered this hall from last night. He walked over the stone tiles, clearing his throat. On the walls the eyes of the few remaining portraits watched him pass, and one of the black cats that seemed to infest the place sat washing, its pink tongue working rhythmically.

He was already regretting his offer to stay for Christmas. Despite Piers's admirable cooking it promised to be a cold, comfortless and embarrassing time. After all, the boy was Venn's responsibility now. And good luck to him, because Jake could be intensely irritating. Also sullen, simmering and mixed-up. But hadn't there been a faint relief through the sarcasm last night? As if he was quite glad not to be left here alone?

Wharton stopped at a glass cabinet. It housed a small collection of pottery figures, elongated and crudely painted. He recognized them as Cycladic, very ancient. One of Venn's areas of expertise. Venn was another mystery. How could a man who had seen so much and travelled so restlessly bear to shut himself up in this cold, silent house?

Wharton shook his head. Then he saw the newspaper. It lay folded on a small table by the door; Piers must have got it from the village because it was today's. The local rag, but something. He flicked the pages. He'd read it when he came back, with a cup of tea. It would probably be the highlight of his day.

Then his hand held the page still.

It was her.

He had only seen her briefly, when she'd brought in the breakfast tray, and the photo was very small, but surely that was Sarah. She was dressed in different, dull clothes and her hair was longer. The byline said *Still no sign of missing patient.*

He glanced round.

Then he folded the paper, tucked it inside his coat, and went out.

Sarah sat on her bed, knees up, and wrote quickly with the black pen.

Will certainly try to find J. H. S.'s box again. It has to be the one recorded in the files . . . When will Venn reactivate the mirror? A boy called Jake Wilde has arrived . . . claims to be Venn's godson. He's already disrupting things. Today there was a strange . . .

She stopped, searching for the right word. Vision? Ghost?

The writing faded. Suddenly, out of nowhere, panic and a terrible loneliness seized her; she wrote frantically, in a wild scribble.

Are you left, any of you? Max, Evan, Cara? ANYONE?

What's happening back there?

One by one the letters died away.

She felt numb and empty.

But then, just as she went to close the notebook, something started to appear. A few words, emerging slowly, as if they struggled through some immeasurable distance. Cold with concentration and a growing horror, she watched them form.

YOUR FRIENDS ARE DEAD, SARAH. NO ONE IS LEFT. NO ONE HEARS YOU BUT ME. WE CAN CONVERSE NOW. YOU AND ME . . . SARAH AND JANUS. YOUR LORD. YOUR MASTER.

Terrified, she slammed the book shut and stared at its cover, her heart thudding. For a long moment she sat there, fighting against fear and despair. Was it true? Were they all gone? If so it was all up to her.

She jumped up, crammed the pen and book back into the secret space under the floorboard and raced downstairs.

Piers, wearing an apron with a huge red sauce bottle on it, was peeling potatoes at the kitchen sink. 'Sarah, good,' he said at once. 'Venn wants you to be there tonight. The Monk's Walk, at eight o'clock.'

Her heart missed a beat. 'Already?'

'He's desperate to get the thing working again.'

She began to wipe the dishes and put them away. There was so much to ask; but she had to be careful. 'The thing?'

Piers grinned. 'You'd never make an interrogator, Sarah. If you want to know details, speak to Venn. But he's heading out again, so you'll have to wait.'

'I thought he never left the estate?'

'Maybe the estate is bigger than you think. Maybe it contains the whole universe.' He tossed a peeled potato into the saucepan with perfect accuracy.

Calm, she said, 'I'm really sorry but I'm afraid a mirror got broken this morning. Up in the Long Gallery.'

He turned and looked at her.

'Jake . . . slipped against it. It cracked . . .'

'Thirteen years' bad luck.' He looked utterly dismayed.

'Yes. It's a pity. Especially as there aren't any mirrors anywhere else.'

Now she felt better because he was the one wanting to ask the questions. He said gloomily, 'Damn. Damn damn damn. I was supposed to get rid of them all. If Venn finds out he'll hurl me halfway round the world . . .'

'He won't. Not from me.' She sat. 'Jake said he saw his father's reflection in it. I think he's a bit obsessed with his father, don't you?'

Piers seemed still worried about punishment. So she said, 'Who's the scarred man?'

'What?'

'The scarred man. Something Venn said . . .'

But he was too quick for her; already he was slicing another potato and flicking it into the pot. 'Absolutely no idea,' he said, grinning.

Annoyed at the lie she got up and stalked to the door. 'Suit yourself.'

But walking down the corridor she thought fast. Let herself smile. She'd never have a better chance than now to get at the box.

The small study on the ground floor was empty. She stood inside, listening to the silence. The sun slanted in, a faint wintry glimmer from the window she had climbed through yesterday.

The room smelled of ashes, and the grate held the grey, flaked remains of burned logs.

She closed the door and locked herself in. Then she crossed to the bureau, opened the lowest drawer and felt through the papers and files until she found the box.

She pulled it out. The initials *J. H. S.* gleamed in the sunlight. She took it to the window seat and perched on the faded red upholstery. Then she opened the box and carefully took out the journal.

It was a small fat notebook, much worn. The covers were black cloth, stained with greasy fingermarks. It had clearly once been badly damaged by fire – the edges of later pages were crisped brown and in places whole chunks were burned away.

She opened it. The handwriting was spiky and formal, in flowing brown ink. It was difficult to read at first, until her eyes got used to it. Venn must have made a transcript long ago. But she didn't have time to find that – she'd have to do her best with this.

It was amazing to be holding it here, in her hands.

She read the first page.

December 1846

My name is John Harcourt Symmes. On this day I begin my book of the Chronoptika.

The details of all the processes are in the appendix; my notes on the obtaining of the precious metals and the meteoric materials will be found in the red leather binders which accompany this. Here, I propose to record only my personal observations and the details of every demonstration I conduct with the device, every success and failure, because I have learned that to fail is as important as to succeed. I am determined to write everything down. I am not afraid. It will be a tragedy for the world to lose what I have discovered.

Sarah glanced up. The grandfather clock whirred; now it chimed, eleven soft notes. Piers was busy; Venn out. She had time. She curled up on the window seat and read quickly.

Jake sat on a bench in the cloister. He leaned his head back against the cold stone and shivered, because the morning was bitterly cold. But he needed to think.

Of course Sarah had seen the face in the mirror. So why deny it? Was she scared? Of Venn?

And who was she? Certainly not Piers's niece.

Something tapped his boot and he glanced down quickly. A brown hen cocked its head and looked at him with one bright eye.

'Buk,' it said.

Jake jerked his foot and the hen squawked away.

He needed to find his father's room. There might be something there, some message left for him, some clue . . . He needed to act, not sit here and let the ghost-face and his father's terrified voice eat into his energy.

Venn. Surely he had heard that.

A door clicked. He jumped up and scrambled behind a pillar just as Venn came into the cloister. He wore a long coat, and strode quickly down the arcade, his tall shape flickering through the trefoiled arches. At the end he unlocked an iron-bolted door and ducked out, into the grounds.

Jake moved out stealthily after him. Here was a chance to get him alone. Outside. Make him answer.

Beyond the door was a flight of stone steps. Venn was already down them, brushing through the wintry wastes of a herb garden, the frost-blackened twigs snapping as he passed. Sharp scents of last summer's lavender came to Jake as he slipped along the path. At the end was an iron gate; Venn opened it and it clanged behind him.

Reaching it, Jake saw Venn enter the Wood.

He closed the gate but the clank made him look down, and he saw that the whole thing was hung with metal objects. Rusty bells and crosses, knives, even a broken pair of shears clattered against each other like some bizarre charm bracelet. He stared at them, noting the iron strip hammered down across the threshold.

What was Venn keeping out?

He ran to the edge of the Wood, and crept in. It was dank and chilly. Venn was far ahead; Jake slunk after him, wishing he'd brought a coat. The track led down between gnarled bare oaks, their heaped leaves slabbed with frozen puddles. He stepped on one; it wheezed and cracked.

Venn looked back.

Jake froze, deep in shadow, praying the low sun

would be in the man's eyes. After a moment Venn turned and walked on. Jake followed more warily. Now, he didn't want to catch up. He wanted to see where Venn was going.

What if his father was being held prisoner somewhere in the Wood? If Venn was heading there now?

The path led deep into green gloom. Soon it was no more than a narrow trail, soft with humps and hollows. He slowed, eyes and ears alert. The Wood darkened around him. It had become a thicket of thorns and brambles, impassable; above him the canopy of branches a closed lacework against the sky. Great roots sprawled across the track; he could hear only his own breath and the soft trickle of water in some hidden ditch to his left. His foot splashed in a muddy spring.

Breathless, he stopped. Venn was too far ahead to see.

Suddenly panicky, he turned. To his astonishment there was no way back. Branches clustered behind him; he took a step towards them. Brambles blocked his way. He reached out and pushed them and they snagged at his hand.

This hadn't been here before.

Was he even facing the right way?

Strange disorientation came over him; he had no idea which way was forward or back, in or out, north or south, as if the Wood had wriggled and twisted. Even the air was as dank and smoky as a November night, though it had been a sunny morning outside.

'What's going on?' he whispered. 'Where is this?'

'This is the Wintercombe, mortal. And you're inside it.'

Jake turned, fast. A boy of his own age was leaning against a tree-trunk. He wore a lichen-green tail-coat and his skin was as pale as ivory.

'What did you call me?' Jake demanded.

The boy smiled a bitter smile. 'You heard. I called you *mortal*.'

CHAPTER EIGHT

He was as cold as far Iceland,

His heart a frozen splinter.

He was as dangerous as the dark

   On the deepest night of winter.

            Ballad of Lord Winter and Lady Summer

All my life I have been an enquirer after strange and singular knowledge.

I was orphaned early; my father, Charles Harcourt Symmes, being killed in an uprising in India. I was left a child alone with his fortune – wealth gained from the slavery of men and women in his factories and mines; their squalid lives in his cholera-ridden slums. What can you do to rid money of such dark origins? As soon as I came of age I sold everything and had the houses torn down, but perhaps my doom was already fixed. My life already cursed.

Certainly my career at Oxford was not a success. I was a lonely, bookish student. I had the money to fill my rooms with arcane volumes and pursue research into subjects that would have shocked my professors. I attended no parties, did no punting on the river. I worked steadily and gained my degree, but made no friends, and after I had left, I doubt many in the ancient town ever knew I had been there.

I bought a large house in London and began my pursuit of dreadful secrets. The truth is, I lived two lives. By day I was a member of polite society. I attended meetings of scientific academies, was to all appearances a young amateur gentleman about town. My interests were in the new wonders, the electric experiments of Galvani, the hypnotic mysteries of Mesmer. I was calm, quiet, popular with the ladies. I was known as a collector of phonographs and chronographs and all the modern paraphernalia of science. My only eccentricity was believing the earth might be hollow.

But by night!

By night I was a tortured soul.

It is true that my mother died in an asylum for the insane. I never knew her, but perhaps I inherited her corrupted blood. How else can I explain how I have such a dark shadow inside me?

The city made me evil. Something about the lurid twilights of London, the slow lighting of gas lamps down the

111

Strand, worked the change in me. As soon as darkness fell I would put on a long cloak and leave the house, walking till the early hours. I roamed the teeming streets of the poorer districts, flitted down the dank, unspeakable alleys of Soho, explored the warrens of filth that were Wapping and Whitechapel.

I desired secrets. Magic. The occult arts of darkness. I desired to enter the deepest depravities of the soul, down ways too terrible for science and too unholy for religion. Above all I desired power – over men and women and beasts. A power only I, of all the world, would possess.

Sarah looked up. A door had opened somewhere in the house. Frozen, she heard Wharton's steady tread squeak past the door of the study. She waited a while, but there was no other sound. She leaned further into the narrowing sliver of cold sunlight. This was it. This was where it had begun.

I dare not write much of this, lest you think me mad. I made expeditions to the corpse-yards of London, so heaped with the dead that the ground oozed with their reek. I explored deep crypts, assisted in dissecting the bodies of gallows-hanged murderers. I joined weird sects and strange covens. I allowed vampyric women to feed on me. And all the time I sought my own secret source of power, and found only cheats and charlatans and depraved souls.

Until I met the scarred man.

It was an obvious question but Jake had to ask it. 'If I'm a mortal, what are you?'

The boy straightened. A flicker of amusement crossed his pale face. 'That's my business. I'm curious about you. I watched you all come to the Dwelling last night, first the girl, then you and the big man. Venn doesn't let strangers in, so who are you?'

Jake said, 'The girl? Last night?'

The boy shrugged. 'In your world, last night . . . I saw her hunted by a wolf. A wolf of frost and snow . . . So, why do you follow Venn into the Wood? He must have warned you . . .'

Jake said shortly, 'Maybe that's *my* business.' He wanted to hurry back, get away with the surprising knowledge that Sarah was a stranger here too, but the boy stepped in front of him. 'You can't. There's no way back without my help.'

Eye to eye they measured each other. Then the boy said, 'Gideon.'

'Jake Wilde.'

Gideon's green eyes widened in sharp understanding.

113

'So you're the son!'

In the twilit forest the moon was a silver fingernail through the branches. Jake's hands gripped into fists. 'You know about my father?'

'Only what I've heard. They don't tell me anything. She and Venn, they keep the secrets.' Elegant, he flipped his coat tails and sat on a fallen branch. His hands, Jake saw, were as brown and lichen-stained as the bark of the trees.

Jake took a breath. 'Is he . . . do you know if my father is dead?'

Gideon shrugged. 'He's not dead, weakbrain. He went *journeying* . . . And they can't get him back.'

It happened like this. In November 1846 I was passing a small shop in Seven Dials and heard a tap on the window. I stopped and turned. Between the stuffed heads of a fox and a badger in the window a wizened Asian man of some ancient age was beckoning to me.

I looked around, but as it was indeed me he seemed to mean, I went in.

The shop stank of glue and unknown potions. It was dark, and on every shelf glassy-eyed beasts stared out in hideous rigidity. Great stags loomed from the walls. Under domes, mummified birds were fixed in unfluttering flight.

114

I said, 'Such things hold no interest for me.' I turned to go, but he reached out a hand like a dried claw and laid it on my sleeve. I shook him off – I confess it – with a shudder.

'Death and life,' he whispered. 'The arrest of Time's decay. These things hold no interest for sir?'

I looked at the fellow. 'Perhaps. But . . .'

'Sir requires more than the captured life, the feathers and the bones. Sir requires, perhaps, a machine.'

A thud went through my heart. 'What machine?'

He shrugged, an insolent gesture. 'A device of great power. So strange and terrible, only an adept of the deepest arcana might dare to use it. One such as yourself.'

This was surely a ruse to rob me. And yet there was something in the dark gleam of the man's eye that ensnared me.

I looked round. 'Where is it?'

'Not here.'

'The price?'

'It is not mine to sell.' He leaned over and pressed a small token into my hand. 'Tonight, at eight, sir must go to Solomon's Court, off Charnel House Alley. Find the house with the pentangle. Show this token. And you will see.'

Then he turned and walked into the shadows of the shop.

Outside, on the wet pavement, I gazed at the thing in my hand. It was one half of a gold coin – a Greek stater, with the face of Zeus, his nose and eyes cut jaggedly away . . .

115

Jake said, 'What do you mean? Journeyed where?'

But before he could ask any more a glitter of light flashed deep in the Wood. Gideon leaped up – a movement so fleeting that he seemed to vanish and reappear in the same instant. He grabbed Jake and hauled him down among the nettles and bracken. 'They're coming! If they see you here they'll take you. Don't even breathe.'

Astonished, Jake curled in the bracken. The urgency in the boy's voice was all too real. He kept still, cold mud soaking his knees and fingers.

No one came. He glanced at Gideon; in the moss-green gloom he seemed perfectly camouflaged, though they crouched right next to each other. Gideon pointed, through the trees.

Jake turned. A tiny shimmer caught his eye. He stared at it; saw a patch of glossy leaf, a lichened tree-trunk.

And it became them.

He breathed in, felt Gideon's warning grip.

They were almost people.

Where they had come from he couldn't tell; they were so much part of the shadow and the foliage. Tall and pale, male and female, it was as if they had always been there, and just some adjustment of the light had revealed them to him. Their faces were narrow and beautiful, their hair silvery-fair. They sat and lounged and leaned on branches or fallen logs, their clothes a crazy collection of fashions and fabrics, green and gold, modern and aged and patched. Their speech, from here, was the murmur of bees.

'Who are they?' he whispered.

Gideon was silent. Then he put his lips to Jake's ear. 'Don't be fooled. They look like angels but they're demons. They're the Shee.'

Jake had no idea what that meant. But he did know, quite suddenly, that this was no longer his world. The twilit Wood was impossible, because it was only midday, and the moon that hung here unmoving should not be so young. His glance flickered. He saw oak leaves and rowan berries, and the flowers of creamy meadowsweet, all together, every season at once.

And yet it was winter.

Then, along the path, a young woman came walking. She strolled out of mist, wearing a brief, simple black dress. Her hair was black too, cropped short. Silver glinted at her ears. Her feet were bare, her lips red. She seemed about eighteen.

Behind her, to Jake's astonishment, strode Venn.

The girl came to the Shee and turned lightly on her toes. She sat on a fallen log with her knees up and smiled as Venn stood over her and snapped, 'If that's all you'll do for me . . .'

'Why should I do more? What do I care about any human woman?'

'She's my wife.' His voice was low, as if he fought to keep it steady.

'Was. She *was*.' The girl smiled, heartless. 'And as you boasted yourself, you don't need me any more. You have your precious *machine*.'

He shook his head. 'I was wrong to say that. The machine . . .'

'. . . is a failure.' She laughed, stretching out her bare foot. 'I know. A chaos of forces that you have no chance of controlling. It's already cost you your friend . . . now you'll experiment on this new girl. How long before she, too, disappears from your world?'

'I don't care about the girl.' He watched her, his eyes cold. 'Are you really still so jealous?'

'Of a dead woman?' She laughed, and some of the Shee laughed with her. It was a sound like the ripple of a hidden stream, and there was no humour in it. It chilled Jake. 'Why should I be jealous?' She stretched out her hand and touched Venn's face. 'I could bring you back to us at any moment I choose. Is that what you want, Venn? To come home?'

He stepped back. He said quietly, 'I don't need you, Summer. Leave the girl alone. The boy too. Leave all of us alone.'

She stood, graceful and slender. 'How can I do that, Venn? Light and Shadow. Sun and Moon. The winter king and the queen of summer. We belong together and we always have. You know you can never exist without me.'

He glared angrily at her, but at the same instant Jake's hand slid in the mud. A twig cracked.

The Shee turned like cats.

Summer was still. Then she took a step forward on her bare feet, and lifted her hand and pointed directly at him. 'Who dares to spy on me?'

It was a whisper of venom. The hairs on Jake's neck prickled. Her eyes were dark as an animal's, without anything he recognized as human.

Then Gideon muttered, 'Leave a window open for me,' and stood up, leaves and dust falling from him. He walked out among the Shee.

'I do, Summer. Just me.'

Summer watched him. She let him come close, with no change of expression. She said softly, 'Anyone else, Gideon, would pay dearly for that.'

'I know.' He glanced at Venn. 'I'm sorry. Just curious.'

'Well, as it's you, I forgive you. As the cat forgives the sparrow. As the owl forgives the mouse.'

Gideon gasped. As Jake watched, he crumpled as if the breath had been struck out of him by a terrible blow; with a cry he fell on hands and knees into the forest mud, gasping and retching.

Venn said, 'Stop that!'

'So you do have some feelings for them.' Summer came and stood over Gideon. 'I envy you, Venn. Most times, they just bore me.'

Gideon kinked and squirmed in agony. His fists gripped mud. Jake wanted to leap out and stand there shouting, 'Not him. Me,' but he didn't, because Gideon gave a low, dragging moan and lay still.

Summer bent over him. She put her arms around him. She kissed him, over and over, on the hair, the forehead, the eyes, and her remorse was sudden and baffling. 'Dear child. Sweet child. Help him everyone. Help him up.'

The Shee clustered like flies. Their thin hands pulled at Gideon, tugged leaves from his hair. Their fingers, delicate as antennae, felt and picked at his clothes.

Then Venn dragged him away. 'Get your vermin off him. Let him alone.'

Gideon gasped in breath. He seemed still dizzy with the shock of pain, but he stood upright and tense, as if ready for anything that might come next, and Jake realized that there was no such thing as safety in Gideon's world.

Summer's mood changed with breathtaking speed. 'Time to go.' Now she was coy and amused. She took Gideon's hand and dragged him down the path. *'Come away, O human child, To the waters and the wild* . . . Goodbye, Venn.' She blew him a kiss, walking backwards. 'Guard your lovely machine, Venn. Guard your darling children. Lock your doors and enchant your thresholds, Venn. Because one day, very soon, we will get in.'

He said, 'Not on my watch.'

She vanished. They all vanished.

Jake just couldn't see them any more. It was as if they had turned sideways and slipped through some slit in the air, even Gideon. Become sunshine and shadow.

Only Venn stood in the clearing, ankle-deep in nettles.

For a moment he waited, as if making sure he was alone.

Then he turned, towards Jake. 'Get up,' he snarled. 'Let's get out of here.'

Sarah flicked over a few pages, desperately impatient. The paper had been rubbed with fingermarks, as if it had been read over and over. The writing was spiky and jagged with excitement.

* * *

. . . dank and dismal. Even with my experiences of the filthy rookeries of the city I found it fouler than foul. The cabman I had hired said, 'Are you sure about this, guv?'

'Sure,' I said. 'But remember. Thirty minutes, no more. My life may depend on it.'

He nodded at me and said, 'Trust me, I'm no tommyflit.' Then he turned the cab and the horse clopped away into the night.

I groped down the alley, cane in hand, slipping in the running sewage, holding my handkerchief firmly to my face. Even so, the stench was stomach-churning. I came to an opening in the dingy wall and a solitary gas lamp flickered over the sign. SOLOMON'S COURT.

Excitement made my heart thump. I fingered the half-coin in my pocket, and the loaded revolver next to it. Then I edged into the courtyard.

It was black as pitch. The houses – or warehouses – reared high into the fog. My footsteps seemed to shuffle and multiply in the enclosed space, as if there were others here, behind me.

The pentangle was scratched on the wall beside a very small door down a few steps running with noisome liquids. I descended carefully, and rapped on the wood with my cane.

I was breathless with excitement and avid for danger. These moments were what I lived for.

The door opened.

A sickly smell enfolded me, which I recognized immediately as opium. It was a vice I had sampled, but I loathed the way it robbed men of their intelligence, and had long abandoned it. I ducked inside. A stout woman in a red dress held out her hand. She no doubt expected money, but I handed her the broken coin. She brought it close to her eyes, and then, seeing what it was, thrust it back at me with almost a hiss of fear.

'Follow me,' she croaked.

The den was crowded, heaps of rags that were men and women lying sprawled, the pipes through which they took the drug spilling from their fingers. Some moaned. I wondered in what nightmare of horrors their souls wandered. The woman brought me to a dismal corner at the back; she pulled a heavy curtain aside and stepped back, gesturing me to go on. I groped my way along a stinking corridor, and at the end, found an open door. Beyond that, a room.

A small fire burned in a dark grate. Next to it a man rose to meet me.

He was the strangest of creatures. A handsome dark-haired man, until he turned, and the flamelight revealed a jagged scar down the left side of his face, a terrible curve, as if some sword had slashed it. His eyes were dark as a rat's, his hair long, his hands delicate and slender. He lifted one, and *held it out; I gave him the half-coin and he spared it one glance, slipping it into his pocket.*

'Mr John Harcourt Symmes,' he said. His voice was curiously husky.

I bowed. 'You know of me, sir?'

His calm stare unnerved me. He said . . .

'Sarah! Are you in here?'

A banging on the door. Sarah jumped. The sun had gone and the window seat was icy. She shoved the journal into her pocket and hustled the box back quickly into the drawer.

'Sarah!'

'Yes . . . wait . . . coming,' she yelled, then hurtled out through the door. Straight into Wharton.

He gasped. The girl had run out without warning. There was a crash and a flutter. He looked down and saw the newspaper with a small fat black-backed journal lying splayed on top of it on the wooden floorboards.

'I'm so sorry,' he began, and she said, 'No it's me . . .'

They both dived for the papers but Wharton was quicker; politely he picked up the notebook and arranged its scattered and damaged pages to smooth order. Words and phrases caught his eye. He stopped, turned back.

Surely he had seen . . .

. . . *Chronoptika* . . .

He looked up. Sarah had the newspaper and her face was flushed. She handed it back to him, quickly. 'Yours.'

'Piers's really.' He took it. Then he said, 'Sarah, listen. I've just read an article in here and your photo is . . .'

'Please.' She looked up at him with blue, urgent eyes. 'Don't tell anyone. I mean outside the house.'

'Venn knows?'

She nodded. 'I ran away because I'm not mad . . . I'm not violent. I just need some time to sort myself out. Where they can't find me.'

Wharton felt deeply uneasy. What was Venn doing harbouring a girl so disturbed? He shrugged. 'Well, it's none of my business. I'm just en route to Shepton Mallet.' He realized he was still holding the journal, and she was looking at it with an anxious, hungry look. He held it out. 'Yours.'

She took it, just too quickly. He said, 'Have you seen Jake?'

'Not since earlier. We managed to break a mirror.' She moved to go past him, then paused. As if she'd made up her mind she said, 'Mr Wharton, do you think his father is really dead?'

Wharton folded the paper absently. 'I have no idea.

But if he is, I don't think Venn murdered him.'

She looked at him calmly. 'Neither do I.'

'That makes three of us,' Piers said, behind them.

They turned and saw he was standing at the end of the corridor watching them, a black cat tucked under his arm. He grinned his sidelong grin.

'Lunch is served.'

CHAPTER NINE

What is a reflection? Where doth it exist . . . in the eye, or in the glasse? What properties in the light return us to our selves? Is it divine revelation, or doth the devyl taunt us with our imperfections?

Above all, this. How can any man be certayn that what he sees in the mirror is true?

The Scrutiny of Secrets by Mortimer Dee

'That was delicious,' Wharton said.

'So glad you enjoyed it.' Piers piled the dishes on a tray.

'I'll take those,' Sarah said, quickly. She took the tray and went out with it. She hadn't eaten much, Wharton thought, and she had seemed tense, on edge. Once, when something had howled far off in the Wood, she had almost jumped, and gone over to the window and stared out at the bleak day for a long time . . . People must be looking for her. Really, he ought just to phone the police.

He said, 'I'm sorry Jake is so late. He's a bit . . . preoccupied.'

Piers nodded. 'Secretive?'

'Most certainly.'

'Hell to teach?'

'Believe me, you have no idea.' Wharton stirred his coffee. 'So . . . Mr Piers. It must be pleasant having your niece here working with you.'

Piers's smile never flickered. Today he was wearing a butler's outfit, smoothly black over a red waistcoat, the tail-coat ridiculously long. He had already tripped over it once. 'Most pleasant, yes.' Now he leaned against the table.

They gazed at each other; it was Wharton who broke first. He tapped the newspaper, suddenly impatient. 'It's odd then that there's a picture of a girl in here who looks just like Sarah. A young woman who's absconded from . . .'

'I saw that.' Piers swept up the crumbs smoothly. 'An amazing resemblance. They say everyone in the world has a double, you know. A sort of reflection of oneself.'

'Do they?'

'Of course this other poor girl who's run away . . . we

don't know what she's running from. Those places must be hell. Not that His Excellency would care. He's not the sort to hide fugitives.'

'Unless she could be of some use to him.'

Piers smiled, but it was a brittle effort. 'Yes. Unless that.' His gaze fixed on the window. 'Ah. Here they are.'

Wharton stood and saw Venn stride swiftly out of the Wood, and to his surprise, Jake stalk behind him, obviously freezing, and even more obviously, furious.

Piers turned hastily. 'Whoops. I fear lunch might not be wanted, I'll just take the rest of the dishes down . . .' Wharton held the door open for him and he stepped out with the tray, vanishing discreetly as Venn barged into the entrance hall in an icy draught that gusted right up the corridor. Jake hurtled after him, mid-shout . . .

'I'll make you talk to me! First off, you lied. All right, maybe you didn't kill him. But you know what happened to him. This machine she was talking about . . .'

'He's not dead. He's lost.'

'Then find him. You're the explorer. You can't just—'

'*Jake.*' It was the first time Venn had used his name. It stopped him. He saw that the tall man had turned at the bottom of the stairs, one hand on the bannister, at bay like a trapped animal. 'Jake, listen to me. Your father is

129

lost. He's not here. He's not anywhere I can find him. He's lost in time.'

Jake shook his head. 'What sort of rubbish is that?'

'I wish it was. I wish to God I had never meddled with it. But I did and now I have to go on. Whatever it costs.' He looked weary and haggard, Wharton thought. No, *haunted*. He looked like a man who sees a ghost in every mirror. Except that there were no mirrors in this house.

Venn turned away. 'I'll talk to you about this later.'

'You'll talk to me now!' Jake leaped up the stairs, right up to the man, so close that Wharton hurried forward. He had seen too many schoolboy brawls not to recognize the sudden urge for violence.

Venn didn't move. His eyes were as cold as winter. 'I should get rid of you,' he breathed.

There was a terrible moment of silence.

Until the phone rang. It erupted like a small explosion in the charged air.

They all looked at the old black telephone on its shelf in the hall, as if they barely remembered what it was.

Then Piers had slid out of the kitchen and was answering, the abruptly cut-off ringing still echoing in the high vaulted ceiling.

'Wintercombe Abbey,' he said, his voice prim and high. 'Yes. Yes . . . Certainly. One moment please.' He turned to Jake and held out the receiver. 'It's for you.'

Jake stared. Then he came and took it. At once Venn stalked up the stairs and slammed a distant door. Piers glanced at Wharton and went back to the kitchen. After a moment, awkward, Wharton took himself off up the stairs too. At the landing he paused and looked down. Jake was talking quietly into the receiver.

Thank God for whoever that was.

Because, for a moment there, it had all looked very nasty.

'Sorry? Who is this?' Jake snapped.

'You don't know me, Mr Wilde, so my name would mean nothing to you. But I have some information for you. Something you might dearly want to know . . .'

The voice was a man's, quiet, faintly husky.

Jake leaned with his back against the panelled wall. 'Like what?'

There was a small breathy silence at the other end. A scratchy sound. Then the voice said, 'I know where your father is.'

Jake kept very still. His hand shook a little, as if he was holding the receiver too tight. He said, 'Where?'

'I can't tell you that over the phone. The line might not be secure . . . You understand?'

131

Another scratchy sound. Was someone listening in? Piers? Jake said, 'Yes . . . OK. But how do you know . . .'

'I'm calling from the village. From the car park of the pub. Can you get here?'

'Yes, but . . .'

'Come at once, Mr Wilde. Come alone. Then I assure you, I will explain everything.'

A click.

Silence.

He replaced the receiver slowly and looked round. Should he find Wharton? No time. And he didn't want the hassle. He grabbed a coat that hung on a peg and went to the front door. It was warped with damp, and stiff; he pulled at it, but Piers said softly, 'Going out again, Jake?'

He swung round, fast. 'Maybe.'

The tiny, smiling man gave him the creeps. Always that mocking grin. As if he knew so much.

'It's just that Mr Venn would rather you didn't leave the estate at the moment. In your state of mind . . .'

'Venn, or you?' Jake stepped forward. 'Who's really running this place, Piers? Because you seem to be the one in control around here.'

'I assure you, I'm just the slave of the lamp. The controller of the cameras.'

Jake was simmering, but he had to keep calm. He managed a bitter shrug. 'I get it. So that's how it is.'

'That, I'm afraid, is how it is. I'm sure by tomorrow, you'll be feeling a little better about things.'

'You can't keep me a prisoner here.'

Piers shrugged. 'It was you who wanted to come, Jake.'

Jake snorted. He walked past him, down a corridor lined with vases, not knowing or caring where he was going, striding round a corner and past a door that opened. A hand came out and grabbed him. 'Jake. In here.'

Sarah looked worried. She stood in the dim scullery and whispered, 'What's going on? You and Venn . . . ?'

'Forget him. Sarah, listen, I need your help. Someone in the village has information about Dad. How do I get out of here without Piers knowing?'

'You have to be invisible,' she said softly.

'What?'

'Nothing. Sorry. Well, there's a side door that leads out by the Wintercombe. But the gates at the end of the drive will be locked, and Piers . . .'

'I'll climb them. I don't care if he sees me. Show me.'

She led him through a tiny stillroom to a black-studded door. It took both of them to grind back the rusty bolts; when it creaked open they found they were looking into shrubbery that had grown thickly over the door. Jake suddenly remembered what Gideon had said, and stared at her curiously. 'I know you only came here yesterday. How did you know about this?'

She shrugged, irritated. The movement slid a small medal on a chain around her neck. It was one half of what seemed to be a broken coin. 'Maybe I know this place better than you think. Jake, listen! Try and get back before eight. I need to talk to you, because . . .'

He slipped out, impatient. 'Because you lied about not seeing my father in that mirror? Get out of my way, Sarah. Tell me later.'

He had to hurry. Whoever made that call might not wait.

He was gone before she could explain, rustling into the dimness. Annoyed, she spared one glance around for traces of the wolf and then slid back in and closed the door, making sure the bolts were rammed tight. He was breathtakingly selfish. She needed an ally here. Someone to talk to.

She made herself stay calm. It was his loss. Because she would have shown him the journal. She kept it stuffed in her pocket now, afraid to leave it in her room, since Wharton had seen it.

And because she was afraid Janus would come looking for it.

She crept down past the kitchen and into the room called the Blue Closet. There she perched in a faded chair and looked at the gilt French clock, as it pinged out three high notes. She had five hours, before . . . what?

The Chronoptika?

Suddenly cold, she pulled out the book and hastily found her place.

I said, 'As you see, I've come.'

The scarred man nodded. 'I was quite sure you would, Mr Symmes. And I have the device, which, I assure you, is quite unique in this world.'

He indicated a veiled object on a table in the darkness, and moved an oil lamp, so that the slot of light fell across it. My eyes fixed on it, and I dare say my greed was perfectly visible to him. I whispered, 'What is it?'

He did not answer. Instead he drew away the velvet cloth.

I saw a black slab. At first I thought it stone, but then as I moved a thousand reflections of myself slid across it and vanished, and I realized it was glass, black glass, high as a man, smooth as a mirror. As I stepped closer I saw my features strangely slanted and shadowed. It was held upright in a narrow frame of silver, an angular design incised with letters of some alphabet unknown to me.

The man said, 'It is pure obsidian. Volcanic glass forged in the deepest furnaces of the earth.'

I was fascinated. I went to touch the mirror but he forestalled me, quickly putting out his hand. 'Not yet.'

I drew back. He waved me to a chair, but I remained on my feet. 'How is a mere mirror a device of great power?' I asked, careful to sound casual. 'Or do you and your confederate think to make a gull of me?'

He just gazed at me. His eyes were dark, his face half demon, half angel. I confess I found myself so mesmerized my voice died to a pitiful silence.

Standing before the mirror he said, 'Let me explain. Some years ago, while clearing ground for building work in a remote district of London, workmen struck stone. Eagerly they uncovered it, and found a tomb. And then another. They had stumbled on a small, forgotten graveyard belonging to some long-demolished church. The tombs were ancient, their very existence lost. There was talk of plague-pits, of disease, and lurking horrors. The men refused to dig further and their employers became uneasy. So they called me in.'

'Why you?'

He smiled. 'Because, sir, I am a specialist in moving the dead.'

I thought then he must be a gallows-crow. A body-snatcher. One who robs graves for the insatiable anatomists of London's hospitals. I said, 'I see. But there would be nothing . . . fresh . . . there, surely?'

His dragging smile. 'The owners wanted the site cleared. I desired knowledge . . . Does that surprise you? Maybe you are a mere amateur in the dark arts, Mr Symmes. I am not. In that place I opened many unusual graves. Monks and nuns, soldiers and merchants. But one tomb was special. In it, I found this.'

His hand went out and gently caressed the mirror frame. I felt a shiver of jealousy, as if it was already mine.

'It was buried with a body?'

'No. That was the strange thing. There was no body, not even the smallest fragment of bone. But the tomb slab had a few words still legible upon it, including the name MORTIMER DEE and below that ALCHEMIST AND PHILOSOPHER. Alchemist was a word that interested me deeply. The grave I would date from the 1660s or perhaps earlier.'

I stared, astonished, at this beggarly man who could read and who spoke like some scholar and yet was obviously a practised rogue. Then I walked cautiously round the mirror. It gave a disconcerting twist to my reflection, as if some other Harcourt Symmes peered out of it. 'And what does it do?' He gazed at me. For a moment I thought I saw the depths of a

137

great despair in him. He said, 'It allows a man to walk through the doorway we call Time.'

Sarah looked up. She gazed out at the darkening estate where the wolf and its handler waited for her.

'And make a hole in the world,' she whispered.

Jake kept out of the Wood. Whatever the Shee were, he had seen enough of them. He half expected Gideon to be waiting for him behind some oak tree, but the drive was dim and gloomy and only the rooks looked down at him with their beady eyes.

He ran. It was already getting dark; the brief December day fading to a smoky twilight. Tomorrow was the shortest day, the solstice. Dad's birthday. Dad always said it was his luck to have less daylight than anyone else, and to be so close to Christmas. He'd always insisted on having breakfast in bed to make up for it. Jake had had to bring it up on a tray – toast, usually burned, and black coffee. Once, when he was about nine, he'd put a picture of Mum on there and a rose in a thin vase, but his father had just put those aside and said, 'Nice try, old man,' and crunched the toast.

What was the point of remembering that now?

He raced all the way up the foggy drive, stopping only

to gasp for breath, sure he was watched. The bare tree branches interlaced over his head. Finally he saw the dark metalwork of the gates emerge from the fog.

He avoided the small camera. It clicked and whirred – maybe Piers was searching for him. The fog was lucky; curling out of the damp ground, it would keep him hidden. He climbed the wall, his boots scraping against the mossy bricks, and jumped down the other side into the lane.

Then he took out his mobile and called Rebecca.

Wharton stood rigid on the landing.

Of course he totally disapproved of eavesdropping, but there was no way he was missing this.

Piers and Venns' voices were muffled by a heavy black baize door. He approached it carefully, praying the floorboards wouldn't creak. He kept still, his hand on the doorknob, and glanced back up the Long Gallery. Then he crouched and put his eye to the keyhole.

'I should throw you into the river!' Venn was pacing, glaring at Piers. 'Are you mad or just stupid? You bring these people here now, just when we're ready, when we've found a subject . . .'

'I didn't know that when I sent the e-mail. Besides, it was David. I was thinking of David.' Piers came up to

Venn and sat on the floor before him, squatting like some eastern sage. It was a posture that astonished Wharton. 'Think, Excellency! The boy is a connection to his father. That might be vital. It seems clear that the device responds to emotion as much as anything else.'

'It doesn't respond to mine.' Venn's voice was bleak. He moved; for a moment Wharton saw only blackness blocking the keyhole. Then Venn was slumped in a chair by the window. He drew his hand through his tangle of hair. He looked weary.

Piers crouched by him. 'I worry about us using the girl.'

'Not that again!'

'We might lose her too. We have no right to put her in such danger.'

'Don't we?' Venn's voice was so low Wharton had to press against the keyhole to hear. 'There's no other way. After David went . . . I dare not use it on myself . . . If I vanish in there before we can calibrate it I'll never see Leah again. Otherwise it would be me. You know that.'

'But a girl we don't even know.'

Venn looked up, staring at the door so intently Wharton jerked back, suddenly sure those ice-blue eyes could see straight through to him. 'That's the strange thing. I do know her. As soon as I saw her, I felt as if I did. I can't explain it. But if it's her life against even the chance of getting Leah back I'll take the risk a hundred times over. There's nothing I wouldn't do, Piers, no one I wouldn't sacrifice! And remember, you work for me. I own you, body and soul, and you will do whatever I say.'

He was out of the chair and striding towards the door.

Wharton leaped back, looked desperately round for somewhere to hide. There was an alcove with a curtain across it; he dived behind it and stood there, the dusty folds against his nose and mouth. Even as he was trying not to sneeze Venn swept past him, the curtain billowing.

He waited. He heard a click, as if Piers had followed his master into the corridor. Then the small man said, 'Wharton knows about her.'

Venn answered but Wharton didn't hear the words . . . His heart was beating too loudly. Then a distant door slammed, but a few creaks of the boards told him Piers hadn't gone. Carefully he edged the curtain aside and put one eye to the slit. The small alert figure was standing only feet away, with a laptop in his hands, but he wasn't looking at it.

He was listening.

His eyes were bright.

Wharton shuffled back into the darkness.

Piers turned instantly towards the curtain. 'Sarah? Is that you?'

He waited a moment, then walked over and tugged the material aside.

The alcove was empty.

Rebecca pulled the car up near the bridge and dimmed the headlights. 'Here?'

'It'll do. He must be parked up in the pub yard.'

They both gazed out. 'Look at it!' she muttered.

The fog had thickened as night fell. Now it was a grey swirling freezing mass against the windows, even the village lights reduced to barest pinpoints. 'I can't see any car. I can't see anything.'

'He's there.' Jake opened the door but she said quickly, 'Oh, I don't like this. It's scary . . . Maybe I should come with you.'

'I have to go alone.' He was already outside. 'Thanks for the lift. I can find my own way back.'

'You must be joking.' Rebecca leaned over and turned music on, a blast of rock. 'I'm not going anywhere. Look, I'll give you ten minutes, then I'll drive in next to you. Or sooner, if you scream.'

He managed a smile. She was so excited, in her tilted blue beret. 'OK, Superwoman. You can come in and rescue me.' He slammed the door, turned his collar up against the freezing night and walked towards the car park.

It was a grey vacancy. He felt he was walking into nothingness, into nowhere, that he might crash into a wall or a door or stride off the edge of the earth and fall for ever . . .

Headlights flashed, once, to his right.

He groped towards them and found a vehicle – something low and dark, but he couldn't even see the make, or find the handle, until a door swung open and the husky voice said, 'Please get in, Mr Wilde.'

He hesitated. Then he slid into the warm interior.

The stranger in the driver's seat clicked on the inner light. He was a dark-haired man, astonishingly handsome, until he turned, and Jake saw the scar that furrowed the left side of his face.

'So you came, Jake,' he said.

CHAPTER TEN

I felt most uneasy. I was in a desolate place and only the cabman knew my whereabouts. But I kept my voice calm. 'I fail to see how one can walk in Time.'

'One thousand guineas, Mr Symmes.'

'This is ridiculous. Do I look such a gull? It is simply a mirror.'

'Buy, or leave. Others will be desperate for it.'

An old line; I put on a scoffing look, but I was tormented. The name of Mortimer Dee was known to me – he had been an astrologer in the reign of Elizabeth. Anything belonging to him was of great interest. But a thousand guineas! I said, 'Five hundred.'

He came close, his face twisted in sudden anguish. 'I'm not here to bargain! Do you think I would sell this treasure to a fool like you if I wasn't utterly so deep in danger I cannot survive!'

Affronted, I stepped back. 'Very well.' We would see who was the fool. I put my hand to the revolver in my pocket.

But at that moment, in the next room, a woman screamed.

Journal of John Harcourt Symmes

Jake knew at once he shouldn't have come. The situation prickled with danger. He said, 'Where's my father?'

The stranger stared straight ahead. 'On the phone you asked my name. It's Maskelyne. Does that mean anything to you?'

'No.'

'They really have kept you in the dark. You haven't read Symmes's journals?'

'Who's Symmes?'

Maskelyne nodded, weary. 'It's a pity. We could have been useful to each other.'

Jake kept his hand on the door. 'Tell me what you know or I leave now.'

'This place is too public.' Before Jake could even object the man had started the car and was backing swiftly out of the car park into the lane. Jake said, 'I could jump out.'

'You won't.'

He glanced back, imagining Rebecca's total panic.

This wasn't working out as they had planned. 'Where are we going?'

'Nervous, Jake?' Maskelyne glanced across. 'Please don't be. Soon, at least one of us will have everything he wants.'

Piers tugged the curtain wider and looked at the empty alcove. Then he balanced the laptop in one arm and tried the handle of the door leading to the Monk's Walk. It opened. He looked inside – a tilted, listening scrutiny. Then he closed the door, locked it securely and walked away.

Wharton watched the small shadow vanish from the gap under the door. He came out from the dimness, took out his handkerchief and mopped his face. Stupid. Stupid! But it would have been so embarrassing to be caught out there peering through keyholes. When he was sure Piers had gone he tugged the door but it didn't move. 'Oh, bloody hell,' he said hopelessly to the darkness.

He was trapped in the Monk's Walk.

He turned. There was a great emptiness at his back, a long stone corridor, with mullioned windows along the right side, the left a bare stone wall running with green damp. Forbidden territory.

He crossed to the nearest window and opened it.

The river ran several metres below, crashing through

its gorge, a surging swollen torrent, leaves and boughs snatched away in its roar. Reflected in it was the moon, a circle fragmented by branches.

No way down.

He looked up the stone arcade. Sarah was in danger – he needed to speak to her and quickly. There must be some other way out. He just had to find it.

Five minutes later he was shivering with cold and totally lost. The remains of the medieval Abbey were tangled under the house – a warren of low halls and cellars, stairs and storerooms. Moonlight slanted in through the few windows, and damp had caused acrid yellow moulds to accumulate over the carvings of faces and wide-winged beasts. Worm-riddled angels regarded him serenely.

And the fog seemed to gather here. The rooms and corridors were full of it. Descending three wide steps, his footsteps loud in the stillness, he came to an archway with the stone mask of a snarling devil on each side. Beyond, wide and dark, seemed to be a vast space. He put his hand up and groped along the wall. Surely there must be some electricity . . .

His fingers found a round switch. He clicked it down. Lights crackled on above him, and then all down the length of a great hall, and he stared in astonishment.

It must once have been a refectory, or maybe the monks' dormitory. Now the pillars were roped with wiring, the roof festooned with cables. Every inch of the floor was cushioned with a layer of soft carpet, so thick his feet almost sank into it. There were banks of storage cabinets; in one corner a powerful generator hummed. But what puzzled him most was the netting. It hung, like the cobweb of an immense spider, from all the vaults and pillars of the room down to the floor, fixed into pinions, stretched rigid. Gazing up he saw that the stuff was like thick wool. It was a dark malachite green, and had a bright, sticky sheen. He reached to touch it, and then stopped, overcome by the ridiculous idea that if he did, he would be glued to it for ever, unable to pull away until Venn came and found him.

Carefully, keeping his head low and his hands at his sides, he ducked under and between the mesh. There was a way that led into it, a clear pathway that twisted and turned back on itself. It reminded him of a maze of box hedges he had once been lost inside as a boy.

It was a labyrinth.

When he finally reached the clear space at its centre, he stared, amazed at the money Venn must have spent on this. State-of-the-art computers, monitors and screens, radiation counters. The area was spotlessly clean, the floor vacuumed dustless.

And in the centre, as if it was the focus of this obsessive attention, a mirror.

He walked around it, considering.

It seemed a slab of black glass, high as a man, wafer-thin, smoothed to perfection, held upright in an ornate silver frame. Cables were attached to it at all four corners. At its back, he stared at a confusion of older machinery – rusting wires, clockwork cogs, some Victorian contraption with a cranking handle and a dial with one snapped finger. As if Venn had imposed modern technology over older.

In a locked glass cabinet next to it he saw a single silver bracelet, resting on a black cushion. Its design was similar to the spiky letters on the frame. Small red lights showed it was alarmed. Wharton didn't touch it.

He came back to the black mirror. His own face, wry and puzzled, confronted him. The mirror was concave, surely; it seemed to be curved, the reflection all wrong, but yet the glass was flat. And the clock face had numbers, but they were not the usual ones.

They said, *1600 1700 1800 1900*.

'What the hell is this?' he whispered.

* * *

Maskelyne swerved the car off the road and into the Wood. They bumped down a track and stopped. He turned the engine off. Sudden silence wrapped them.

Tense, Jake waited.

Maskelyne turned, the leather seat creaking. 'I'll tell you the truth now, Jake, because no one else will. Your father and Venn have been experimenting with a device – a black mirror – that has the property of subverting normal chronology. That is, altering space-time. They've been working on it obsessively. They got it to work and they made a few trials with objects and animals. But then they needed a test with a human. Twice David Wilde volunteered to enter the mirror. The second time, he vanished. Venn and his slave have not been able to get him back. He was, as we say, *journeying*. So I'm afraid your fears are right, in one sense. Your father is dead. Depending on how far back he went, he may have been dead for centuries.'

'That's not possible. How can—'

'I'm afraid it is.' The flat conviction in his voice stunned Jake.

He sat still, numbed. Then he said, 'But how do you . . .'

'. . . I know all this?' Maskelyne stared into the dark trees. 'Because the mirror was mine once. It belonged to me, and it was stolen. And I intend to get it back.'

150

The scream rang out; I moved at once.

As the police whistles split the night I shoved the man aside and grabbed the mirror. He came at me fiercely but I drew my revolver and pointed it at him. 'Back, sir!' I commanded. He stood still.

In the opium den the screeching of the woman was astonishingly loud. A door splintered. Men's voices rang through the squalid court.

My cabman had done his errand well.

The scarred man's face was white with dismay. 'You've betrayed me,' he said.

The device was in my hands and I confess I laughed. 'I'm not such a fool to pay a thousand guineas for a mere warped mirror!' I raised my voice and yelled, 'Help, ho! In here!'

His eyes were black with rage. I knew he would be caught by the peelers, and it would go hard with him, that he would be transported at least for body-snatching, or even climb the gallows.

The door shuddered. A hefty shoulder burst through.

The scarred man stepped towards me and I jerked back in case he had a knife. But all he did was spit words in my face. 'You have no idea how many lives you will destroy by this.'

And then . . . imagine my astonishment! Then he made a rapid run towards the mirror, and as the police crashed in and the door burst wide he threw himself at the glass and into its blackness.

And vanished!

A great, silent, ringing explosion filled my head. I dropped the gun and almost swooned, because the room was a wild, deep vortex that dragged at the very throbbing veins and nerves of my body. Then I lost consciousness, and knew no more.

Sarah closed the journal, threw it down and looked at the clock. Jake hadn't come back. It was getting very late. She put her hand to the jagged coin that hung at her neck and fingered it, then held it still.

So this was how Symmes had got hold of the mirror. They'd always wondered about that, about his claims to have made it himself, but no one had known for sure, because Janus had the journals, locked in some deep vault, secret and guarded.

Janus.

Where was he? The young, lank-haired Janus, already plotting his future behind those blue spectacles. Was he prowling the grounds now, trying to find a way in? Trying the doors, letting the wolf snuffle every threshold?

Something tapped at the shuttered window.

152

She listened, tense with fear.

One tap. Then another.

She stood, crept up to the dark wood and stood staring at it, her heart thudding. Was he out there? Could the wolf smell her in here?

'Who's there?'

'Let me in.' A whisper. A voice against the glass, like the wind in a crack of darkness. 'Please.'

She jumped back, just as the door opened behind her. Piers put his head round and said, 'If you're ready, Sarah, we'll set up now.'

For a moment, tight with trauma, she didn't understand. Then she turned. 'Right. Yes. Let's go.'

Symmes's journal lay on the table. There was no way of getting to it without Piers's quick eyes seeing, so she walked calmly in front of it and out of the door. He moved aside for her.

He led the way, his shadow long on the wall. She noticed how strangely thin his hands were, how he pattered lightly up the staircase. But halfway up he stopped her with his spidery fingers on her arm. 'Listen to me, Sarah. Go down to the telephone now and call the Linley Institute and tell them where you are. Believe me, that would be best.'

'No,' she said.

153

'That policeman then . . .'

'Not him!' She glared at him, fierce. 'What's the matter with you? You haven't told anyone I'm here? Venn promised . . .'

Piers shrugged. 'No one has betrayed you. But I'm scared . . . The process is dangerous . . .'

She walked past him, quickly. 'Don't worry about me. Besides, Venn said if I didn't go along with it he'd send me back there himself.'

Piers smiled. A small, unhappy smile. 'He wouldn't do that. I know him. The threat shows how desperate he is.'

'I just want to help.'

He sighed. 'Well, I'll be there. I may be totally useless but I'll try to make sure we don't lose you.'

He led her down the Long Gallery. She noticed how the fog had thickened outside the mullioned windows, and had even crawled into the house, misting the end of the vast room. One of the cats ambled past them, its green eyes slitted, and then there was another, curled tight under a table.

'How many cats are there?' she asked.

'Seven,' Piers said wearily. 'Their names are Primo, Secundus, Tertio, Quadra, Quintus, Sextus and Septimo. They are the plagues of my life.'

As he swept back a curtain to reveal an archway with a small door, the thought struck her that maybe the cats were all Replicants . . . Venn would have had to experiment, after all . . .

Piers unlocked the door, and a damp draught gusted out, chilling her. She saw a bare stone passageway, slanted with moonlit windows.

'The Monk's Walk.' He took her arm with his spindly fingers, and led her in.

'It must be lonely for you,' Maskelyne said. 'No parents. No friends.'

The car headlights showed swirling fog, dark trees.

'I have friends,' Jake said. He was still too devastated to be annoyed.

'Do you? You seem the isolated sort. The sort others find difficult to get on with. You remind me of Venn, and myself. We are all locked into obsessive searches – his wife, your father . . .'

'You expect me to believe in time travel?' Jake turned, fierce, realizing his hands were clenched; his shoulders tight with tension. 'Do I look that stupid?'

'You do believe it. You have the photograph to prove it.'

Jake stared at the man. 'You know about that?'

'I've seen it.' Maskelyne's voice was husky; his delicate hands gripped the steering wheel as tightly as if the car was moving at speed. Jake felt confusion; a sudden astonishing misery. 'You knew my father?'

'I met him once.'

Fog was filling the car, misting them both. Jake had to say it. 'I saw him. Back at the Abbey. I saw my father's ghost in a mirror.'

Maskelyne turned, fast. 'A black mirror?'

'Just a mirror.'

Disappointment flickered over the man's ruined face. 'Well. That is what Symmes called the *delay*. A temporal echo. Or perhaps more like a ripple. It means nothing. Your father isn't there any more.'

Jake shook his head. 'Look. Tell me about this thing. The Chronoptika. Tell me everything.'

Gideon landed lightly on his feet and turned his back on the Dwelling.

So much for leaving a window open. He walked swiftly into the trees, simmering. He had taken Summer's punishment for this Jake, this spoiled arrogant child. Had thought, after all the timeless eternity of his captivity, that maybe this could be a friend.

A human contact.

Summer was right about them. They were boring.

The moon balanced over the Wood. Snow was coming. He could sense its cold, silent approach.

And something else.

He stood still, listening, one hand on a bine of ivy.

Something uncanny had entered the estate.

He could smell it. All the hairs on the back of his cold hands could sense it. An intrusion from some dark place. A rank, animal stink.

He slipped into the undergrowth, crouching low. And then, so abrupt and close it made him shiver sideways, he heard it howl.

A long, eerie, spine-chilling wail.

A wolf's anger.

He breathed out dismay into the frosty air. Leaves crackled. A shadow ducked out of the trees.

Still as winter's most frozen corpse Gideon saw the man flicker by; a thin, lank-haired man, his eyes hidden by small blue lenses that seemed to reflect everything.

A man with no substance.

A man like a wraith, an echo. And slinking at his heels, white as paper, the soft-padding wolf.

Safe in his Shee-craft, Gideon let them pass. He watched them merge into the shadow of the house. They left a darkness on the night, a vacuum.

Gideon breathed out. Maybe Jake had been wise not to open the Dwelling. 'Because Shee I know,' he breathed to himself. 'And humans I know. But what sort of creature are you?'

A starling flew down and landed on the branch beside him. It fixed him with a black sidelong eye and said, 'She asks is there anything to report?'

Gideon kept his face calm – they were experts at reading the slightest expression. He made up his mind then in that instant. He would escape them, even if he had to die. She would not own him for all time.

'No,' he said. 'Nothing to report.'

Wharton heard voices coming, froze in his examination of the mirror, swore once and slid hurriedly behind the clockwork. He crouched behind a bank of levers just as Piers ushered Sarah through the labyrinth. Venn was close behind them.

Venn looked at her. 'There's nothing to worry about. Piers and I are both here . . . in case . . .'

Sarah stared round at the crude webbed labyrinth, the alien, crowded machinery. Then she saw the mirror. 'It's OK,' she said. 'I'm not scared.'

It was a lie. To see it again, this terrible device, the shadowy warped reflection of her face in its depths, terrified her. It was festooned with trailing wires and monitors and she knew far more than Venn about the devastation it could cause . . . She tried to sound calm. 'Is this it?'

Venn came and stood beside her, so they were both reflected. 'This is it. The Chronoptika. An impossibility in itself – a concave mirror that seems flat. It was obtained by a Victorian eccentric called John Harcourt Symmes, back in the 1840s. He claimed it could warp time. But his results were generally failures, though we don't know for sure. One volume of his journals is missing. His last experiment may have worked.'

She said, watching Piers test systems and flick switches, 'What happened to him?'

Venn shrugged, unhappy. 'Forget him. We won't be trying anything as stupid. Just getting the thing calibrated.' He looked at Piers. 'The bracelet?'

'Not yet. Stand just here please, Sarah. I need to run some tests – your height, weight, and so on.'

She stepped on to a small perspex platform. 'This mirror. How did you get it?'

'A long story.' Venn seemed so tense he couldn't keep still; he walked round to Piers and watched him impatiently. 'Will she do? She has to.'

'Two minutes.'

'And David Wilde? He worked with you on this, didn't he?'

Venn raised his head and his eyes were hostile. 'I suppose Jake told you that. Leave it, Sarah, I don't want to talk about David.'

I'll bet you don't,' she thought. What about her! She was the one facing the risks. But she bit her lip and told herself to stay calm. This was what she was here for.

And she was so close!

'Right.' Piers scuttled round the mirror. 'There were a few rather strange readings there, but nothing the system can't handle. I've been trying to build in a reflex barrier – a sort of safety function. We didn't have it when we lost David, so you should be safer.'

Venn watched, motionless. 'She's ready.'

She said, 'Yes.' Defiant, her eyes on his.

'Then put this on please.'

Piers held a wide silver cuff of metal. *The bracelet.* She stared at it, then held her arm out, tugging up her sleeve. The bracelet was icy round her wrist. It hung a little loose. Her heart thudded, like a tiny vibration in the glass.

'Good. Now . . .' Piers turned, but Venn grabbed him.

'Wait.' Venn was staring at the shadowy corner behind

the generator. Sarah turned quickly but Venn's voice was a roar of anger.

'JAKE! Get out from there!'

Nothing.

Then she saw it too, a shadow, lurking close. For a moment she knew the Janus Replicant had crept inside, that it was here. Then it detached itself. Something clattered and Wharton stepped out, looking guilty and dismayed and determined. 'Actually, it's not Jake. It's me. And I'm afraid I can't let this charade go on for one second longer. It all stops now.'

'So you see,' the scarred man said quietly, 'the mirror is a dangerous thing. Venn is working blindly, with no second chances; he's lost the bracelet your father was wearing and has only one left. No margin for error. Yet he is obsessed. If he had a subject he considered expendable, he might . . .'

Jake looked up. 'Subject?'

'Someone to experiment on. Someone young, healthy. Expendable. He may ask you. If he does you must refuse . . .'

Jake wasn't listening. '*Sarah*.'

'What?'

'She had something she wanted to tell me, and I didn't

listen. But it shouldn't be her, it should be me!' He grabbed at the door handle, furious. 'Let me out of here! Or drive me back, now.' He whipped round. 'We have to get back there before . . .'

He stopped.

Maskelyne was facing him, the scar cruelly obvious now, the dark eyes clear and sad. 'I'm sorry to be crude, Jake. But that's not possible.'

He had a small strange weapon in his hand. It looked like a long-barrelled duelling pistol, but it was made of transparent glass. The muzzle was pointed directly at Jake's head.

Jake stared in disbelief.

'I want my mirror back. You are all I have to trade with. Venn's beloved godson.'

Jake almost laughed. 'Are you crazy? He can't stand me! You'd be doing him a favour!'

His scorn was scathing. Just for a moment, Maskelyne froze in doubt.

And Jake attacked.

He grabbed the gun; the man twisted away. Jake's fingers were tight over Maskelyne's; he tugged, forcing the weapon up, his other hand gripping the man's throat. Maskelyne was stronger than he looked; they grappled, breathless. Then Jake shoved and kicked, the gun

162

slipped, he touched the trigger. An explosion of brilliance flung him back in the seat, rocking the car, knocking all breath out of him. For a strange, timeless moment the world was splayed darkness, a bruising crash in his ears that became a steady, fierce hammering on the car door. He struggled up.

He got the door open. Sudden bitter cold.

'Jake!'

He was outside. Rebecca was dragging him, holding him up. 'What happened?' she gasped. 'Are you hurt?'

He could taste blood. He swallowed and the roar in his ears popped; the night was a fog around him. He was shivering with cold and shock.

'Jake! Can you hear me!'

'I'm not hurt.' His lip was cut, his hands too. She stared into the car, her face white.

'Is he dead?' It was a whisper of dread.

The windscreen was a cobweb of shattered crystal, its centre a neat circular hole. Maskelyne lay slumped head down over the wheel.

She leaned inside and touched him, feeling chest and neck. 'Oh, thank God. Thank God. He's alive.'

Jake grabbed the weapon. Whatever it was it had fired light, not a bullet. But Rebecca hissed, 'Leave it, leave it!'

He dropped it, reluctant. 'OK. Let's go. Before he comes to.'

'Shouldn't we call an ambulance . . .'

'He tried to kidnap me. And I have to get to Sarah . . .'

Maskelyne's hand twitched. He moved, and groaned. Instantly Jake and Rebecca were out and running, between the trees, leaping branches, fleeing down the track to the road. Rebecca was faster; she had the car open and the engine fired up before he got there; breathless, he threw himself inside. 'Go. *Go!*'

The tyres screeched. Mud flew. Jake was thrown back in the seat.

'Where?' she screamed.

'The Abbey.' He was up on his knees, staring back. The forest was a foggy gloom. He slid down, and took a deep, sore breath. 'Let's hope we get there in time.'

'You will sit there,' Venn said, savagely, 'and you will not interfere. Or,' as Wharton opened his mouth, 'even speak a single word!'

'Nonsense. It's my duty . . .'

'My God!' Venn was eye to eye with him in seconds. 'Tell me why I shouldn't put you into the thing instead of her!'

It was a real threat. Wharton sat silent.

Piers said, 'Excellency. We have to do it now.'

Sarah said, 'It's all right. Do it. Get it over with.' She looked down and saw that the bracelet was slowly closing tight around her wrist, shrinking like a locking handcuff, or a snake devouring its own tail. Venn pulled her hurriedly inside the green strands of the web.

Power clicked on. Deep in the obsidian glass, a charge flickered. Light slid and glimmered.

Sarah held her breath. *This is for you, Max*, she thought. *For Cara. For all of you. For Mum and Dad.*

For ZEUS.

Voices.

Doors slamming.

The bracelet locked. Venn turned.

And then the darkness of the mirror stretched itself out for her, and she gasped. She was wrapped in it. The surface was gone; it was a great black hole of darkness, sucking everything in and down. For a second the way was there, she saw it, it lay open and wide and clear, the way home, the way back, and then with a spark of agony it collapsed, and she was caught and tangled and trapped by a mesh of sticky threads, held by them when she wanted to crumple on her hands and knees, giddy and sick.

The bracelet fell off and rolled into the dark. She

struggled up into Wharton's grip and saw Jake was there, shouting and arguing with Venn, a tall red-haired girl running in behind him. Their voices were all confused in her head, mixed with the echo of carriages, the stink of horses, the mirage of the city on her retina and in her ears.

She tugged herself out of the sticky maze, away from Wharton's concern, letting the terrible disappointment fade down into a dull ache of failure. She sat on a chair Piers hastily fetched and put her head in her hands. She was shivering with cold.

Then she saw they were all staring at her, silent.

'What?' she whispered.

Venn crouched, urgent. 'I said, did you feel anything? Anything at all?'

She swallowed. Wharton said, 'She looks so pale . . .' but she ignored that and said, 'Yes.'

Venn flashed a glance of triumph at Piers. 'I knew it! The bracelet triggered it!'

'No.' Sarah's voice was a croak; she swallowed and stood up, wiping her face with her sleeve. 'No. Not the bracelet. Nothing was working until Jake burst in. It was Jake that triggered it. And then I saw . . . *I saw another world.*'

It was worth the failure, she thought, worth the loss. To see the astonishment in Jake's eyes. And the joy in Venn's . . .

Like the hectic in my blood he rages

CHAPTER ELEVEN

Interviewer: And how do you feel about conquering a summit like Katra Simba and going where no one else ever has? Does it give you a great sense of freedom?

Venn: That's a stupid question.

Interviewer: Well ... um ...

Venn: You don't conquer mountains. They conquer you.

Interviewer: Yes, but I mean ...

Venn: You don't have a clue what you mean. If you'd ever been up there, you'd see why. A place like – a mountain like that – doesn't set you free. She chains you to her memory for ever.

BBC interview: *Volcanoes – Hills of Fury*

Sarah knocked again on the door. 'Jake!'

There was no answer, but she knew he was in there. 'It's me.' She opened it and went in.

Jake said, 'Leave me alone.'

She sat on the unmade bed. It was a four-poster, with red damask hangings, ridiculously grand in the panelled room. 'You didn't come down for breakfast. Wharton was worried.'

'I'm devastated.' He sounded bone-weary. He was sitting, knees up, on the wide window ledge, wearing a coat over pyjamas, gazing out at the white frost that had stiffened the lawns. Beyond, the Wood loomed dark.

'Venn wants a meeting. All of us. About last night.'

His eyes flicked to her. She gazed round at the tumble of his clothes, the laptop, the monkey's mess of crumbs and stolen nuts. It seemed like he had stumbled to sleep last night as exhausted as she had, after Venn had ordered Rebecca home and the rest of them to bed.

She said, 'We need to get things straight. If we're going to succeed in finding your father we need to be working together, not as enemies. You and me. You and Venn.'

It made sense. He still hated it.

'And you've got to get rid of this idea that he's responsible for your father's . . .'

'He is responsible.'

'You know what I mean. Let go, Jake.' She got up and came over to him, looking at his fragmented reflections in the tiny windowpanes. 'He wants to get David back as much as you . . . He's desperate. He's not the person you think he is.'

He didn't move or answer but she sensed a change, the slightest of thaws. As the marmoset swung down and settled cosily on his lap she said, 'Do you believe him? About the Chronoptika?'

He shrugged.

She squeezed on to the seat beside him. 'It is true, Jake! Last night, when I was looking into it, I saw it. I saw the past.'

Silence. Finally he said, 'What did you see?' and she knew she had won. She stood up. 'If you really want to know that, come downstairs. We'll talk about it all together. You'll get nowhere skulking up here by yourself.' She took a small cloth-bound book from her pocket and thrust it at him. 'And when you get a moment, read this. It's Symmes's journal. It'll explain a lot.'

She went to the door and out, and he let her go without a word, his fingers deep in Horatio's fur, watching her reflection vanish.

Then there was only the blue sky to stare at.

He was cold, and alone. The hot excitement of last night, the fight with Maskelyne and the amazing story of the mirror seemed like a dream now; it had evaporated into restless sleep and listless bewilderment and he felt that all his energy had gone. That he almost didn't care.

And yet.

What did she mean, that she had seen the past?

Suddenly, he had to move. Pushing the monkey off, he ducked its wild screechy swing and went over to his crumpled pile of clothes, pulling on the black jumper and dragging a comb through his hair. For a moment he wanted to look at himself, to see if he looked older, paler, but of course there was no mirror and maybe that was good, because he didn't want another vision like the last, another ghostly hand clutching at his. He pushed the small journal into his back pocket.

'Stay here,' he said. 'And don't wreck the place.'

Horatio bared his teeth and climbed the curtain.

Jake walked the creaking corridor and ran down the stairs. The house was in its eternal silence, the dark panelled rooms deserted, only the clocks ticking. Then he caught the low mutter of voices from far along a stone-paved passageway at the back that must have once been for servants.

He walked down there and paused in the archway.

Heat struck his face, and the sweet smells of tea and toast and baking bread.

It was the kitchen. A vast hearth opened in the roof and under it – inside it really – a fire was burning with inglenook benches on each side. Wharton was sitting on one, his feet stretched blissfully out. Sarah perched opposite, her eyes on Jake. Venn was talking to Piers by a big table littered with dishes and books. When he saw Jake he stopped. 'So. We're all here.'

'Except our friend Rebecca,' Wharton said.

'I escorted the young lady arm in arm back to her car last night.' Piers set out five striped mugs on the table. 'Although she would happily have stayed. She was *so* curious, so breathless. Her voice has registers. She's not quite the ditsy scatterbrain she appears. Perhaps we should be careful about how much we tell her.'

'I don't want her here again.' Venn's gaze was on Jake.

'Don't tell me who I should see,' he growled.

'See her if you want. But not here.'

Jake shrugged.

As if that was a signal of some sort, Sarah came over and sat at the table. Piers carried the huge brown teapot, its handle wrapped in a tea towel, and carefully poured hot tea into all the mugs. 'My own biscuits,' he said, proud.

They were Christmas-tree shaped, and decorated with

swags of icing and small pearly spheres. Wharton dipped one into his tea. 'Magic, Piers.' He crammed the rest into his mouth. 'Makes most biscuits taste like cardboard. But how on earth do you get the time?'

Piers shrugged, sly. 'As you say. Magic.'

'You must give me the recipe.'

Jake sat. Ignoring the others, he turned to Sarah. 'Tell me . . . tell us . . . exactly what you saw. Please.'

She stirred sugar in the tea, considering.

Venn came and sat opposite. She felt enclosed by their need, squeezed by their desperation. She knew they were both taut with nerves, but so was she. So she said, 'At first there was nothing. Even when the bracelet started locking itself. It closed in on my skin – it was so cold it hurt. Then I felt the mirror change. It became less . . . solid. It's difficult to describe, because I think it was at that moment that Jake came running in, and it was as if the mirror . . . *imploded* . . .'

'How . . .' Wharton began but Jake said, 'Shut up. Go on, Sarah.'

'It just wasn't there any more. It became a vacuum. A sucking emptiness. It was so powerful – it pulled at me, as if it would drag me in. It was a sort of . . .' she shivered, her voice grim, 'black hole.'

Venn flicked a glance at Piers, who said, 'Like David.'

She looked up. 'If it hadn't been for your spider web I would have been pulled right inside. I felt as if my ears and nose were bleeding; as if there was some tremendous build-up of pressure . . . And then I saw the street.'

Venn said, 'I didn't see anything . . .'

'I did. Houses. Big, like tenements or warehouses. A dull grey sky. People, running out of the rain. Umbrellas. The noise of horses' hooves and cartwheels, a terrible clatter. A stink of dung.'

'People?' Venn was leaning close over the table now, his ice-eyes points of fever. 'What sort of clothes?'

'Old-fashioned. The women had long dresses. Bustles. There were horse-drawn omnibuses.'

He stared at her, astounded. 'Was it London?'

'Maybe. I don't know.'

'My God.' He glanced at Piers, then back, his fingers grabbing hers and gripping them so hard it hurt. 'Are you saying this was the 1840s? 1850s?'

She had no idea. She said, 'It was definitely Victorian. From pictures I've seen. But it was only there for a second. A blink of light. And then it was gone, and I felt so sick and giddy I couldn't even stand up any more. And you were yelling at Jake and the bracelet fell off and rolled away . . .'

To her own surprise she felt upset; almost tearful. Wharton said, 'Take your time,' but Venn just snatched his hand away and leaped up, pacing to the fire.

Piers slid the plate of biscuits towards her. 'Eat up.'

She took one automatically, glancing at Jake. She had thought he would argue angrily in disbelief, but his stare was considering, and she felt sure all at once that he knew more than she'd thought. Who had phoned him last night? What had they told him? Suddenly she needed to know it wasn't Janus.

Wharton said, 'Well, this clearly doesn't mean . . . that is . . . you obviously imagined you saw it. In that dizzy moment . . .'

'The rain was on my face. I could have stepped through. Gone there.'

'Oh surely . . .'

'I'm not a liar!'

Wharton didn't flinch. 'No?' he said quietly.

'Leave her alone.' Jake's mutter was hoarse. 'She's right. She saw the past . . . That's where Dad is.' He swivelled in the chair, to Venn. 'You got him there. You can get him back.'

Venn was near the fire. He turned his head, winter-sharp. 'Have you been talking to anyone about this?'

'Like who?'

176

'I don't know. But you seem very ready to accept it all of a sudden.'

Jake shrugged. 'Maybe I believe Sarah more than you.'

Venn's stare was level. Then he came and sat at the table. In the silence only the fire crackled, and a ripple of tea as Piers poured himself another mugful. 'Tell the boy, Excellency,' he said quietly. 'Tell them all. It's time.'

When Venn spoke again he didn't look at any of them. He looked at the fire and he spoke steadily, to the flames.

'According to Harcourt Symmes, the mirror allows entry to time. I have a theory that it curves space-time, but that doesn't explain . . . well. Never mind that now. The fact is we inherited the wreckage of an eccentric's dream, and had to rebuild the thing almost from scratch. David found it. He was at an auction sale in Durham, one time, and this thing was in the catalogue. Lot eighty-six. *Box containing a Victorian mirror, wiring, associated machinery etcetera*. Etcetera turned out to be a journal kept by Symmes, two silver bracelets and some files of calculations and notes. It seemed to be just junk, but David was interested enough to bid and he got it all for twenty quid. He brought it here, and he read the journal. Stayed up all night reading it. He got really excited about the thing – the Chronoptika, Symmes calls it. I was . . . Well, I didn't care about anything. Maybe he thought at first it might be something to take my mind off Leah. Then he began to get this strange obsession that it might actually work.

'I didn't need much persuasion. I was living in a terrible arctic darkness, on and on, for months. This was like a gleam of hope. Like the day you realize the sun will rise soon.

'We needed help. I summoned Piers up – he's clever with his hands. He and David worked on the thing. They read and experimented and were up all hours. It was a long, difficult process, and they had to look after me too, because at that stage I was . . . suicidal.' He was silent a moment; Sarah flicked a look at Jake, who sat, arms folded, listening, pitiless.

'The first time we used it, it almost exploded. Then, the next time, David wore one of the bracelets, walked through the mirror and back out, immediately. At least, that's how it seemed to us, but he said he had been back to 1965 and spent two days there. His clothes were dirty, he was unshaven, and he had a photograph of himself holding a newspaper. I remember how I just sat there, staring at it . . . We were so amazed . . . We thought if we can do that we can do anything. Change time. Change history. Avoid the accident . . . *Bring her back.*' He gripped his fingers tight together, a knot of tension. 'I can't tell you what it felt like to be given a glimpse of that. We drank, we dreamed, we flung all the windows of the house open and whooped and whistled for joy. But then. Two days later we tried again. After our pride, the fall.'

Suddenly he stood up. 'I can't do this. Tell them, Piers. Give him the key to David's room.' Abruptly, he went out, ducking under the low arch.

Piers cleared his throat in the awkward silence. One of the cats leaped on the table and head-butted him; he stroked it idly. 'Ah. Well, it hit him hard, you know. So much hope, so much despair. But your father is a determined man, Jake, and he was desperate to help his friend. I advised against another attempt until we had the web finished, because it was clear the power of the machine could drag us all into it without some safety device. But David wouldn't wait. He put on the silver cuff and we activated the Chronoptika. There was a tremendous crack of sound, and every one of the lights in the house blew out. I knew then. We tried . . . believe me, Jake, we really did. But David was gone. And the mirror was black and hard and empty.'

Jake was silent. Without looking up, he turned the mug with his forefinger. 'What did you do?'

'Waited. And waited. He never came out.'

Wharton leaned back, squeaking his chair. 'I have to

179

say, it all seems incredible.'

'No,' Jake said. 'It doesn't.' He took out the crocodile-skin wallet, pulled the photo from it and placed it on the table. 'It explains this.'

Sarah swivelled the photo round and stared at it. She looked astonished. 'He had this taken?'

'It came with the note from my father. Someone sent them to me.'

He turned to Piers. 'It was you, wasn't it?'

Piers shrugged, shifty. His small body seemed to shrink. 'Well, yes. But for God's sake don't tell Venn. I'm in deep enough doodah as it is.'

'Stand up to him. He doesn't own you,' Wharton growled.

'Actually he does.'

'Why send it?' Sarah asked quietly.

'Because it would get Jake here. And I thought his presence would affect the mirror. I was right.'

'Venn lied to the police,' Jake said, grim. 'My father never left this house.'

'Depends on how you define left. But we couldn't have the plods ferreting around here. I'm really sorry, Jake. I'm an expert at getting things wrong.'

'Venn wouldn't have cared.'

Piers stood. 'He was in no fit state to care about anyone.'

He went to the wall, took down a bunch of keys and selected one. 'I saw him spend nights sitting before that mirror, drinking, waiting. It's taken months to get back to where we were. But last night showed me that there is still a chance . . . So tonight, I'm sure he'll try again.'

Sarah looked up, alert. 'So soon?'

Jake slid the photo from under her fingers and put it back into the wallet. 'Well, this time I wear the bracelet. Not her. And not Venn.'

Piers slid a key over. 'That's for you. It opens your father's room.'

Jake took it, but before he could answer the rapid high peeping of an alarm startled them all; bursting out like a pulse in the silent house.

'What's that?' Sarah leaped up so fast her chair fell over.

'The gate.' Piers flitted out of the room and she ran after him, quickly, through the old scullery and into the dairy, though now its cold marble counters held only TV monitors and a keyboard.

Piers's long fingers flicked on the keyboard. Sarah stared at the screen. She was looking down at the wrought-iron gates from a high, awkward angle, through a camera grimy with dirt. No one was there.

'Odd.' Piers clicked the camera; it panned left and right, up and down. They saw the rutted lane, a high hedgerow, bare brambles, some mud slashed with tyre tracks. Then the left-hand pillar with its stone lion . . .

'There's no one there,' she said, anxious.

'Well, something set it off.'

'A fox?'

'Maybe.' He touched a switch and the image flickered; she saw by the digital clock in the corner that he was running the footage backwards.

'So we really can go back in time,' she said, trying to joke.

'Mortal time is only an image. The capture of images.' Piers stopped. 'There! See! What's that, I wonder?'

A figure. The edge of a dark shape, standing in the untidy tangle of the high hedges. Someone motionless, blurred in the grainy image, there and then not there, so swift they might have been a movement of branches and thorns.

She stared at it, knowing it was Janus.

Piers looked grave. 'Houston, we have a problem. Tell me, Sarah, did that look like a man with a scarred face to you?'

'Why?'

'We've had such a man hanging around in recent months. Maybe one of Summer's but I fear he knows something.'

'Who's Summer?'

Piers giggled, nervous. 'You don't want to know.'

She didn't answer. She was peering at the mud in front of the gate, where the tyres of cars had flattened it. Even in the dim image she could make out the prints. Broad splayed paw prints.

'It could be anyone,' she said, in a whisper.

CHAPTER TWELVE

Throughout the early days of the Revolution Janus worked stealthily behind the scenes. He gathered power, began to denounce former colleagues. We do not know how he gained possession of the Chronoptika, but at some stage he began experimenting with it. As a result we believe that he created as many as a thousand Replicants, including several of himself. The youngest known is a 19-year-old self. It displays its Original's cunning and ruthless nature. But it hasn't yet developed his full maturity of evil. Like all Replicants, it appears to be immortal.

Illegal ZEUS transmission: Biography of Janus

'For a start, she's not Piers's niece.'

'I gathered that.' Jake turned the stiff key in the lock of

his father's room and opened the door.

The room was dim, the curtains drawn. He crossed the room and dragged them open.

Pale winter sunlight lit the bed, a neat dressing-table, its shaving things set out carefully. A comb and brush, snagged with a few hairs, lay under a thin film of dust.

He didn't touch them. Instead he opened the wardrobe.

'Yes, but I've discovered exactly who she *is*.' Wharton sat thoughtfully on the bed. 'And I have to warn you, Jake, this isn't good.'

He wasn't listening. The scent of his father hung in the clothes; it came out and seemed to enfold him, and the memories it brought caught in his throat like choked breath. The aftershave, the cheap French cigarettes, the indefinable musty mix that had made David Wilde. Always joking, always full of dire puns and stupid pranks.

He reached out and touched the stiff, hanging clothes, the old tweed suit from some charity shop in Oxford, the check shirt, the black overcoat that Dad had thought made him look like a pre-electric Bob Dylan. Underneath, in casual pairs, his boots and shoes, his trainers standing as carelessly as if he'd just stepped out of them.

'Jake?' Wharton was behind him. 'Are you OK?'

He wasn't. The clothes blurred. He wanted to rub his hands through them, push his face against them, breath in their scruffy, warm Dadness. He wanted to go through the pockets and pick out every rolled sweet paper, every torn train ticket that his father had touched. But he couldn't, not with Wharton here. That would have to wait.

He said, 'I'm moving into this room.'

'Well, I suppose Venn won't mind that. But, Jake, please. This is important.'

Reluctant, he closed the cupboard door and turned.

'I saw it in the local paper,' Wharton said, and held out a torn article. Jake took it and stared at the photo.

'It looks like her, but . . .'

'She's cut her hair. Read it.'

He stood still and let his eyes race over the words . . . *psychiatric . . . criminal . . . still missing . . .* By the end he was taut with attention and surprise. 'This is crazy. She's on the run and he's hiding her here?'

'Not from the kindness of his heart.' Wharton looked uncomfortable. 'I heard him yelling at Piers. He wants her for this series of tests because no one will come looking for her if she disappears. It's cold-blooded, Jake. Venn is so desperate he'll do anything to succeed. Does he really believe he can get his wife back this way?'

Jake said, 'His wife?'

'It's perfectly clear.' Wharton stared gloomily at his

shoes. 'His wife died in the car accident and he was driving. It was his fault. He must be eaten up with guilt and remorse. That's enough to send any man a little insane – and he was an extreme personality before that . . .'

Jake went to the window and stared out. 'He thinks he can change the past? Go back before the accident and make sure it never happens? That's like a fairytale. Something out of a Greek myth.'

'Fairies don't exist. The Chronoptika does.'

Jake, thinking of the Shee, wasn't so sure. But he turned and said, 'Why would she go along with this? Sarah, I mean.'

'He may be paying her.'

'But she saw the past. You heard . . .'

Wharton was looking at him pityingly. 'Oh come on, Jake. Do you really believe her? Think about it! She wants to stay hidden here. She gives him what he wants. A little fanciful description. Anyone who's seen a period drama on the television could do as well. No, she's humouring Venn, and Piers seems happy to go along with it all, though that slave of the lamp stuff is a mystery to me, I must say.'

Jake frowned. He went up to the chest of drawers and opened the topmost one. Folded T-shirts. And, face down, a silver frame. He said, 'That reminds me. How come you were in there with them? Did Venn ask you?'

Wharton cleared his throat. 'Ah yes. Well . . . I . . . was worried about the girl. I insisted on being there.'

Jake shot him a quick look. 'What a hero.' He turned the silver frame over.

The zoo.

A cheeky seven-year-old Jake Wilde eating chocolate ice cream, licking a fragment of the cone. The baby chimp in the keeper's arms. A woman, slim, in white jeans and a blue shirt, her hair short and dark, laughing.

Her hand on his head.

He stared at it. He had not seen his mother for so long she seemed like a stranger.

This was the past. The only past left. Captured by light, frozen in a rigid image. Gone. But if you could re-enter it; if you could go back to that place and be that person again, if you could live that moment again, better, without the stupid remarks, the arguments, the mistakes, wouldn't that be a thing worth taking all the risks in the world for?

Very slowly, he set the frame upright next to the others on the dressing-table. He turned, suddenly. 'What happens now? What's our plan?'

'Venn will try again tonight, it seems. We'll both be there. I won't allow him to exploit Sarah, or you.'

Jake shrugged. 'If what you say is true, she's exploiting him.'

A knock. Sarah put her head around the door and said, 'It's the phone for you, Jake.'

He ran down after her, wondering if she'd caught any of the conversation. Then he thought of Maskelyne, and stopped. 'Is it a man?'

She glanced back. 'It's Rebecca.' She pulled a coy face. 'Being oh-so-very secretive and oh-so wanting to talk *only* to you.'

He wanted to say, 'Jealous?' But that would be stupid. Instead he watched her walk down the passageway before he picked up the receiver. 'Hi.'

'Jake! Are you all right?' Rebecca sounded relieved.

'Fine. I told you to ring my mobile.'

'I tried! There's not one scrap of signal down there. Listen, have you told Venn about Maskelyne? I mean, about that gun . . .'

'Not yet. Don't talk too much, because anyone might be listening. Piers has this place wired up like NASA.'

'Well, I just want to say don't say a word! I've found out something, it might be nothing, but . . . we should meet.' He heard something rustle. A voice, close by. A dog barking.

'Where are you?'

'Wintercombe. At the post office. I think it's going to snow, but can you get here?'

He looked wearily at the sky. It was no longer blue. Heavy cloud lidded the valley. 'I'll come but I'll have to walk. Is there any sort of short cut through the Wood?'

Silence. Then she said, 'Jake, you don't go in there. Ever. Do you hear?'

'You sound like Venn.'

'He's right. If you were a local you'd understand . . .'

'About the Shee?'

She laughed, but it was nervous. 'Well, OK, they're just legend. But people do disappear in there. Stay on the drive and come along the lanes. I'll meet you here in say half an hour. OK? Bye!'

The phone clicked to silence.

He held it a moment, listening, but there was no sound on the line, and he put it down, just as Piers came through the hall carrying bikers' leathers and a helmet. Jake stared.

'You ride?'

'A Harley. Lovely beast. Puts a girdle round the earth in forty minutes.' He hung up the jacket and shrugged into the worn lab coat. 'Weather's closing in.'

Jake nodded, and walked up the stairs. As soon as Piers had gone, he ran back down, felt in the pocket of the leathers and pulled out the key of the bike.

He tossed it with one hand. And caught it in the other.

Sarah put the kitchen phone down as gently as she could. She sat for a moment, considering. Had Jake read the journal? And who was this girl, this Rebecca? But she knew why she was restless. Hearing Jake talk about his father had hurt. Because she had a father too, and a mother, locked deep in one of Janus's dungeons. And she could never talk to anyone about that.

Resentful, she slipped up the back stairs to her room.

Jake didn't even know he was born.

It was bitterly cold. She was already wearing two jumpers that Piers had found for her, but now she pulled a coat on over them, and then opened the secret panel in the floor.

She took out the notebook and the black pen. For a moment she hesitated, fighting dread.

Then she wrote

I'm not afraid of you.

YOU SHOULD BE. The answer was prompt, eager, as if he had been waiting for her. It spread in bold letters diagonally across the page.

AND DON'T LIE, SARAH. YOU ARE AFRAID. YOU ARE THE LAST OF ZEUS – THE OTHERS ARE ALL DEAD. YOU MUST KNOW THAT.

She clenched a hand over her mouth. But no. He was trying to break her. It filled her with hot fury. *Liar*, she wrote, *Liar. Liar. Liar.*

DO YOU THINK YOU CAN SAVE THE WORLD? BE THE GREAT HEROINE? MY REPLICANT KNOWS WHERE YOU ARE. HE WILL ENTER THE HOUSE SOON.

YOU'RE ALL ALONE, SARAH. ALONE AND AFRAID AND FAR FROM HOME. IF YOU SUCCEED IN YOUR PLAN YOU WILL NEVER SEE YOUR PARENTS OR YOUR WORLD AGAIN.

She wrote so fast the pen tore the paper. *I think you're the one who's scared. If even one of us is alive you're in danger. Tonight I'll be close enough to the mirror to touch it. And then*

AH YES, BUT WHAT IF VENN FINDS OUT WHAT YOU MEAN TO DO?

She slammed the book shut.

Was that another tap at the window? Suddenly wild, she leaped up and flung the shutters wide.

Snow was falling gently against the window, a soft crystal scatter. She stared at it, entranced.

August 1847
I have spent too many pages detailing my frustrations with the machine, my failures, my long nights of work. Suffice to say I have become a stranger to my old

haunts, and my obsession with the mirror grows. Someone else is equally obsessed. Burglary has been attempted at my house at least twice. Last week, as I walked down New Bond Street, a hansom cab came from nowhere and deliberately attempted to run me down. Had not a warning been shouted to me by a stranger, and had I not been quick and agile, I should have been killed. This was Maskelyne, surely, or his Oriental accomplice, because I am certain Maskelyne entered the mirror.

Tonight, however, something amazing has happened. I can barely describe it steadily even now for excitement. I have had to take cordial and stand outside in the cool garden, breathing the night air. I have had to make myself inhale slowly, to calm my racing heart.

I note it down here, carefully.

The date is 11th August. The moon is full, the weather warm. The time 12.34. This is what happened.

I repeated my operations of yesternight with the rewired machinery and this time something sparked. A peculiar smell of burning filled the room. And then I felt a great sucking pain in my chest and leaped back, because it seemed to me that the mirror had become hollow, a bottomless chasm. It was no longer . . . here.

Then I saw a figure.

It was standing within the penumbra of the mirror, darkened and warped, but it was most certainly a human figure, despite the barbaric clothing it wore. A figure of some ancient, primitive time.

It moved, lifted its head, looked at me. I saw this was a girl. A young woman, her hair hacked off, as short as a boy's. The shock was so great I stepped backwards, and as our eyes met I forgot all scientific discipline and cried out. I recorded nothing, I just stared.

She spoke. It was a whisper through the dark glass. She said, 'Where is this? Who are you?'

She seemed as terrified as myself. I was to her, perhaps, some savage god, some angel of the Old Testament, dark and vengeful.

I wish now I had raised my hand and been benevolent, had made my voice wise and reassuring. Instead I was so astonished I had only breath to foolishly gasp, 'My name is Symmes.'

'Symmes.' She intoned it like a syllable of prayer. Then she smiled.

And the mirror was solid and empty.

At the edge of the lake, Gideon watched the snow.

He saw how it fell with silent intensity, how the fallen trunks and briars and thorns took on its whiteness with such a gentle cruelty you couldn't even see it happen. Just, after minutes, the clotting and accumulation of death.

He understood this. This was the way the Shee worked, this relentless coldness, the slow burial, the freezing of his soul. He knew they had almost won with him; that he had forgotten nearly everything of his human life, that he was far more one of them than he even dared think. They had made him immortal and his humanity was a lost thing, far away and in a forgotten place.

He looked back.

They were playing the music.

He stepped, quickly, out of the Wood, into the world. The music was dangerous, the most lethal spell they had. If you listened to it it devoured you; you sickened for it like a drug. Once you had heard it – and he had heard it for centuries – you could never forget it . . . Never.

'Gideon?'

Summer stood in front of him. Her short dress had become blue today, an ice-blue shift to fit the world's weather, her arms and feet bare. 'Where are you going?'

He shrugged, bitter. 'Where can I go? You've trapped me in this forest . . .'

'The forest contains everything.' She came up and put

her arms around him, hugging him close, smaller than he was. 'Always so moody, human child. Always so sad. But you know, you can go anywhere, do anything. We've given you freedom. Far more than the other poor souls out here have.'

He opened his mouth to speak but she laid a cold finger on his lips. 'Do you want songs, Gideon, or dancing? Rich clothing? Food from far lands? To fly with the jay and scurry with the mole? All that's yours. You'll never age, never be old, never be sick or corrupted with some cancer. You have the life that humans dream of in their religions and their myths. You have eternity. What more is there?'

He wanted to say *Love. Pity.* But she wouldn't understand what the words meant. He wasn't sure that he did either. He wanted to shout out that it wasn't enough, that he wanted people, people with all their faults and irritations and compassion and arguments. He wanted a place where fear had boundaries.

Instead he said, 'Why did you choose me, Summer? Out of all the children in the world . . .'

She laughed, stepping back. 'You were mine from the start. We'd play our music to you even when you were in the cradle. When you were older, you wandered for hours in the Wood. They couldn't keep you in their cottages, their tiny dull family. You were too bold for that. Too beautiful. Then I decided to bring you to me. To make you mine, Gideon.'

He remembered that day. The kindly girl in the green dress who had taken his hand and drawn him away, deep and deeper into the Wood, and how tight her slim white fingers had been round his, and how at first he had turned because he could still hear his mother, fainter, always fainter, calling and calling his name. How he had tugged and pulled.

How she had never let him go.

Now he shrugged. 'Let me go back. You could, if . . .'

'It's too late.' She smiled at him, perfectly calm. 'Our time is not their time. Out there, centuries have passed. Your mother is dead, Gideon, your father, your brothers, anyone who ever remembered you. Dead for centuries. You've become a story. A legend. The boy who wandered away never to be seen again. A picture in an old book. A warning to mothers not to let their children out of their sight.'

She shrugged, a slight, careless movement. 'You can never go back. Take one step out of Venn's estate and you crumble into dust. To fine desiccated bone. You don't exist any more, Gideon. You are eternal, yes, but you are also long dead.'

CHAPTER THIRTEEN

The Wintercombe estate has been in his family for centuries. Orpheus Venn, a Cavalier nobleman loyal to Charles the First, reputedly received the land as a reward after the Restoration, and the family have lived there ever since. The valley lies between Dartmoor and the sea, and has a mysterious air. The locals believe the Faery Host inhabit it, and that one of Venn's ancestors once had an amour with the Faery Queen, and that the family are now only half human. When asked about this once at a book festival in Bremen, Venn gave his ice-chip stare, snatched off the microphone and stormed out.

His temperament is legendary.

Jean Lamartine, *The Strange Life of Oberon Venn*

Rebecca watched the dusk through the twinkling lights in the post office window. 'I'm dreaming,' the postmistress sang, 'of a White Christmas . . . Can I get you anything else?'

'No. Thanks.' She went out reluctantly on to the pavement, the shop bell ringing behind her, and stood looking up the street. The half an hour was long gone. Obviously, Jake wasn't coming.

It was already getting dark. She idled down towards the bridge, seeing how the heavy lid of cloud was a weight on the village; how the old houses and the church and the pub seemed to cower down under it. It was colder than yesterday. Her breath frosted in the air, and the river, when she came to it, foamed over rocks that gleamed with frozen spray.

She leaned on the parapet and gazed down.

The Wintercombe was a haunted river. It drew her always, its dark peaty water emptying from the moor, cutting its fast deep gorge to the sea. Leaning out, she took a small object from her pocket and held it over the water.

It was a memory stick, and on it were all her notes from uni, all her seminars and assignments. A whole year's work. A whole year's absence.

All she had to do was open her fingers.

And let it go.

Something touched her face. She gasped and jerked back, clutching the piece of plastic, but the touch came again, and as she stared up she saw the long expected snow had come at last.

It fell in the silent, relentless way she so loved, and as the flakes landed on the stone parapet they melted very slowly into stars of damp.

Wintercombe would freeze tonight.

Another movement. This time it was behind her, and she turned to complain at Jake for being so late.

Instead she saw a man standing on the bridge.

He was a metre away, wearing a dark coat and a hat that shadowed his face. In the glimmer of snow he stood still, watching her.

The bridge was narrow. There was no way past him. She took one step back, and he said, 'Rebecca.'

Snow blurred him. She glanced back quickly; the village street was empty.

'Is he coming?' Maskelyne stepped closer.

'I don't think so,' she said. Then, 'What were you thinking of! That gun! Are you stark mad?'

'Probably. It was . . . a desperate gesture, though it wouldn't even have hurt him . . . Have I scared him away for good?'

201

Impatient, she shrugged. 'Jake's not the scaring type. But you shouldn't be here. If he sees us together . . .'

He took the hat off and his dark hair was damp with the snow. 'Rebecca, what was that in your hand?'

In her pocket, her fingers tightened on the memory stick. Then slowly she took it out and laid it on the parapet. The wind edged it; he came and grabbed it quickly.

'Your university work.'

'It's not important.'

'Yes. It is.' He gave it back to her. 'Don't give up your life for a dream. For me. Don't lose everything for a man who intends to leave as soon as he can.'

She shrugged, wordless.

Maskelyne leaned on the parapet. 'Does Jake suspect you?'

'No.' Rebecca shoved her gloved hands deep in her pockets. 'But they might be stopping him from coming. Venn might. Should I phone again?'

He shook his head. 'Venn has the caution of a man used to danger. And, if, as you say, the Chronoptika even flickered with life last night, how agitated he must be. How eager to try again.'

He looked up. 'It will be tonight, because he thinks he can force the mirror with his guilt. With his pain.

He has no idea at all of the damage he might do . . .'

'And you do?'

'None better.' He turned his face and she saw the terrible scar that cut its jagged way down his cheek.

She said unhappily, 'Jake thinks I'm his friend. I *am* his friend. I don't like . . .'

'You don't have to blame yourself . . .' He stopped. 'I should never have involved you in this.' She saw how his eyes suddenly focused, sharp, over her shoulder. He said, 'Listen.'

She turned. The village was lost in a soft blizzard. She heard nothing but the crisp hiss of falling snow. And then, oddly magnified, a sharp bark. Quick and stifled. Footsteps. The panting of some large fevered animal.

Maskelyne grabbed her arm, and she saw the fear in his face. 'Come on. Quick!'

The raw urgency in his voice made her move; before she realized it they were running over the narrow bridge, their shadows shrivelling under the solitary lamppost. In the centre, down three steps, was the tiny stone lock-up, used centuries ago for drunkards to sleep it off overnight. Maskelyne jumped down and flung himself against the ancient, graffitied door; it lurched and split, and instantly he was in through the crack like a shadow, tugging Rebecca behind him.

The space was barely big enough for them both, a pitch-black, stinking hole. Alarmed, she turned, but he was already jamming the door back fiercely. 'Help me! Before it gets the scent.'

She shoved the wood with her foot. 'Scent? A dog?'

'A time wolf.'

He'd pressed back against the curved stone wall, breathing hard.

Her heart pounding, Rebecca watched the faint slit of twilight under the door. Snow drifted; then she saw a flicker of darkness.

Maskelyne's breathing stopped. They were both utterly silent.

In the blackness only the numbers on her watch shone, a tiny circle of time. She was tense against the icy wall. Every muscle rigid.

The shadow snuffled under the door. It pawed and clawed.

Then, so close it made her jump, a voice said, 'I know you're in there.'

Jake got as far as the fallen tree before the bike's engine sputtered out and it slewed to a stop.

He whipped the helmet off and stared at the gauge.

Empty.

Unbelievable! It had been full. He was sure.

Snow fell on the glass gauge; he wiped it off but the small red line was quite clear. Disgusted, he flung the bike over.

'Oh I don't think that's called for.' Piers sat on the fallen tree-trunk, ankles crossed, watching, his eyes bright as coins.

Jake stared. 'How did you get here?'

'Maybe I took a short cut.' The small man stood, his white coat dusted with snow. 'Did you think I was that stupid, Jake?'

They faced each other. Then Jake breathed out, hauled the bike up, wheeled it round and began pushing it back.

Piers grinned. 'You're learning. 'That's so good.'

An hour later Sarah snapped, 'Of course I'm ready.' She rinsed the potato knife under the tap and gathered the peelings into a tidy heap. Then she dried her hands, while Piers watched.

The small man scratched his tiny beard. 'I know it's a bit soon after yesterday's scare. If it was up to me, we'd wait, but . . .' He shrugged.

Sarah looked past him. 'Some people can't wait.'

'Some people have waited too long.' Venn watched from the archway across the kitchen. His eyes were on her. Ignoring Piers he said, 'This will be the last time for you, Sarah. If it works I'll wear the snake myself. You'll be free to go.'

The dismissal alarmed her, but she smiled. 'You're so sure.'

'Try to describe what you see as it happens. Piers will prolong the exposure as long as possible, until the web is under pressure. We aren't risking losing you in there.'

'You mean you aren't risking losing the bracelet.' She turned, bitter. 'I know how much I'm worth.'

'You agreed to this,' he snapped back.

'I did. But what about Jake? It's personal for him.'

Venn didn't move. Then he said, 'I'll find him.'

Piers picked up the tea towel and refolded it neatly. 'Excellency, something else. The alarms. There was someone watching the gate earlier. We should be careful. If it's . . .'

'I don't care if it's the Devil himself.' Venn turned. 'Five minutes. And we test this thing to its limit.'

He went out. She stood, looking after him.

Piers said quietly, 'You've been reading Symmes's journal.'

It was so sudden she couldn't even bluster. 'Yes . . . I found it . . . I haven't got to the end. I gave it to Jake.'

'There is no end. It stops in the middle of a burned

page. Symmes vanished too, they say.' He looked up. 'If you're not happy . . .'

'I'm fine.' She stared at the empty doorway. 'I'm ready. It's what I signed up for.'

The handle of the lock-up door turned softly. Rebecca swallowed a gasp. Maskelyne, an edge of shadow beside her, did not move.

The wolf growled, a low sound. They saw its claws, long and sharp, slide under the door, its long nose savouring their scent. Then it was dragged away. With a crash that made her heart leap, someone kicked the door. 'Is that you, Sarah? But then how could it be?'

The voice was so close Rebecca felt she could have touched the speaker, if the door had not been between them. It was a young man's intrigued whisper.

'The wolf smells you. Are you some village ghost? Some echo from the delay?'

The door shuddered again. The wolf whined.

'Are you some Replicant? Or are you a journeyman, straying in time?'

Maskelyne's fingers held her in silence.

Yelps and scratches.

The purr of a passing car.

The tiny, tiny hiss of falling snow.

Neither she nor Maskelyne moved a fingertip, because they both knew that the stranger was still there, listening, a faint dimness beyond the threshold of the door.

Finally, after a long moment, his voice whispered, 'If so, my advice is to *journey away* and do it at once. Because this time is not a safe one for strangers.'

Then there was just the snow.

After five full minutes Maskelyne whispered, 'Gone.'

He leaned over and eased the plank away. When he tugged the door open snow gusted in, and they saw that darkness had fallen on the bridge. He stepped out, and after a moment, beckoned.

Climbing through, Rebecca saw that despite the chilly wind the snow was thick. The bridge was white with it, the footprints of a man and a wolf rapidly filling, leading away towards the Abbey.

She breathed out. 'Who was he? What was that creature?'

He shook his head. 'That wasn't a man. *That was the copy of a man.* It seems I'm not the only one looking for the mirror.' He turned to her, and she saw his worry. 'Apart from Jake and his tutor, is there anyone else at the Abbey? Anyone at all?'

Rebecca shrugged. 'Just that girl.' She frowned. 'Her name's Sarah.'

* * *

The door opened.

Jake looked up from the pages of Symmes's journal, his mind full of the scarred man and the mirror, over the scatter of his father's books across the carpet. Each was open, and he had out all the letters he could find, and notes, and photos, because he had begun by searching for anything about the Chronoptika and ended by just sitting and reading and remembering.

Maybe the bleak loss showed in his face as he stared up, because Venn stood silent a moment, his glance around the dark room swift with discomfort.

'We're trying again. Now. If you want to be there.'

It was grudging. But Jake nodded. He pushed the books aside and stood up. 'I'm surprised you want me.'

Venn shrugged. 'I don't. But David would.'

CHAPTER FOURTEEN

He conjured snow, he summoned ice,

He frosted lakes and rivers,

He killed the birds in the elderwood,

   He blackened toes and fingers.

He said If I can never rest

Then all the world will suffer.

I will destroy both man and beast

   Until I find my lover.

       Ballad of Lord Winter and Lady Summer

The silver snake closed around her wrist like an alien hand but this time Sarah was ready for it. She stared into the obsidian mirror.

In its convex darkness she saw the room, warped and unfocused, a blur of shapes in the gloom of the winter afternoon. She saw the soft, relentless snowfall outside the mullioned windows.

They were all watching her – Piers at the computer, Wharton perched on a broken armchair, Jake leaning against the stone wall, his arms folded in rigid defence, after his bitter argument with Venn that it should be him.

But Piers had told them both to shut up, and he had clasped the bracelet on her wrist . . .

Venn stepped back. 'Anything yet?'

'No.' Sound was muffled in the soft carpet. It was there to protect the mirror if it fell. She frowned. What if it did fall? Would that be enough?

Venn turned on Piers. 'Now?'

'Less response than before. The temporal axis is steady. No fluctuations.'

Her hands were sweating. She stared into the mirror, willing it to change, praying something would happen to its stubbornly solid surface. Glancing at Wharton, she sensed the rising silence of his disbelief. He was a lot shrewder than he looked. Had he told Jake about her?

The room was gloomy, woven with the dense web of cables between her and the Chronoptika. Its pillars rose into darkness, their capitals adorned with clusters of crumbling ivy leaves and carved acorns. Under some the faces of green men peeped through brambles, tendrils of leaves sprouting from their mouths.

They were watching her too.

Piers sighed. 'Nothing. Maybe we should take a break.'

'No!' It was her own cry, echoing Venn's.

'No,' he said, walking round behind Piers. 'We increase power.'

'I don't think that's wise, Excellency. It's already at the maximum we . . .'

'Don't argue with me! Just do it!'

Wharton was on his feet. 'I don't think . . .'

Venn turned, lean and ominous. 'No one asked you.' He came and stood in front of Sarah. 'Be ready. There might be a strong reaction. If you feel anything at all, just say. If you can't speak, raise a hand, and we'll switch it off. Understand?'

Wharton said, 'I want you to know I heartily disapprove of all of this. Jake. What do you say?'

Jake was looking at Sarah. Quietly he said, 'We should go on.'

He knows. The knowledge flickered through her fear, her swift sight of Wharton's shock. *He knows I'm not who I say. And he'll sacrifice me if it means getting his father back*.

Venn was already at the controls, that mishmash of Victorian wiring and dials, roped with modern cables. He adjusted a few dials, said, 'Now, Piers,' and turned to watch the mirror.

Nothing seemed different, but at once the air changed. It seemed sharper, tasted of metal. Jake peeled himself off the wall. A whine he had barely been aware of before was growing, inside his ears, inside his skull. It was climbing to a shrill, subsonic needlepoint of intense irritation.

Sarah was still, focused on the mirror.

She made a small movement, as if of pain.

Jake said, 'What is it?'

She didn't look at him, her gaze caught by her own curved reflection.

'It's starting,' she said.

Gideon lay on the top of the high wall of the estate and watched the snow settle on the flat roof of the car below. All he had to do was slide his legs over and jump. He would land safely, ankle-deep in the snowy lane. He would be free.

He didn't dare.

Between him and that safe landing lay centuries of days and nights, sunrises, moonsets. So many lifetimes that almost nothing was left the same from the place he had been born. He dragged dirty hair from his eyes and lay with his chin on his hands.

Was it true, or one of her lies?

Would he crumble to dust, would old age fall on him as soon as his foot touched the outside? Was Venn's estate really a protected outpost of the Summerland, with nothing but death beyond its borders?

There was only one way to find out. He stood up, balancing.

From here he could see the weather vane on the church tower at Grimsby Deep, miles away. That was the church he had been baptized in; vaguely he remembered a gaunt, echoing space. It had stayed with him, but it must be very different in there now. For him seventeen years ago. He had not changed by as much as a lost eyelash.

Everything else had rippled through fast, inexplicable changes. Houses appeared, almost overnight. Carts had crawled, then cars had sped up the lanes. Small planes had fought each other in the sky. Pylons grew. Strange wires that the swallows gathered on every autumn hummed in the frosty wind. What were they all? When had they come? He couldn't remember. And he had never been beyond, to the places where cars and people arrived from, where the planes sailed from, the small fascinating silver birds that flew so high.

He had asked her once, what they were. She had kissed his forehead and said, '*They are the enemy, sweet boy.*'

A voice said, 'You would be a fool to jump.'

He wobbled, then crouched and turned, furious. 'Don't creep up on me!'

The Shee, waiting in the dark branches of a pine, smiled its charming smile. It was a male, gracefully dressed in blue and silver, its long hair tied back. 'What are you looking at? May I see?'

They all had this childish curiosity. He said, 'A car. Someone's parked it here. And I think they've come inside.'

He could see from the snow that the car had been here a while. It was a dark, sleek machine, and its skin gave out no heat.

The Shee wandered over to the gates and Gideon jumped down beside it. The creature indicated with a long finger. 'Look.'

The gates were open; as far apart as a man could slither. They swung slightly, in the icy wind. The camera was already clotted with snow. Gideon said, 'What is that thing?'

'Venn's scrying device.' The Shee gave a languid grin. 'It will see nothing today. Not even these.'

They both gazed at the footprints that led through the gap between the snowy gates, and up the dark, clogged drive.

A man's. And the splayed spoor of the wolf.

The whine rose in Jake's teeth and nerves. It shivered down his spine. He wanted to yell for it to stop, but he forced himself to keep still, his eyes fixed on Sarah. She was gazing into the mirror. He moved so he was behind her, but saw only blackness.

'Nothing.'

'Exactly.' Venn's voice was breathless with triumph. 'Nothing. *No reflections*. Nothing.'

Sarah said, 'A room. A man, thickset, with a moustache. He's seen me. He's talking to me.'

The whine rose to screaming pitch. The web vibrated. Piers said quickly, 'Shutting down . . .'

'*No!*' Venn's eyes were on the mirror, searching. 'Not yet. Not till I see it. Where is it, Sarah? Where?'

But she spoke, not to him but to the mirror. 'Where is this? Who are you?'

The answer came from no one in the room. It was a thin, pompous voice, oddly quailing. It said,

'*My name . . . my name is Symmes.*'

The Shee knelt and touched the footprints, sniffed them. Then it raised its hands to its ears. 'What *is* that terrible whining cry?'

216

Gideon was wondering that too. 'Is it the world freezing up?'

He had been with them so long they had taught him to hear as they did. He could hear the cold night coming down, puddles on the gravelled track hardening infinitely slowly, the icy crystals lengthening and creaking to a pitted surface. He could hear the birds edging on their frozen roosts, the blown barbs of their feathers, the blinks of their beady black eyes. He could hear the frost crisp over the windowpanes of Wintercombe.

But this whine was worse than all of that.

'Sounds like a human machine.' The Shee rose, disgusted.

Gideon nodded. The creatures' aversion to metal still pleased him, even after all this time. It was their one weakness. The Shee listened, snow dusting its thin shoulders, its moonpale hair glimmering.

'Summer will want us to investigate.' Gideon turned.

The Shee's eyes went sly. 'Enter the Dwelling? Many have tried. Venn is too careful.'

'For you, he is. But I might be able to . . .'

'Summer forbids it.'

It was a risk. They were treacherous beings – this one would betray him in an instant. So he said, heavily, 'You're right. And after all, tonight, there's the Feast.'

The creature grinned, as he had known it would. 'The Midwinter Feast! I'd forgotten! We must get back.'

Its quicksilver mind would be full instantly of the promise of the music, the terrible, tormenting, fascinating music of the Shee. The music that devoured lives and time and his own humanity, the music that enslaved him and haunted him and that he hungered for like a drug.

'You go,' he said. 'I'll come later.'

'I have to bring you. She'll be furious.' Its bird-eyes flickered. He saw the small pointed teeth behind its smile.

'I'll follow you. I just want to see where these prints go.'

It hesitated, tormented. Then nodded. 'Very well. But be quick!' It turned, and its patchwork of clothes ebbed colour, a magical camouflage, so that now it wore a suit of ermine and white velvet, the buttons on its coat silver crystals of ice. It stepped sideways, and was gone.

Gideon kicked the gates shut.

He ran, fast and hard, towards the house.

The screech ratcheted up the scale, a nightmare howl that made Piers snatch his hands back and swear.

Sparks cracked in the dark.

'Turn it off!' Wharton yelled.

Sarah was sucked flat against the web. Behind her,

grabbing her arms, Venn said, 'I can't see him! Is he there? What does he look like?'

She screamed. 'I'm falling. I'm falling!'

The mirror was gone. It was a wild, gaping rent in the world. A scatter of objects lifted from the desk, flew, and were sucked straight in. With a vicious crack part of the web came free, one green cable whipping past Jake's head and vanishing with a bright blink like lightning.

'Stop it!' Jake yelled.

'Not yet.' Venn shoved him off. 'I've got you, Sarah.'

But she was fighting him, struggling back. Jake yelled, 'Let her go!'

He grabbed her. A fusillade of rivets cracked past him; he dragged her down. For a terrible unbalanced moment he and she and Venn were one tangled person, dragged and flung forward. The green web held them against it, but the force of the hole was too strong, it pulled hair, hands, breath like an immense invisible magnet, and then just as Jake could feel the agonizing suffocation rise to his throat the whine cracked, and with an explosion that flung him backwards off his feet the mirror came back.

He staggered. The room roared with smoke. Wharton was yelling, 'Fire!' In the corners of his eyes brilliant crackles of red were spurting up . . .

Sarah pulled him up. She screamed something, but his ears were ringing.

Flames whoomed into the roof. He saw Piers and Wharton appear and vanish through clouds of steam, a ferocious hissing, and then something seemed to pop in his head and his hearing came back, and the fire extinguishers were pumping fierce cascades of foam, over the sparking cables, the flaring embers of books and circuits.

And then, in a terrible sudden silence, there was only his breathing.

When I came to I was lying in my room with my Indian servant applying stimulants to my brow. The room was oddly dark and stank of burning, with some of the furniture overturned, but strangely nothing seemed severely damaged. A few objects were strewn on the floor, smouldering.

I sent Hassan out, righted my chair and sat on it gaping vacantly at the mirror. I had seen a girl from another time and had spoken to her.

We had conversed, across ages.

It was then that I realized that not only had my life changed, but that the world had changed utterly. Out there gas lamps were being lit, men were hurrying out to taverns to buy their evening meal, theatres were opening their doors, the vast populace of London was teeming in the rainy streets. Yet here, in this solitary room in a house among a million others I, John Harcourt Symmes, had broken open the boundaries of time and space.

So when the brick crashed through my window I almost screamed with the sudden shock of it.

It landed on my mahogany desk, scattering papers and books, and I leaped up and ran to the smashed star of the window and stared out.

In the dim shrubbery to the side of my gate a dark figure flickered and was gone.

Hassan came racing in, with the men I had hired. 'Get out there,' I snapped at them. 'And do your duty!'

Quickly I closed the shutters and picked up the missile. It was a half-brick, and I shuddered as I thought how it might have smashed the mirror itself to pieces. Tied to it with a length of dirty string was a note, which I unfolded. It read:

You have stolen from us and we will have our payment. And until we do you will never sleep soundly again.

I crushed it in my fist and smiled. The poor wretch from the shop, perhaps. The first thing I would do was have him sought by the officers.

And then, believe me, I would amaze the world.

Soft steam hung in the dimness. Jake looked at Wharton,

who stood breathless with his empty extinguisher, surveying the wreckage.

Burned-out wires glowed like cigarette tips.

Ash drifted in an icy draught.

Sarah hugged herself, the snake bracelet tight in her fist.

Venn picked himself up and pushed past Jake. Ignoring everyone he ducked through the safety web to the mirror, and when he reached it he put his hands against it, meeting his own contorted reflection.

Piers came from the controls, a zigzag of soot on his forehead.

'The mirror itself is undamaged,' he said. It was almost a plea. 'It's not the end.'

Venn was staring at himself. His hands, maimed by frost, gripped the black glass. For a second Jake was sure he would grasp it tight and pick it up and throw it to the floor, shattering it in a million pieces. But all he did was stare into his own blue eyes, his hands flat on the solid, unforgiving surface.

He seemed to Sarah to be staring at the torment of his failure.

And of hers.

CHAPTER FIFTEEN

If a speculum is polished sufficiently, it becomes invisible. For it doth reflect all about it, so that the eye sees only that which is shown, not the devyse that showeth it. And if a man become hard as diamond, faceted and flawed, he too will show nothing of himself, onlie the fractured images of his world.

The Scrutiny of Secrets by Mortimer Dee

'I'll take it,' Sarah said.

Piers looked at her closely. 'You've had as much of a shock, invisible girl, as him. You should go and rest. It's almost midnight.'

'The last thing I want is sleep.' She took the tray with the mug on it and turned to the door. The house was silent, its long corridors still. Wharton had finally gone to

223

bed, and where Jake was she had no idea. Failure seemed to hang in the air, as acrid as the lingering stench of smoke. She was tired, and as she walked along the dim corridors she still felt the terror of the mirror, dragging at her.

But this had to be done.

She knocked on the door.

No answer. 'Venn? It's Sarah.'

She knew he wasn't asleep. She said, 'Let me in. Piers has sent you tea. He's worried stiff.'

She balanced the tray and groped for the handle, her wrist encircled with a white ring where the snake had grasped it. She eased the door open.

His room. She had expected a mess, like Jake's, but it was spartan. Nothing on the shelves, no clothes, none of his prized ceramics. The furniture was black, modern, glossily lacquered. In all its surfaces reflected snow was falling.

'Leave me alone, Sarah,' he said, his back to her.

'You are so like Jake. Anyway, you don't mean that. Part of you must be excited about what we did.'

'Must it?' He was sitting in a chair facing the window.

She put the tray on a table and turned. 'I spoke to someone in the past. It's a breakthrough! Piers will repair the damage . . .'

'It's over,' Venn said. 'Burned out. Finished.'

His voice chilled her. She walked over to him. 'He says it looks worse than it is.'

'He's lying. You can take your money and go tomorrow. Where the hell you like.'

'I don't want to . . .' She stopped. Because he was holding a small revolver in his right hand, loose and careless. As she watched, he cocked the trigger back, and turned its muzzle into his stomach. The tiny click leaped in her heart.

Tap.

Tap, tap.

Snow was falling on the window. Jake ignored it. He stared into the dim embers of his bedroom fire, the marmoset curled cosily on his lap.

Had Sarah been lying? Maybe the first time, but this time he had heard that voice, that querulous question. Hadn't he? After the confusion of the explosion he wasn't even sure any more.

Was she really some mixed-up patient dragging them all into her madness? Not that Venn needed dragging. And if the Chronoptika had really swallowed his father, could they ever get him back again, especially after this disaster? Piers had been upbeat, but even he could see the damage. If only he could get close to the device on his own, maybe there was some way it would respond to him.

Maybe now, tonight!

Tap. Tap.

The small noise filtered through his drowsiness. He focused on it, realizing suddenly that it was too regular for snow or wind. He put the monkey on his shoulder and went quickly over to the window and listened.

Tap.

Carefully he unlatched the shutter. Nothing. The sill was cluttered with his father's books; he pushed them aside and knelt up there, Horatio's arms wrapped firmly around his neck.

Outside, snow fell in slow diagonals, twirling out of the dark. The Wood was a black emptiness against the sky.

With an abruptness that made him yell and jerk back, a figure hauled itself over the sill and gazed in at him. He glimpsed a flicker of eyes, then the bang of a fist on the glass.

Jake opened the casement.

Gideon crouched outside, gripping tight to the ivy. He was white with cold.

'You!' Jake stared.

'I thought I told you to keep a window open!'

Jake shrugged. 'Get in before you fall.'

'I can't. You have to pull me in.'

The wind roared between them. 'Why the hell should I?' Jake snapped, irritated.

'Because no one has, for centuries.' Gideon's fingers slid, bone-white on the ivy bines, his eyes green as the leaves. 'And because I saved you from Summer and I paid for it. You owe me.'

Jake stared at him.

Then he leaned out and gripped the changeling's hand, and hauled him in.

Very quietly, so quiet she barely heard her own voice, Sarah said, 'For God's sake, be . . .'

'. . . careful?' Venn didn't look at her. 'Too late. I should have been careful three years ago. Now maybe I should finish it here. Who would care?'

'I would. And Piers.' She sat on the bed, stubbornly calm, staring him out. 'Don't be insane.'

'That from a girl who thinks she can become invisible?'

She didn't smile. Instead she said, 'Tell me about Leah.'

It was an enormous risk. For a moment she thought he would really lift up the weapon and fire right in front of her, but then he waved it a fraction to the right. 'There she is. Look at her, Sarah.'

The portrait was positioned so it could be seen from the bed. It was modern in style, a woman's face, dark hair, high cheekbones, laughing at some private moment. Not beautiful but intelligent, and full of life. Sarah stared, fascinated.

Venn said, 'My family has a reputation. Half human, half Shee. Difficult. Untrustworthy. Since I was a boy I'd been used to loneliness. I didn't care. I was consumed by ambition – I burned with curiosity about the world, wanted to go everywhere and see everything, to cram it all into me, to fill up the emptiness. I was never satisfied. Even after Katra Simba, after the honorary degrees and TV series and money and fame, I was empty. Not fully human. Until I met her.

'It was up on Dartmoor. I was driving home, late one night, and it was raining hard. Just up by the crossroads to Princetown the headlights raked over a car, with someone leaning over the open bonnet.

'The rain was lashing down, so I pulled up behind and kept the headlights on full. Then this figure in a black hooded waterproof straightened up and yelled at me. "*Don't just bloody sit there. Get out and help!*"'

'That was her?'

He nodded. 'Oh that was her. Caught in that flash of light, behind the rain. Caught like a hare in the headlights. Wild and free.'

He was silent, shuffling the gun loosely in his hands, so Sarah handed him the mug of tea. He took it, absently.

'We were married for two years. I was a different man. It was as if some old nagging pain had been healed. Can you imagine that?'

'I think so.' She curled up her legs and glanced again at the painting. Then at Venn. He laid the weapon on the table and the mug of tea next to it. He sat back. She could almost feel him gathering strength for what would come next.

'The last time I saw her was beside a car too. But it was so different. Hot, dry, arid. A blazing sun. A road that looped around the mountains above a sea scored by luxury yachts and ferries. Wild and free, yes, and I was driving too fast. And the bend went on and on and my foot went down and then a lorry was in front of us and I twisted the wheel . . .' His voice was a whisper. 'The things you wish you could forget are the ones that stay with you. Her hair, all tangled in the grass. A small fly crawling on her forehead. Her eyes, looking at me. Not seeing me.'

Sarah couldn't move. It was as if the horror of his memories had woven a spell around them, had invaded the dark room.

Snow piled and slid on the window. She forced her

voice to the cliché. 'You shouldn't blame yourself . . .'

'Blame?' He turned his gaze on her. 'You have no idea. I don't *blame* myself. I don't exist any more. I haven't drawn a breath since that day. I'm buried as cold and as deep as she is.'

His self-loathing filled the room with a numb despair. She glanced at the door. She desperately wanted Piers to walk in, or even Jake. Anyone. And yet this was her chance and she had to take advantage of it, now, without pity.

'And so you think, with this device . . . ?'

He looked at her, sharp. 'Always the device, Sarah.'

'Well, I'm the one you're experimenting on. Who made it anyway? This Symmes, he wasn't the inventor . . .'

He shrugged. 'Maybe this man Maskelyne. Maybe Mortimer Dee. Maybe it's even older. But I know Symmes got it to work.'

He looked up. 'So I had to have it, Sarah, because I'm even more insane than you. You're just invisible. I intend to bring my wife back from the dead.'

Wharton dived out of his bedroom and grabbed Piers as he passed, just as the clock downstairs began to chime twelve. 'I have to talk to you.'

Piers looked worried, less sparky than usual. His lab coat was scorched. 'Tomorrow. Something's wrong . . . it looks like the gates are open. Maybe it's just the snow, but . . .'

'I know she's not your niece. I know who she is. What the hell do you think you're playing at? I have a good mind to phone the police myself right now and . . .'

'That's another thing.' Piers shook his head. 'The phone's dead. The lines must be down. Or . . .'

Wharton felt a cold chill in his heart. 'Or what?'

'Someone cut them.' Piers shrugged, his gold earring glinting in the hall lamps. 'I don't suppose you know how to load and fire a shotgun, Mr ex-army teacher, do you?'

Wharton stared.

In that instant the doorbell clanged, loud and urgent.

'What's that?' Gideon looked round, startled.

'Someone at the door.' Jake threw him a towel. 'You're soaked.'

He was more than that. He was saturated with water, a trickling creature of moss-green and ivy, dirty as a gargoyle, gazing in greedy wonder at the room around him. He looked at the towel as if he had no idea what to do with it.

'How long since you've been in a house?' Jake asked quietly.

'There is no time with the Shee. There's just now. And

now is always hungry and usually cold.' He wiped his face. Livid moss stains smeared the material. Then he saw the plate of nuts on the table and went straight for it, grabbing and crunching a mouthful.

Horatio shrieked a horrified protest from the curtain.

Gideon turned, whipping out a sharp flint blade. He levelled it at the monkey and hissed, a savage, eerie sound. 'What monster is *that*?'

Jake came and shoved the blade down. 'My familiar spirit. You're eating his food.'

Gideon stared. 'In truth? Your familiar? You're a sorcerer?'

Did he believe it? Jake shrugged. 'I am a sorcerer of great power. And maybe I can save you from the Shee. But first you have to do exactly what I say.'

Piers unbolted the front door cautiously and Wharton, behind, leaning on the bannister with the shotgun ridiculously aimed at the rectangle of snow, saw a tall red-hooded figure duck inside, wipe its feet, and say, 'I thought you'd never answer. I'm so sorry it's so late.'

She tugged her hood off.

He lowered the shotgun quickly and came forward. 'Rebecca? What on earth are you doing here? However did you get through?'

She laughed. 'It wasn't easy. It's coming down in blizzards out there! But I had to warn you.'

'Of what?' Piers said darkly.

She tugged off her coat in a shower of snow. 'A man and a wolf,' she said.

Venn walked to the window, looking down. 'Call me insane. I am insane. But only the device has kept me alive. We all caught David's enthusiasm, and we worked like slaves on it. But there were so many setbacks. Losing David was the worst.'

He turned, his eyes palest blue. 'And yet it worked – *it worked* – even though it cost me my only friend to find that out. A cruel exchange. But now . . . You've seen the damage. Now it's over. And all hope with it.' He looked at the pistol; but she put her hand on it, firmly.

'Don't give up. Don't stop.'

'I told you, it's over.'

'You'll succeed. I promise you . . .' It was clear to her, quite suddenly, that she had to keep him alive. Her own mission needed this to work. Then, afterwards, she would be free to act.

He stared. 'How can you promise?'

'I can. *I know*.'

A bang and a clatter downstairs. Venn flicked a glance

at the door. Then he came over to her. 'Sarah . . . who are you? Why are you here?'

She didn't answer. Instead she reached into her pocket and touched the diamond brooch. She said, 'There's something I need to tell you. I'm not from this institute. I'm from another place altogether. You need to know about Janus . . .'

At that moment the door crashed open. Piers seemed to appear from nowhere. 'Trouble. Come now.'

'Wait!'

'Can't wait. Intruders, in the grounds. We need to secure the house.'

Sarah turned in instant alarm. 'Who are they?'

'Not sure. Man and a wolf, Rebecca says.'

'*Rebecca?*'

Downstairs, shutters were slamming. She raced out and looked over the bannister and saw Wharton and Rebecca wedging a great bar behind the front door.

'Where's Jake?' Venn roared.

In the Monk's Walk Gideon stared around at the green web and whistled. 'But I'm telling you if Venn comes, I vanish. He'll tell Summer and then . . .'

'Leave Venn to me.' Jake shoved past him. 'Listen. You stand there and push this switch when I tell you. Understand?'

Gideon shivered with elegant distaste. 'I don't trust these devices. The Shee can't touch metal. They say it has demons inside.'

Jake ignored him, fastening the snake bracelet on his own wrist with feverish haste. Its clasp was icy, and light. 'OK, OK, I'm ready. Quick. Do it now!'

The complexity of the machine had daunted him. He had switched everything on and there was a faint hum. So something was working. He ignored the safety web and the charred wires and stood directly before the mirror, hands clenched on each side of the frame.

'Dad,' he whispered. 'It's me. I'm here. I'm coming.'

Gideon stepped back warily. 'It may not be a demon but it's making a howl like a fox in a trap.'

Jake could hear it, a terrible cracked, broken whine. He could hear crackles and snaps around him, distant bangs in the house.

His skin tingled. A charge like fear built up in him. Snow swam in his eyes. The bracelet tightened like a vice around his wrist.

It was happening.

The mirror was folding, collapsing in on itself, over and over, like an origami of glass, and into its emptiness was the only way left in the world. He staggered, was dragged a step forward.

He said, 'Now!'

Did Gideon press the switch? He had no idea. Because everything in his mind was gone, sucked into the dark void, all his thoughts, all his memories. Everything that was him. Until all that was left was his body.

'*Jake!*' The yell of anguish came from the door and Gideon instantly leaped back into shadow, snatching his fingers from the magic lights and howling moan of the metal.

Venn tore through the webbing like a madman, shadows flickering behind him. 'Jake. Step back! Now!'

His voice was sucked down the vortex.

Jake couldn't turn. 'Can't. Can't hold . . .'

He let go, but Venn was faster. With a yell of anger he ran across the room and grabbed Jake, just as the whole inner core of the Chronoptika became the utter blackness of a vacuum, the nothingness of infinity.

Of silence.

Sarah, breathless, leaned on the stone wall and gasped. Wharton and Piers and Rebecca came racing in behind her.

The mirror was black and silent. The room was empty.

Wharton stared. 'Did they . . . ? Oh my God they haven't . . . No, surely . . . Jake?'

Sarah was numb with anger. She whispered something, and for a moment he thought the words were 'Me. It should have been me.'

At that moment every light in the house went out.

If like a crab you could

go backwards . . .

CHAPTER SIXTEEN

There was always something strange about the boy. He laughed at shadows, he sang different songs. When the other children were merry he was still and silent. More than anything he loved the music of pipes and viols.

His mother's anxiety about the Shee made her stern. He was never to enter the Wood. He was never to stray from the cottage and the lanes.

But one winter twilight, when the stew was simmering on the fire, she went out to call him, and he was gone. It was said he had been seen hand in hand with a woman in a green dress.

He was never seen again.

The Chronicle of Wintercombe

Jake lay crooked and sore against a slimy brick wall.

His neck was bent at a painful angle; his right leg was numb. Something was sticky and wet on his fingers.

He moved, and groaned as pain shot from his ankle.

'He's alive,' a voice said.

Jake froze. His first instinct was to open his eyes, but what he saw made him close them at once and play dead. There were two figures bending over him, and one had a knife. He'd caught the dull glimmer of the blade, the dirty thumb on the hasp.

He held his breath.

'Finish him.' Hands grabbed him, hauled him over, rummaged quickly through his pockets and jacket, a quick rough search all over him. He felt something – his watch? – dragged from his wrist.

'Useless.' A coin jangled on the wet cobbles. 'Filthy foreign tin.'

'Take it anyway. The siller ring will fetch.'

Jake's fear was becoming anger. Then, sharp as a squealing rat, a whistle pierced the air.

'Peelers.' The two men jumped up; Jake rolled instantly to his hands and knees and threw himself at the nearest, grappling for the knife that came slashing at his chest.

He got one good kick in before a punch cracked darkness into his eyes; when that had cleared the alley was empty, except for a two-pence coin and a spatter of blood.

He picked himself up, cursing, and looked round.

He was in a narrow place, dark, with high buildings on each side. He took a breath and his eyes widened at the stench of the air. A foetid, gagging smell of sewage and old vegetables, of smoke and sweat, it almost made him retch.

Groping towards light he peered out on to a tiny courtyard, and his hand felt a few letters incised into the stone. He rubbed away soot and black moss to read

SOLOMON'S COURT

It sounded familiar. Dizzy, he tried to remember where he had heard the name, but then the whistle came again, urgent and near. A group of black-suited men charged in from the street against a small door in the corner, burst it open and ran inside, yelling.

Jake stood still, one hand still leaning on the wall.

He had to fight against astonishment. Keep calm. He had entered the mirror. He had *journeyed*. But where was he? He felt so sick it was difficult to think, and his head throbbed. He took a few steps nearer the door.

Screams met him; a large woman hurried out, throwing on a shawl, and after her a stagger of wrecks and drunks fled into the night. Was this some sort of raid?

And instantly the memory of where he had seen the name came back – it was the place Symmes had written of in the diary, the place he had got the mirror.

Was this the same night?

At once, ignoring his blurred vision, Jake raced down the three steps, past the pentangled doorway and into the opium den.

It was in chaos. The police – if that's what they were – were grabbing money and goods for themselves, rummaging in the pockets of opium-eaters too drugged even to notice. The sweet smell of the drug choked the close air. Remembering Symmes's journal, Jake looked for the back room; he raced across, shoving a man out of his way, and burst in through the dingy curtain.

The room was empty. Beyond, a back door banged in the wind . . .

He made two steps towards it before a hand grabbed him. 'And we'll be taking you down too, sonny.'

He was swung around. A huge man in a dirty black uniform grinned at him. 'See the duds on this! Come and take a look, lads. Here's a gallimaufry.'

A few chortling faces grinned through the curtain. 'Let me go,' Jake snarled.

The peeler snorted, 'Very good, milord,' and opened his hand.

It was sarcasm, but it gave Jake an idea. He drew himself up, raised his chin and fixed the man with a glare. 'Take your hands off me, man. Don't you recognize your betters when you see them? How dare you involve me in this disgusting farrago!'

Wharton, he thought, would have been proud.

The man's face lost its grin. He said, 'You mean . . . Lor love you, sir, I . . .'

'I shall have you dismissed without pay for this . . . audacity.' Jake dusted down his clothes. He had too many bruises. Too much dirt for the part. But the man was cringing.

'I 'ad no idea, sir. In this den . . .'

'I'm not here for the opium! I'm looking for a gentleman. His name is Symmes. John Harcourt Symmes. Have you arrested him?'

'We ain't nabbed no toff 'cept yerself, mister . . . ?'

Jake shrugged. 'Jake Wilde. Son of Lord Wilde . . . surely you know my father, man? The personal assistant to the Home Secretary?'

He had no idea if there even was a Home Secretary at

this date but it didn't seem to matter, he was rapidly understanding that just to be haughty and speak in his crisp twenty-first-century English might be enough. As the peeler looked round hopelessly for help he pushed past him. 'He was here, in this room, minutes ago. It was he who had you summoned. He can't have gone far . . .'

'We come on a nark's word.'

'Nark?'

'Grass. Informer.'

Jake frowned. Symmes had set up the raid, he would have been ready. He'd have already taken the mirror in the cab. He turned quickly, past the peeler. 'I have to find him!'

'Ah now, sir, you can't just . . .'

But Jake was already out in the dingy courtyard. The rattle of hooves made him turn; he saw the quick glimpse of a cab rattle past the archway; saw in the flash of the gaslight a plump, rather smug-looking man settling down inside.

Jake raced after the cab. Bursting out into the street he saw it swallowed by fog. He took two steps after it and crashed into a small shape that burst from the alley and grabbed him to stop itself falling.

He looked down and saw the dirtiest child he had ever

imagined. The girl wore a ragged blue dress over trousers and worn boots. She screeched, 'Let me go!'

He dropped her, but the cab had gone; the fog was a silent, greasy swirl. He swore. Then he said, 'Listen, kid, what year is this?'

The girl stared. Her eyes widened. 'You from the Bedlam, mister?'

He pulled out the two-pence coin and tossed it; she caught it, bit it and pocketed it in one smooth move. 'Foreign tin and no good.' She grinned. 'But as I like yer face, I'll tell you. It's 1848.'

Two years.

Wrong raid. Symmes had had the mirror for two years. Jake swore.

He said, 'Listen, I don't have much time. You live here?'

She shrugged.

'Two years ago a man came here. A gentleman.'

She rolled her eyes. 'They all do.'

'Not for opium. He came to buy a mirror. There was someone in the back room, a man with a scar on his face . . .' He groped after the name. Maskelyne. 'Do you know him?'

For a moment intelligence flashed into and out of her face. Then a yell from the den made her twist.

'I knows him. And I knows them as robbed you.' She sounded breathless. 'As took yer siller. Bail me and I'll take you to 'em.'

For a moment he thought she was speaking some foreign language. Then a peeler came out of the door and said, 'You! Girl! Come 'ere.'

The girl snatched Jake's hand. '*Bail me*.'

The peeler came over and grabbed her. 'With me, you.' He dragged her away; she screamed, tugging and struggling, a small thin whine of woe that set Jake's teeth on edge. He shook his head. 'Siller? What's siller?'

Did she mean . . . *silver*?

With a sudden terrified jerk he whipped up his sleeve, and stared.

The only thing round his wrist was a bare white ring in the flesh.

The snake bracelet was gone.

A small yellow flame cracked and flickered in the darkness and Piers's high voice said, 'Don't anybody move. I don't want any injuries. Or accidents.'

The flame moved jerkily across the blackness of the hall; Wharton heard noises of opening, and then the click of a powerful torch beam swept his face. He had a nightmare glimpse of a slot of dark room with

Sarah standing in it before Piers focused the beam on the generator.

'This is our emergency supply. If everything's in order we should get . . .'

Light.

A faint, flickery crackle as the overhead lights came back on, the generator erupting into an efficient hum.

Then it went off, just as abruptly.

Piers groaned and tried again. Nothing. 'I loathe machines,' he hissed.

Wharton took the torch and turned it on the mirror, black and enigmatic in its silver frame. Sarah came and stared into it, and her reflection turned Wharton cold.

She looked devastated.

He hurried across. Rebecca, just a voice behind him, said, 'But where's Jake? What happened?'

'Are you all right?' Wharton caught Sarah's elbow and drew her gently back.

She shook her head. Near the glass the air was charged: it felt as if a great surge of power had somehow drained it; and Sarah too. As Wharton held her arm she staggered; he grabbed her and said, 'Fetch a chair, quickly.'

Rebecca dragged one over.

'I don't want a chair.' She wished the shaking in her fingers would stop – no wonder he thought she was scared. How was he to know it was dismay and sheer fury. Jake – Jake! – had *journeyed*.

'This girl is in shock.' Wharton swung accusingly to Piers. 'And I have to say so am I. What has happened to Jake and Venn? Have we lost them too?'

Piers had lit a candle and was studying the controls. He seemed calm, but Wharton could see the faint sweat on his lip.

'How am I supposed to know! You're the teacher, mortal!' He took a breath. 'OK. They both seem to have entered the mirror, apparently only one fiftieth of a second apart, though only Jake wore the snake . . . I don't know what that will mean. They could come back at any moment. Or not for hours.'

Or never, Wharton thought, catching the panic under the forced control. He drew himself upright.

'Then I'm taking charge. Listen to me now. We need to regroup. Split up and work together . . .'

In the slant of torchlight he caught Rebecca's giggle.

'Well, you know what I mean. We have two emergencies here. This intruder. He seems to have disabled the lights. How?'

'The mains supply comes down under the drive.

There's a control box in the stable block.' Piers shook his head. 'I'll need to get over there and work on it. But after I'm gone you must make sure every window and door is firmly locked.' He glanced at Sarah.

Wharton said, 'Is this intruder anything to do with you?'

She wanted to tell him. But then, 'We know who it is.' Piers came over, wiping his hands on his coat. 'He's been spying on the place for a while. We call him the scarred man. Venn thinks . . . well, you've read the journal, Sarah. You've read about Maskelyne . . .'

Rebecca turned, restless. 'Look it doesn't matter who he is, he could be forcing his way in right now. You should have seen that huge white wolf. It was terrifying. Let's lock this place down!'

Wharton nodded. 'OK. You're with me. Sarah, stay with Piers. No one is to be on their own.'

He hurried out, and Rebecca, after another glance at the mirror, ran after him.

Sarah reached out towards the obsidian surface, and touched its solidity with her hands. 'So where did they go, Piers?' she said quietly.

He shrugged. 'Somewhere near where the mirror is. David told us that he did not actually emerge from it, but it was within a mile or so from his arrival point. They have to find it.'

But his voice was uncertain.

As she turned a flicker of eyes caught hers, a green glimmer in the mirror.

She gasped. 'Who's that?'

Piers grabbed a crowbar. 'Where?'

At first she thought it was one of the cats. Then she reached into the shadows and drew him out. He slid into the candlelight as if he had materialized out of air, a green-eyed boy in a ragged frock-coat, watching her with the wary stare of a trapped deer.

The boy from the Wood.

Gideon said slyly, 'Don't you know me, Piers?'

Sarah saw Piers's eyes widen in disbelief and then raw fear. 'You! How did you get into the house?' He whirled, flashing the torch into all the dim corners. 'Are they here? Is Summer here?'

Gideon smiled. 'Stay calm, little man. It's just me.'

His eyes moved to Sarah's. 'After an eternity in the greenwood, I finally got inside.'

'Wait!' Jake came forward and grabbed the peeler's arm. 'There's no need for this. The kid's . . . the child is perfectly harmless.'

252

His heart was thumping. Terror froze him. Without the bracelet he was trapped here for ever. He would have to live out his life in this stinking century and never see his father again.

The girl watched him through her thatch of dark hair. Her eyes glinted with sly triumph.

'Er, allow me to . . .' Jake's hand scrabbled in his empty pockets . . . A single pound coin remained; he pulled it out and held it up, so that it glittered in the gaslight. 'Allow me to recompense you for your troubles, my man. And leave the child out of this.'

He sounded like a bad actor in a worse period drama but that was all he knew of the past, all anyone could ever know, the thousand clichés of film and TV. All the history lessons in the world couldn't help him now.

The coin gleamed.

The peeler said, 'Well . . . mebbes I could.' His eyes on the coin.

Jake threw it.

It flashed through the dark. The man let the girl go and grabbed for it; instantly she ran, past Jake, so that he had to yell and twist after her, over the slippery cobbles of the yard, under the arch into a street ripe with the refuse of the dark houses that overhung it.

She was fast and fleet as a rat, and he was still aching

from the *journey*, but he caught her at the corner and flung her round.

'Wait, you little brat.' Breathless, he held her off as she kicked and tried to bite. Then he held her in a firm armlock. She screamed.

'Will you be quiet!' Jake looked round nervously. The fog masked the houses; deep doorways. 'Quiet! You said you saw them. The men that robbed me. I paid for your freedom. You owe me!'

She stopped struggling and stared at him. Then she said, 'Leave off.'

He let her go.

She looked up at him through her hair, poised to run. 'You don't arf talk rum.'

'So do you. What's your name?'

'Moll.'

He grinned. 'I'm Jake. Moll, I need to find these men and I need to find them now.'

Behind them in the fog, a whistle blew. The girl gave a quick glance and said, 'Not here, mister. Too many rozzers. We'll go to Skimble's.'

Before he could argue she was gone, running into the fog, and he had to follow, clutching at the pain in his side.

Down dim streets lined with runnels of flowing sewage, through labyrinths of dark alleys the girl led him, and he followed, deeper into the warren that was London's squalid heart, totally lost among the courtyards and warehouses, the occasional flaring naphtha light of a late shop or a tavern where shrieks and shouts echoed. Cabs clattered by him, dark figures in cloaks and tall hats, women with painted faces called at him from doorways. Every wall was a patchwork of peeling advertisements.

Moll slowed to a walk, darted down a passageway between two derelict buildings and clattered down some steps behind a rusty railing.

'Wait,' Jake said, uneasy. 'Why down here?'

'Because this is it, mister.' She pushed at a warped dark door until it opened.

Jake stopped.

She caught his arm, impatient. 'Don't be frit. It's just Skimble's.'

She pushed through into a corridor and he followed, wary. The corridor was dark, running with damp. Once it had been ornate though, because above him were odd swirls of gilt paint, a ragged swathe of scarlet curtain, tied with a fat tassel of silk.

'What is this place?'

She shrugged. 'A doss. A night pad.'

He had no idea what she meant. And then, as they came to the end of the corridor, she ducked under a

CHAPTER SEVENTEEN

I dream of the scarred man. He comes and stands at the foot of my bed, and he is half angel, half demon. He says, 'Don't try to use the mirror. The mirror will possess you. The mirror will devour your soul.'

He is too late. I have already discovered that.

My house is a fortress, locked and bolted and barred. But ghosts and phantoms flicker here, in polished surfaces, in glass and crystal.

And someone is watching every move I make.

Journal of John Harcourt Symmes

'Who is he?' Sarah snapped.

'Like I said.' Piers lowered the crowbar reluctantly. 'He's a changeling. He's with the Shee. Venn knows him.'

Gideon laughed. He flicked his coat tails and sat, as if relishing the comfort.

She was astonished at him. He was thin, almost insubstantial, as if his very being had worn away through centuries. And yet under the fever-bright eyes and the crazy costume there was a lost boy, someone so far from everyone else there was no way back, and she understood that only too well.

Not only that, his presence here was a sudden fierce hope for her . . . The Shee, if they existed, were reputed to be creatures that lived outside time. To them, all times were the same.

She thought quickly. 'Jake brought you here?'

Gideon shrugged. 'Foolishly, I thought he wanted to help me. But he only wanted me to operate the machine. That was all he cared about.'

'And what do you care about?' Sarah quietly watched as Piers turned back to the black mirror.

The boy smiled, bitterly. 'Going home. Though that is not possible.'

'Why not?'

'Because nothing is left. They took me centuries since. Now I can't leave the estate, so Summer says . . .'

'Summer?'

'Their queen. She's told me many times. If I even set the toe of my foot on the unenchanted earth I will dissolve into the dust I should have been five hundred years ago.

She taunts me with it. I have no idea if it's true, or if so much time has truly passed. Living with them — there's no day and night, no seasons. No ageing.'

'But . . . the Wood . . . it's real . . .'

'The edges are.' He shrugged. 'As you go in deeper it changes. You come to a strange place, where it's always warm, the leaves are always green. Another world, not like this.'

She looked at him. 'An ageless land of summer. It sounds perfect.'

Gideon allowed himself a small, hard smile. 'You think so? These creatures, they're not like us . . . Like you. They are beautiful and they think only of themselves, their music, their cold laughter. No ambition, no future, no past. They exist, like the wind. They're like butterflies mostly, but even butterflies die. The Shee don't die. They don't fear death. *They have no fear at all.*'

She shivered. For a moment she had the briefest glimpse of how his life must be, the precarious neverending balance between fear and boredom. And then understanding came, and she stared at him.

'That's why you're here! You think the Chronoptika can get you home!'

Piers turned. 'What?'

The boy's green eyes flickered a warning. For a moment

she paused. Then smooth as a snake she said, 'I was saying the Chronoptika is our only way of getting Jake and Venn home. We have to do everything we can . . .'

'And you think I'm not?' Piers was weary and irritable. 'I don't intend to be a slave for ever! Come on, let me out into the stables and lock the door after me. And you, Gideon, go back to Summer before she finds you missing. No one here can help you, and the last thing I want is her causing mayhem. I can't deal with her. Not without Venn.'

He stood before the mirror, and they saw his warped, curved image stare curiously into its darkness.

'Who may be dead for all we know.'

Wharton slammed and locked the final window. The casements were ancient, the fastenings frail with rust. It would be so easy to break in. Though perhaps the siege of the snow was more to be feared than some prowling stranger and his hungry wolf.

He turned to Rebecca. 'Right. That's the lot. Go and check the cloister, though God knows what passageways and doors there are under this place . . .'

'There's an old story about a tunnel from the Abbey down into the river gorge.' She turned, eyes bright. 'Maybe we should explore! It's a way they might use to get in.' Her eyes were wide with excitement. *She's acting*, Wharton thought.

'What about your family? Won't they be worried about you?'

For a moment she just stared. Then her eyes flickered and she said, 'Oh no . . . that's OK. They won't worry.'

'Phone them.'

'No signal.'

He nodded at the land line. 'Use that.'

She seemed reluctant. But when she picked it up she put her ear to it only for a moment and then held it out to him, and even before he took it he knew what he would hear.

Silence.

'They've cut the line,' she whispered.

'Or the snow's brought it down.' He turned, worried. 'Go on. Check the cloister. Quick.'

When she'd gone he crossed to the study and rummaged in the mess on the shelves till he found the object he'd glimpsed yesterday, a battered ancient transistor radio. There still seemed to be some life in the battery; he tuned it carefully, noticing with a shock how his breath clouded. With the power off, the house was rapidly getting colder. And he desperately needed to find out what was going on in the outside world.

Suddenly a local voice blurred out of static.

'. . . *whole of the West country. Blizzard conditions have forced the closure of the M5 and all major roads across Dartmoor are severely affected. Motorists have been forced to abandon their cars and . . .*'

The voice faded.

'Blast.' Wharton rubbed his numb fingers and tried again.

'. . . *emergency services. Police have advised . . . in outlying areas . . . not to leave home unless their journey is absolutely necessary . . .*'

'Great.' It was clear they were trapped here. The drive would already be knee-deep.

'. . . *Other news. A young woman . . .*'

His hand went to the off switch and stayed there, paralysed, '. . . *missing for two weeks from the Linley Psychiatric Institute in Devon has been found. Sarah Stuart walked into a police station in Truro yesterday, and . . . memory loss . . . she has . . . living . . . uncle in Penzance.*'

He swore, grabbed the radio. Shook it, stared at it.

In a final dying whisper it said, '. . . *Today in Parliament the Prime Minister . . .*'

Silence.

Wharton sat back and breathed out a cloud of astonished breath. Then, to two of the black cats that sprawled on the desk he said, 'What the hell is going on here?'

The cats blinked back at him.

As soon as she was alone Rebecca slipped through the cloister to the small outer gate and dragged it open. The snow was already falling heavily, every crack and crevice dusted with it; it blew horizontally into her face and the cold stung her eyes to tears. She wore a woollen hat pulled down over her ears but still the blizzard sounded like the hissing of endless static.

'Where are you?'

She dared not shout. Wharton was too close. Beyond the gate was nothing but snow, all the overgrown lawns lost in it, the very trees invisible.

And then he was there, a darkness darting out of that blinding white world, and he helped her drag the door shut and click the icy padlock, Rebecca dragging the bar across.

Maskelyne leaned against the wall, coughing.

He looked half frozen, hunched up with shivering, his lips pale blue with cold.

She said, 'Sorry. I couldn't . . .'

'What's happened?' He hugged himself, numb. 'You were so long.'

'It's all gone wrong! You wouldn't believe . . . ! Venn and Jake have . . . *journeyed*. Isn't that what you say?'

His scarred stare was so stricken she had to look away. 'Where? When?'

'About half an hour ago.'

'No I mean *when*? . . . What interval of time?'

'No one knows. Piers is scared stiff.'

So was he. He leaned forward and put his head in his hands, the thin fingers clutching the lank dark hair. 'Rebecca, this is unbearable. To be so close, and to . . .'

'You can still take it. The mirror. I'll help you . . .'

'*The mirror is no use without the bracelet.*' He shook his head. 'I can't believe . . .'

'Rebecca?' Wharton's yell made them both jump.

Maskelyne turned like a cat. He slipped out into the cloister and ducked behind the low wall just as Wharton ran through the inner door.

'All secure?'

'Yes. Fine,' she said, breathless.

'Good. We need to get back. I want to talk to Sarah.' He turned, abruptly, and so tense with agitation she said, 'What's wrong?'

'Apart from everything, you mean?' He shrugged, and she realized suddenly that even this big, bluff man was scared. Scared and angry. 'I want answers, Rebecca.

Because this whole bloody charade is getting dangerous. And I'm worried sick about Jake.'

He stormed into the house and she followed, glancing back at Maskelyne, who rose out of the cloister and watched her like a ghost.

I am desperate to make my first public demonstration of the machine, but I must be so careful! I must do nothing until I am sure of its powers, or I will look such a fool. There are plenty of mule-headed bigots in the Royal Society who would scoff at my claims, so I must proceed with utmost care, and not ruin my triumph by impatience.

Five times now I have managed to create the vortex in the mirror. I have had to supply a vast amount of voltaic energy, and create a magnetic field so powerful its effects can be felt streets away. I have also destroyed two rooms in my house as the result of explosions and a recent fire. But wonderful things have happened.

First, there is a terrible compulsion to enter the mirror. Rather like Odysseus, I have resorted to tying myself down in my chair before beginning the experiment and fastening the chair itself with chains to a pillar in the basement. Even so the drag yesterday snapped the ropes and I was hurled forward with such force I bloodied my head, and only my hand leaving the controls saved me.

Who knows in what time or place I would have found myself?

And then, I see such things in the obsidian glass!

I have seen a green meadow, backed by wooded hills and a small blue lake. Perhaps the Lake District, perhaps Wales. I have seen a room so dark it might be underground, and heard singing there, in some tongue I could not identify, and then a figure garbed in some cloak, for an instant, before the void. I have tossed in meticulously weighed samples of minerals, wood, vegetative matter.

All have vanished.

None have returned . . .

I have analysed the variations in gravity, the harmonics of the mirror's curve, the strange alterations in its weight and mass.

And today, I shall make my first experiment with a living creature.

The dog is one I picked up from the streets; the alleys of London swarm with such curs. It is of some mongrel variety, terrier-like, with a black ear and a great black blob on its flank.

A trusting creature, it allowed me to scoop it up and bring it back in the carriage; it ate hungrily of a whole plate of beef and then composed itself for sleep. Now it lies snoring and snuffling.

But someone has just knocked on the door.

As I look down from the window, I see it is a man. He looks up. He has dark hair.

He is a stranger.

Jake tasted the vile brew again; this time it was infinitely worse. He put the chipped china cup down politely. 'Thanks.'

Moll looked at his face. 'Too sour for you?'

'No. It was lovely. Thanks.'

'Eat then.'

She waved at the selection of faintly rancid pastries, obviously stolen from the bins of some bakery. He picked one up and took a cautious bite. He had no idea what it was, and didn't want to ask.

They were sitting on the floor of a tiny space that Moll called her 'crib' – a heap of dirty blankets and possibly clothes – and they were taking tea. He wasn't sure if the girl was playing some game of make-believe or was deadly serious; certainly her pride in having him there seemed only too real.

The crib was a small balcony or box, high up on the side of the theatre. If he stood up he would be looking down into where the stalls had once been, but now that space was a makeshift squatter camp of flimsily constructed shelters, tents, even small buildings made of poles and partitions and props and scraps of once bright theatre curtain. On the wide stage itself men sat and drank, women roared with laughter, dogs and babies fought. It stank of gin and ordure, the roof greasy with candlesoot.

It was a vision from a nightmare.

'Look,' he whispered. 'I don't have much time. These men . . .'

'Filchers . . .'

'OK. These filchers. I need to find them. Fast.' He had sudden fears of the men selling the bracelet in some dingy pawnshop, of it tossed among a heap of useless metal, slithering unnoticed to the bottom of the pile.

'I told you. I know them and I'll show them.' Infuriatingly complacent, she was eating what might have been half a sausage; she gave a quick sideways jerk of her head. 'They're down there. But watch they don't see you.'

He turned and peered down. 'On the stage?'

'Wiv the drabs.'

'The what?'

'Drabs. Trulls. The tarts!' She slithered up behind him and jabbed a thin finger, and he saw them.

Two men, one thickset, the other, the one he'd kicked, a skinny ferret-thin man. They were sprawled among a pile of broken scenery drinking; one had his arm around a frowsty-looking woman in a torn red skirt and not much else.

'Right,' Jake said. 'I get it. But the stuff they stole – the bracelet – where is it?'

She wriggled next to him and waved the sausage past his nose. 'They'll have the stash up there . . . where they keep all their stuff. See look, a-hanging.'

He saw. High up, suspended from the rickety walkways above the stage, looped with ropes and pulleys, a leather bag swung high and safe.

'No one can get at it there,' Moll said thoughtfully. 'Leastways, they don't think so.'

Jake frowned. The men were drinking immediately below. 'Including me.' He shuffled back and turned round. 'But I have to get it back, Moll. I *have to*.'

She pushed the dirty cup at him. 'It's fine. Don't fret. Drink yer tea and sleep for a bit. I'll keep watch, and soon they'll be snoring. And then, you and me, we can climb up. See? I'll show you a way. Easy as kiss-me-hand.'

Jake took another absent slurp of the brown liquid.

Below, the raucous shouts of laughter broke out even louder.

Wharton stormed into the kitchen.

Sarah turned. 'This is Gideon. A friend.'

The boy's presence threw Wharton right off track. Who was he? How had he got here? He felt for a moment as if the whole tangle was a dream; that he would wake up soon in his narrow bed in the school and see the fresh white Alps behind the pile of books to be marked on the windowsill . . .

Behind him, Rebecca came in, a little breathless. She stared at Gideon.

Then Wharton said, 'Never mind him, Sarah. Who are you?'

'What?' She had that wary, careful glance he was beginning to recognize. 'I don't . . .'

'You've been lying to us since the start. You're not this escaped patient. I just heard on the radio that that girl's already been found. That was just some story you used to get in here.'

'What?' Rebecca said.

'It's true. Look at her face.'

Sarah knew she was pale with dismay and frustration. Rebecca came and stood by Wharton, folding her arms. Gideon perched on the table, feet dangling, watching with interest.

Rebecca said, 'Is this true?'

Suddenly she was tired of pretence, of being alone among them. 'All right. So what if it is.'

Wharton came up to her and stared in her eyes, and his hurt would have made her ashamed if she had let it, but she had to think about ZEUS now, about the others who were lost, about the black hole Janus would make of the world.

'Is that all?' he said.

She shrugged. 'I can't explain. Not to you. To Venn.'

She expected anger but instead, very gently, he reached out and turned something hanging at her neck, and she realized he had the half-coin in his fingers, that it had slipped out of her scarf and that he was staring at it in strange disquiet.

He dropped it and stepped back.

'Lock the door,' he snapped.

Rebecca ran and slipped the bolt, standing with her back to it.

Wharton's eyes were steely. He faced Sarah without moving. 'I want to know exactly who you are, lady. Where you came from, what you want here. No lies, no excuses. And I want to know now.'

CHAPTER EIGHTEEN

That a man could grow quietly into so much power.
That he could plan and scheme and have his
enemies removed one by one, and then his allies,
until finally everyone is too terrified to speak out
against him. Until he rules with a sceptre of steel.

We should have seen this coming. This is history
– it has happened again and again. But if he then
discovers a weapon that can destroy the world.

We are the first to fight against such a terror.

Illegal ZEUS transmission, Biography of Janus

'Wake up, cully. It's time.'

The small hand was shaking his shoulder; he rolled
over and nearly groaned, but the dirty fingers clamped
tight on his mouth.

Moll drew back. Her tangled hair had been pushed

into a man's cap; her eyes were lit with excitement.

Jake sat up. He must have slept for a few hours; he was stiff and sore from the hard floor and his mouth was dry. Scratching his hair, he felt flea-bites. He whispered, 'Water?'

She shook her head.

'Probably just as well. So . . . Where are they?'

In answer she squirmed alongside him, and they both peered cautiously over the balcony.

The thieves had drunk themselves into oblivion. They lay sprawled on the cluttered stage, one on a bench, the other curled in a heap of old coats and cloaks, only his head showing.

The women had gone.

'Right.' Jake glanced up at the swinging bag. 'We need to lower that. Are there some pulleys . . .'

She looked at him sadly, as if he was the child of ten. 'Not as works, cully. You have to climb.'

He scowled. Silently, she pushed him through the door out of the balcony.

The sleeping theatre was a nest of rats. They scattered in rustling scutters as the small girl led Jake, her hand in his, along the rotting corridors. Ancient posters hung in rags, layer upon layer of lost comedy acts and forgotten singers, of plays mildewed into obscurity.

The backstage area was a maze of bedding and rubbish. A woman squatting in a corner turned and stared at them, and Jake saw she held a baby, swaddled tight to her chest.

Moll put her finger to her lips; the woman nodded, blank with weariness.

What had once been the wings stank now; pools of what Jake hoped was water ran on the boards, some of which had been ripped up for firewood.

He paused.

The bag of loot swung overhead. It was at least fifteen metres up, and the rope it hung from snaked down and was firmly tied round the big thief's waist.

Jake swore, silently.

Moll tugged him down; her small lips tickled his ear. 'Look there. You'll have to climb.'

Slung next to it was a thicker cable, rising in a great loop. He gazed at it, then at the men. He said, 'Right. You stay here. If they wake, *they mustn't look up*. Do you understand?'

'Clear as muck, Jake.'

He took the cable in his hands. It was filthy, and the fibres creaked, but it was strong and as he tested it carefully he knew it would support him. He slid his hands up, gripped with his feet and began to climb.

Hand over hand he hauled himself up. The rope's end twitched and swayed; then came loose from somewhere and skittered over the stage, making a soft rustle that froze him in fear.

The big thief snored.

Moll, crouched in the darkness, gave him a double thumbs-up. He climbed on.

Soon his hands were red and sore, his knees and back one fierce ache. The higher he went the more the rope swung, its end kinking and flicking. Up here it was dark, and sweat stung his eyes, but at last he was alongside the bag, its dim shape an arm's length away.

This was tricky. He tried to reach out and grab it. Twice he missed.

The third time, with an effort, he forced the cable to swing, and as the swing brought him close he caught at the bag and this time held it, the leather soft and yielding. Gently, he drew it towards him.

The cord leading down strained tight around the fat man's belly. He snuffled and muttered something in his sleep, flinging out one arm.

Carefully, gripping only with knees and ankles, Jake eased his hand inside the bag. He felt cloth, the greasy edges of coins. He felt the solid round lump of a gentleman's watch. And he felt the bracelet.

Its snake form was cold under his fingers.

He tugged at it.

Coins slid and clinked. He had it but it was tangled on something in there; he pulled it again with more force.

The rope swung, the cable swept. In a sudden dizzying moment he lost his grip; his ankles slid, he grabbed wildly at the rope and at once he was upside down, gasping, the snake bracelet ripped from the bag of loot that tipped out all its contents, crashing, tumbling, an iron rain, on to the sleepers on the stage.

Sarah said quietly, 'I never actually said that girl was me. I let you believe it. I saw the report in the paper and the photograph was like me. It was too good a chance to waste.'

They were all gazing at her as if they didn't know her any more. It was hard, but she fingered the short hair at her neck and floundered on.

'My name is really Sarah . . . just not Stuart. I . . .'

Wharton pointed to the coin. 'Explain that. In the journal, Symmes is given it as a token. ZEUS. Why is it significant?' His voice betrayed his anger.

She stared. 'You read the journal?'

Wharton looked slightly red. 'Well, I went into Jake's room and there was all this stuff . . .'

She nodded. 'The journal is about the past. I don't come from the past. I come from the future.'

Rebecca stifled a grin; Sarah's eyes flickered to her. 'Don't laugh at me.' She glanced back at Wharton. 'He believes me.'

He shrugged. 'Yesterday . . . an hour ago . . . I would have laughed too.'

'She's telling the truth.' Gideon's voice was cool and disinterested. 'I've seen her – she was a little girl. They took – will take – her parents away.'

She stared at him, dizzied by the way all time was one for him. Then she said, 'I will be born here. But my Wintercombe is a ruin. A place of ghosts. A colony where ragged people lived like rats, and where I hid my secrets in a hiding-hole in a brambled room.' She shrugged, and went and sat on the inglenook bench, staring into the flames. 'I can't tell you all of it.

'But there was a man in the camp called Janus. He started off as one of us. One of the revolutionaries. Gradually, he changed. Became one of them. My father said, "He's going too far. Thinks he's more important than the cause." One night, in winter, we heard him on the radio. TV was long gone, the Internet dead. We heard Janus and we knew he was all that was left. My mother laughed, but my father was afraid. It only took an hour after that for the headlights of the lorries to come roaring down the drive. They took my parents away. I don't know where. They took me to the Labyrinth.'

Gideon came softly and sat next to her. 'A place of terror?'

She laughed, softly. 'A place where I learned to be invisible. A place of secret experiments and strange procedures. A place where they studied humans, how to make them more than mortal.'

He laughed too. 'More than mortal!'

Rebecca shivered.

'But a few of us were stubborn.' Sarah looked up. 'We formed a resistance cell. We called ourselves ZEUS – because of the coin, and because of the story . . . the legend. In Greek mythology . . .'

'What legend?' Rebecca asked.

Wharton nodded. 'I see. Chronos – that is Time – was a titan who murdered all his sons one by one. Until Zeus was born. Zeus was the one who defeated Time.' He looked at her. 'How many of you were there?'

She shrugged. 'Six. Six friends. Angry, disaffected kids with no hope. No plan. Until we found out about the mirror.'

Wharton got up and put a new log on the fire, pushing it well down into the hot red embers. 'So you get yourself in here, you make us feel so sorry for you, you lie and pretend, and all the time you want to steal the mirror?' His anger was sharp as a wasp. He stood there and dusted his hands and held her with his annoyingly honest stare.

'Not to steal,' she said quickly.

'Then . . .'

'To protect it. From Janus ever getting it.'

She glanced at Gideon. He sat in the inglenook, watching the crackling fire. His hands were around his knees, his whole body twisted away from the ironwork. He was listening intently.

She hurried to escape the lie, maybe too quickly. 'He's experimented with it. We don't know details, but we do know that it works and that he's *journeyed* because . . . because of the Replicants.'

Wharton said, 'All this is fascinating but . . .'

'No, please, listen.' She turned to him, her blue eyes fierce. 'This is important. If a journeyman makes a mistake . . . if you come back at the wrong time . . . that is, if you come back before you leave . . . don't you see? *There will be two of you*. We call it replication. Janus must have done that because he has several Replicants. One of them is here, outside, in the grounds. Now.'

'And the wolf,' Gideon said. 'Don't forget the wolf.'

'He breeds them. They smell out the tracks of a traveller in time.'

Wharton frowned. 'But, the snow . . .'

'Won't stop him. He'll use it. He's already cut the power.'

Rebecca shook her head. 'All this . . . it sounds crazy.'

'Who asked you?' Sarah swung round, irritated. 'What are you doing here anyway?'

The tall girl shrugged. 'I came to warn Jake . . .'

'Why?' Sarah said, suspicious. 'About Janus? Then how did you . . . ?'

'Look.' Wharton's voice was sharp. 'The house is secure. Any minute now Piers will get the lights working. No one can get in. I assure you.'

The crash silenced him.

He stared at Sarah. Then they were both out of the archway and running down the frosty corridor, under the bells. Hurtling into the hall, Wharton stopped dead, seeing the front door had been burst wide open, the lock still smoking. Snow swirled over the black and white tiles of the floor.

Behind him, Sarah said, 'He's inside.' She turned to him, her face pale. 'Get to the Monk's Walk. Quickly. Or we're finished.'

'Oh I intend to. But not you.' Wharton blocked her

way. 'I'm afraid you're not going anywhere near that mirror, Sarah. Because everything you've told us could still be a pack of lies.'

Deep in the lightless house Maskelyne heard the crash. He had crouched, shivering, trying to rub feeling back into his arms and shoulders for long minutes; then had explored carefully, opening doors, peering into rooms, working his way silently into the heart of the ancient building, its scents of wax polish and old lavender.

He knew the device was here. In some inexplicable way he could sense its waiting presence, feel its tingling aura in his nerves. The mirror recognized him. He moved towards it, down passageways, up stairwells, treading stealthily down the long, empty expanse of the Long Gallery.

The crash stopped him, under a portrait of a long-dead Lord Venn. Someone had forced open the front door. For a moment he heard the blur of anxious voices, then he ran, up a narrow spiral stair that led to the first floor.

He walked stealthily down the corridor and turned a corner.

Piers was waiting for him.

The small man smiled, satisfied. 'So. It is you after all.'

He stood in his grubby white coat, the red waistcoat

bright under it, his small feet planted firmly. He had no weapon, but Maskelyne knew he didn't need one. This was no human servant.

He stopped. 'You know me?'

'You're in Symmes's journal. You're the one he stole the mirror from.' Piers strolled down the corridor. 'I've seen you on the cameras. You've been trying to get in here for months.' He came up to Maskelyne, curious. 'Did you *journey*? Did you come straight from that night in the opium den?'

Curiosity. The bright eyes were wide with it. It was the one weak point Maskelyne understood. He let his shoulders slump; allowed exhaustion to cross his marked face. He said, 'I'm lost in this time. I just want the mirror. My mirror.'

There was a small blue and white ceramic pot on the wide windowsill. That would do, if he could reach it. Quickly he drew the slim glass weapon from his pocket.

Piers laughed, as if surprised. 'That won't hurt me.' He came right up to it; let the barrel rest against his chest, almost friendly. 'I'm not the sort of being that can be destroyed with a weapon.'

Maskelyne nodded. 'I know that,' he said. Then he spoke, so fast, so low, the whisper was barely intelligible; a rapid spell in ancient Latin and lost Celtic, the words garbled backwards, forwards, inside-out and opposite, a web of knotted sound, a rattle of power.

Piers gasped.

He looked down at himself, howled a syllable of rage, flung out both spidery hands.

Maskelyne sidestepped, made a sigil of his fingers.

Piers was an outline, a glimmer. He was a faint after-image in the air of the corridor. He mouthed curses but no words came.

Maskelyne took the jar and lifted the lid. It smelled of the ghosts of roses. He stopped the spell, took a breath, and commanded.

'Enter.'

Piers, faint as dust, fixed him with a furious glare. And then he was gone, though Maskelyne felt scorched, as if that wrath had burned right through him.

Hands shaking, he put the weapon away, fixed the lid on the jar and stood it on the sill. Then he sat down beside it so fast he felt as if his legs had given way, and put his head in his hands.

He had not made such a dark magic for centuries.

He was surprised to find he still had it in him.

The noise was terrible. Coins fell like rain, bouncing and rolling, rattling on the bare boards. The thieves were awake in seconds. Moll screeched, and Jake only managed to stop his fall by grabbing the twisted cable so tight the snake bracelet bit into his hand. Hot rope scorched him.

The men saw him; they swore and yelled. One – the smaller – ran and grabbed the end of the rope and jerked it so ferociously Jake could hardly hold on. If he fell he was finished. If they had a weapon he was finished.

Then Moll struck.

She came out of the ruined wings like a spitfire, kicking, spitting venom. She had some sort of cudgel of wood; she cracked the thin man from behind across the back of his knees so that he staggered and fell, howling. She dragged her weapon up and turned, but the big man was there.

With one back-handed blow, he floored her.

Jake roared with rage. Forgetting safety, he slid down the rope, hitting the stage so hard his knees buckled; in seconds he had the thick cable looped round the man's throat and was hauling him back, throttling, dodging the flailing fists and clutching fingers.

The thief made choking, animal noises; he scrabbled desperately at the rope. Jake clung on, but the man's strength was too much; with one convulsive jerk he turned, and a knife slashed so close to Jake's neck he felt the whistle of air.

Moll yelled, 'Jake!'

He leaped back.

Breathless, he confronted the thief. The man tossed the knife into his right hand and plucked another from his back pocket. The blade slicked out. Menacing, grim with anger, he moved in.

'Down, Jake!' Her screech was so shrill it sounded like the monkey's. He gave one glance back, then threw himself aside with a yell, and the vast stage curtain swept over him like a smothering tidal wave of darkness and dust. For a moment he was drowned in it, and then he had rolled free and she was grabbing him, dragging him up. 'Run! *Run!*'

Half blind, he crashed into the ramshackle scenery; through lopsided battlements, through a tilted doorway cut in a cardboard cottage. Behind, the big thief roared and floundered under the curtain, swearing death and revenge, but already they were fleeing through heaps of painted graves, tombs adorned with skulls and crossed bones, through flimsy flats of gnarled trees and fairy rings and a vast sprouting beanstalk.

Moll giggled.

'You're crazy,' Jake gasped. 'He could have killed you!'

'He never. And he won't.'

She grabbed him away. 'Down this way. Smart now.'

A narrow grating in the wall. She had tugged it open and was swarming through; Jake slid after her, feet first into a pitch-black stinking space, a slit barely wide enough to squeeze inside, descending at a steep angle.

As they scraped themselves down and down they slowed, gasping in the foetid air, until at last they stopped, and Jake heard, far behind, the big man slamming at the tiny grid with chilling rage.

He heard a small creaky sound in the darkness beside him. Moll, it seemed, was laughing.

He realized he was sore, one hand badly rope-burned. But the bracelet was safe. He touched it, in the dark, then shoved it deep in his inner pocket. The thought of how close he had been to losing it for ever turned him cold. He gazed up the filthy tunnel.

'How far does this go?'

'Into the gutters,' she said, snuggling up tight to him. 'All the runnels and sewers, the new ones, they all meet down here. This is where the meat-men live, and the rat-boys, too. But don't fret. I knows a way up that will bring us near the posh streets, the ones you want.'

'Why should I want them?'

He caught the glimmer of her grin, patient and knowing. 'Because that's where he lives, don't he. The one you want. The cully what took the mirror.'

Sarah paced the tiny scullery, furious.

Wharton had been polite but utterly firm. He had taken her arm, marched her in here and locked the door. She gave a small scream of frustration. *They had no idea what they were dealing with.*

She stopped.

Taking a glove off she pulled the grey notebook from her coat pocket and, for a moment, stared at it. Reluctant, she opened it. The page was covered with the sloping script of Janus.

I'M SORRY, SARAH. MY REPLICANT IS IN THE HOUSE NOW. AND THANKS TO THAT LITTLE SUBTERFUGE OF YOURS, WHICH OF THEM WILL TRUST YOU ANY MORE? THE BLUFF TEACHER, THE LITTLE GENIE, THE REMARKABLY CURIOUS LOCAL GIRL? GIVE UP, SARAH. OR YOUR PARENTS WILL PAY.

Icy with dismay she stared at the words, then slammed the book shut and flung it from her as if it was infected.

She had to get out!

She ran to the door and rattled the handle, strained at the lock. Maybe if . . .

'Girl from the future.'

A quiet, amused voice. She stood very still. She said, 'Who is that?'

'Gideon.'

Her hands clasped tight on the handle. She said, 'What's happening? I have to . . .'

'You can't get to the mirror. Rebecca and Wharton have gone down there and he's armed.'

'You could let me out.'

He sounded as if he was laughing, a cool, rare laugh. 'Why should I?'

'Listen to me, Gideon. Open this door. Take me into the Wood. Take me to Summer. That's what I want you to do. And in return, if I get Jake and Venn back, then I promise I'll get you home. Back to your family. Before this nightmare ever began.'

He was silent so long she thought he had gone. When he said, 'Summer is far too dangerous,' she almost cried with relief.

'I have to try. Please.'

A rattle of sliding bolts. She stood back. The door opened and he stood there, in his moss-green ragged coat, looking at her.

'Will you betray me too, Sarah?'

'Of course not,' she lied.

CHAPTER NINETEEN

And you would not believe the pleasant happenings! On Christmas Eve the waits came and sang, and then late at night, the mummers with their old play, all dressed in ragged costumes, and then – rather eerie this, my dear – the Grey Mare, a horse's skull on a pole, carried by villagers. And all the while the land lies deep in winter snow under the roundest of moons . . .

Letter of Lady Mary Venn to her sister, 1834

Like a shadow, Maskelyne crept down the Long Gallery.

Again he stopped and looked back, swivelling the weapon.

The house was dark, and only moonlight slanted through its casements, reflecting here and there in dim polished wood, the angled smiles of framed faces.

Twice he had thought he had heard a footfall, the

faintest tread. And once, a snuffle. A sinister, animal breathing. Quietly he said, 'This will kill you, Replicant. Do you hear me?'

Nothing.

He hurried on, letting the mirror draw him. He felt its disturbance like ripples in his mind, like an ache in his bones. It was close now, closer than it had been since that night when the stout, pompous man he had thought such a fool had tricked him out of it.

And he had thrown himself in, guideless.

He came to the covered alcove and drew the curtain aside. There was a door, and it was locked.

He worked quickly. Years in the thieving underworld of London had taught him many skills; he had the door open and closed behind him in seconds.

The Monk's Walk, its grim cold Gothic stone, made him smile, because this was familiar. He had explored many vaults like this, broken through all too many crumbling sepulchres.

He walked on, carefully.

The room beyond was vast, and dark. He paused in the doorway listening. Had they left the mirror unguarded?

Because there it was. He could not stop himself, he pushed hastily through the feeble remnants of Venn's safety web, ducking under broken threads and snapped green cables.

After years, after centuries, after Symmes's betrayal and his own bitter, stretched arrival, here it was.

His Chronoptika.

He walked right up to it and it showed him his own warped reflection, his face twisted and ugly, and then in a shiver of moonlight, handsome and whole.

He leaped back. 'Rebecca?'

She had been there, a slant of anxious eyes. He turned, saw her, took one step towards her when a voice said, 'Stand perfectly still and drop that weapon. Or you get both barrels.'

The big man, Wharton, had a shotgun pointed right at him.

Maskelyne took a breath. He crouched, and slowly laid the glass weapon on the floor.

'Move away from it,' Wharton barked.

He took one step.

'Rebecca. Get it.'

She slipped out from the shadows and ran and picked it up, gingerly, as if it was hot.

'Now.' Wharton came forward into the light, cradling the shotgun; he took the weapon from her and looked at it, grim. 'I want to know how you got in here. And who the hell you are.'

Maskelyne was silent. He felt so weary he wasn't sure if he could speak.

It was Rebecca who spoke up. Facing Wharton she drew herself up and she was nearly as tall.

'Actually, he's sort of from the past. And he's with me.'

Symmes's house was a large one, in a wide London square. From the darkness of the gardens opposite, Jake staked the place out, noting its pillared porch, the black-railinged servants' area in front with its worn steps, the lofty windows – one, on the first floor, cosily lit behind its looped curtains.

Moll breathed noisily at his back.

They had crossed a London of nightmare, that he had barely recognized. Great rookeries of filth and squalor, sudden tangles of slums, and then at a turn of a corner a gracious street, a wide avenue he knew in his own time. But the foul stench of the place, its rumbles and clanks, even its voices, had an alien note; they seemed to hang too long in the air, to be pitched too high. The books he had read – Sherlock Holmes, even Dickens – had not prepared him for the sheer brutality, the hundreds of horses, the opulence of the women's dresses, the scrawny crossing-sweepers with their sickly, pocked faces.

Now he looked down at Moll. Her breathing was harsh after the running. What would happen to her? Consumption? Smallpox? He had a sudden mad idea of getting her back through the mirror with him, seeing Piers's astonished alarm, when she said, 'He's got a visitor.'

He turned.

The house front was lit by a solitary gas lamp; in its cone of light he saw a man walk along the street and pause at the steps, then stride up and rap impatiently at the doorknocker.

'Closer,' he muttered.

They crossed the road. Tree-shadows from the gardens rustled over them.

The man was tall; he wore a dark hat, and as he swept it off and the hall light fell on his fair hair and lean face, Jake took a breath of surprise.

'Who is it?' Moll whispered.

'It's Venn.'

He was intensely relieved, and then filled with bitter envy. Venn obviously hadn't been set on by thieves; judging by his Victorian outfit it had been he who had done the stealing.

Jake moved along the railings. 'Venn!' he breathed.

Venn turned, fast, but at that instant the door opened and a servant in a dark suit said, 'Yes?'

Venn swung back. 'My name is Oberon Venn. I'd like to see Mr Symmes.'

The butler looked doubtful, but Venn's height and bearing seemed to reassure him; still he said, 'Mr Harcourt Symmes does not receive visitors at this hour.'

'He'll receive me.' Venn took out a small card and wrote something on the back. 'Give him this. Tell him it's urgent I speak with him now.'

The butler vanished. Instantly Venn turned. 'Jake? Where the hell have you been!'

'Where have I been? Getting robbed, beaten up . . .'

Venn's icy glare took in Moll. 'Listen. Get inside. Through the servants' entrance. I need to look at Symmes's set-up for the mirror, and . . .'

The door opened; he turned. Jake shrank into the shadows.

'Mr Harcourt Symmes will see you, sir.'

Venn flashed one look back into the dark street. Then he ran up the steps and the door closed behind him.

Jake turned, against the damp railings. He breathed out in anger. 'How am I supposed to get inside?'

Moll looked at him, pitying. 'Watch and learn, Jake, luv. Watch and learn.'

* * *

294

The Wood was a network of ice. Frozen branches criss-crossed above Sarah's head; in the black sky the stars were brilliant as jewels. Gideon looked back. 'Not far now. Are you cold?'

'No,' she muttered, sarcastic.

He grinned.

They had slipped out of the house and run; though she was wearing coat, gloves and Jake's school scarf she was still shivering, hugging herself against the terrible, knife-sharp winter.

It was Christmas Eve, but here in the deep tangle of greenwood it could have been any time, a pre-pagan neolithic silence, of cracking branches and crunched puddles of ice aslant the path.

She gasped. 'How do you . . . stand this . . .'

'I don't.' He reached back and took her hand, leading her through the briars. 'I live in the Summerland. See?'

Between a step and a step, the world changed.

She crossed a threshold that wasn't there and the Wood was green, the sky blue. Bees buzzed in the throats of flowers. Warmth enfolded her, a relief so deep she wanted to cry out with the delight of it.

'Incredible!' She turned, staring. 'It's like paradise! Where are we?'

And yet there were rooms in it, and buildings, that

seemed to obtrude at crazy angles, corners of temples and museums and libraries, slabs of castle. As if these places began in some other dimension and ended here. As if they had slid in here, coming to a halt in the tangled Wood, snagged in brambles, held by honeysuckle.

He didn't answer, and she saw he was gazing over her shoulder, with a dismayed, defiant look.

She turned.

Summer stood there in a dress of red, a brief, floaty thing. Her feet were bare. She smiled, charming. 'Who have you brought me this time, Gideon?'

He shrugged. 'She brought me.'

Sarah went to speak, and found she couldn't. She tried to move, and nothing would work. In silent, suffocating panic she stood trapped in an immobile body, even unable to turn her own eyes and watch as Summer slowly circled her.

'A strange child indeed. So old, and so young.' Summer came round, reached out a finger and jerked Sarah's chin up, studying her face. 'A plotter and planner. A mad girl, of water and weeds.'

Her hand dropped. Then Sarah felt the lightest of touches, and realized the faery woman had lifted the broken coin from her neck and was examining it carefully.

'Zeus. I met him once. Another fool who came to nothing.'

She looked up, and Sarah looked for a moment deep into her eyes, and they were green and no light reflected in them.

Then, as if she had lost interest, Summer turned and Sarah, with a gasp, could move.

She looked round. The clearing was grassy. There were fallen trunks and a sweet cascade of honeysuckle. Under it a fountain splashed into a deep well where salmon swam; hazelnuts fell from a bush above and floated in the water. On the grass a selection of chairs stood, rough and wooden, an ornate gilt stool, a toppled plastic garden chair, a faded painted throne that might have been Egyptian or from some film set. Summer sat on the stool and spread her bare toes luxuriously in the warm grass. 'So. Sarah. What do you want with us? Not many mortals have the gall to come here.'

'I need a favour.'

'From the Shee?' Summer laughed. 'We don't do favours. Bargains, perhaps. Is this about Venn?'

She nodded, trying not to sound too anxious because she sensed already how this creature seemed to feed on that. 'Last night Venn and Jake entered the mirror. They haven't come back.'

Summer's laugh was a tinkle of spite. 'So he finally got to seek his lost love. How I hope he rots in some brutal age for ever.'

'He won't,' Sarah said quietly, 'and you know that. Your jealousy . . .'

Summer stood, swift as a cat. 'I am *not* jealous. Of a woman!'

'Did you ever meet Leah? Did you know her?' Sarah's curiosity was sudden and real; she saw Gideon glance at her quickly, a warning.

Summer shrugged. 'Human women are all the same. I don't remember.'

'But Venn . . .'

'Venn is one of us. Our music is in him. When he gets tired of his obsession with the mirror, he'll come home.' Summer frowned. 'Don't I know you? Haven't I seen you somewhere before? Among the ruin of Wintercombe maybe, the burned hall, the ashes of the Gallery?'

'No.'

'I think I have.'

Sarah went and righted a garden chair and sat on it. It was yellow plastic, from some cheap supermarket. Angling it to face Summer she said, 'You seem to know about the past.'

'All times are now to us.'

Sarah nodded. This was a huge risk, but she had to take it.

'Do you know Janus?' she said.

'What do you mean, he's with you?' Baffled, Wharton lowered the shotgun.

Rebecca eyed the slim glass weapon. 'I'm sorry. It was me that let him into the house.'

He stared. Even her voice was different.

'He and I are friends. It's a long story . . . But I know about the mirror, and, well, Maskelyne's not dangerous. He just wants what's his.'

'Don't we all.' Wharton took a step closer. He looked closely at the man. 'I remember you. You were on the plane. You followed us here.'

'I did.'

'Are you really the one in the journal? All that time ago?'

Maskelyne shrugged. He looked wary.

'Well, then you can operate this thing! Get Jake back . . . ?'

'Maybe. At a price.'

They exchanged a long glance. Wharton said, 'I have no idea what to do here. They're all gone – even Piers seems to have vanished. There's only me left to guard this thing, and I don't know the first thing about it. I need help.'

Maskelyne faced him. His eyes were dark and troubled. 'If I get them back, I take the mirror. It will be best – for Jake, and Venn.'

'They won't think so.' Wharton frowned, blew out his cheeks, glanced at Rebecca. 'I must be mad to trust you two. But do it. Do what you can.'

Rebecca laughed in relief. Maskelyne said, 'I'll try.'

Wharton turned.

'Where are you going?' Rebecca said, alarmed.

'To get Sarah. I think we need to be all together.'

Venn walked into the drawing-room and saw a stout man in a red dressing-gown standing before the fire in a hastily adopted pose. His moustache was bushy, his face florid.

He held the visiting card in his hand.

Venn said, 'Mr John Harcourt Symmes?'

'Who on earth are you?' The voice was peevish and suspicious. Symmes held up the card. 'What is the meaning of this? This is the card of a fellow member of the Royal Society; I know him well, and you, sir, are an imposter.'

'My name's Oberon Venn. We're not acquainted. I'm an explorer and, some say, a man of science.'

300

'Well I've never heard of you, so . . .'

'I've come about David Wilde.'

Symmes stopped in mid-bluster. He stared at Venn and then, as if in a sudden weakness, groped for the chair behind and lowered himself slowly into it. 'Bless my soul,' he whispered. 'Are you from . . . that is, have you *journeyed*?'

Venn nodded. 'I also have two companions with me and by now they're probably causing havoc in your servants' hall. Could you have them sent for please.'

It was a command.

Symmes seemed helpless with surprise. He rang the bell, and even as the butler entered Venn caught Jake's voice from far off in the house.

'You have some . . . people down there,' he snapped. 'Bring them.'

The man looked at his master. 'Sir? These are an urchin from the streets and a young man in the most bizarre clothes . . . The girl at first pretended to be ill, and so . . .'

'Fetch them,' Symmes growled. 'Do it.'

While they waited he said, 'I would appreciate . . . just a few words of description. Your time . . . how has London changed? Are there flying machines? Do women have the vote?'

Venn said quietly, 'David never spoke of it then?'

'He said it would be best if he did not.'

Venn smiled. That was David. As the door opened and Jake strode in with a small ragged girl trotting at his heels he suddenly saw the resemblance again between the boy and David, that sharp awareness. That rapid taking-in of everything around them.

Moll's eyes were wide. She went straight to the fire and crouched there, almost purring. Jake faced Venn. 'What's going on?'

'This is Harcourt Symmes. He met your father.'

Jake said, '*What?*' He turned fast. 'When?'

Symmes's answer devastated him. 'Three months ago.'

Venn sat on one of the armchairs and nodded to Jake to do the same. 'I knew David would come here. He must have realized that if we managed to *journey* after him you'd be the one we'd search out.'

'So he said.' Symmes seemed a little more at ease. He settled comfortably in the chair, and began to talk, and Jake caught the self-satisfied tone of the man that he had read in the journal.

'I . . . er, obtained the mirror and worked on it for two years with limited success. It was obviously a portal to some other existence; I sent inanimate objects through, and then a rat and even a dog, but I dared not use it on a human, least of all on myself. A scientist should perhaps be bolder, but . . .'

Jake couldn't wait. 'Dad came through the mirror?'

'Oh no. Not at all. In fact, like you, he simply knocked on my door.'

Moll's fingers slid over the table and took an apple from the bowl. She began, quietly, to crunch it.

'It was this May. I saw a thin, rather worn man of premature age . . .'

'Age! My father was thirty-eight!' Jake stared at Venn. 'How could . . .'

'I don't know!' Venn's impatience was savage. 'We don't know how long he'd already been living here. Let him talk.'

Anguished, Jake sat back. His father was young, lively, always laughing. A joker. The thought of him growing old and alone in this squalid, noxious city, desperate and lost, was terrifying.

'He told me he was a traveller from the future, from the twenty-first century, which I scoffed at, until he showed me a small object which he called a mobile telephone, and which, quite frankly, I found amazing. It did nothing, but he said that in your time he could speak to distant people upon it, and certainly I had seen nothing like it. Still, he might have been a Bolshevist or a Prussian spy, so I was about to hand him over to the police, when he described my mirror. My mirror, in my study upstairs, my greatest secret. That convinced me.'

Venn nodded, bitter. 'David can be convincing.'

'He explained his plight. He wanted to get home, as he put it. He promised me access to untold secrets if I would help him do it. He said his son would be worried about him.' Symmes glanced at Jake. 'I assure you, you were all he thought about.'

Jake couldn't speak. Moll whispered, 'Told you.'

'What happened?' Venn's voice was dark, as if he guessed.

'We worked together for two months. He did many things I didn't understand. Finally he said the mirror was ready. He gave me a sealed paper and made me swear not to look at its revelations until he had gone. Then, we activated the device. I shook his hand – we were quite friends by then – and he strode into the black vacuum of the mirror.'

Into the silence he said, 'He has not come home?'

'No.' Venn sat still a moment, then lifted his head. 'The paper?'

'Ah yes, the paper. I had fondly imagined it a list of the secrets of the future. It was nothing of the sort.' Symmes got up and limped goutily to the sideboard and opened a drawer. He brought out the paper, but instead of giving it to Venn he handed it to Jake, who snatched it and read it avidly and then was silent so long Venn's patience ran out.

'What is it?'

Jake looked up. His face was lit with a bitter happiness. 'A letter. To me.'

CHAPTER TWENTY

Part of the charm and the fascination of the man lies in his obsessive nature. His great friend, David Wilde, once said, 'Venn is like one of those ferocious jungle snakes that won't let go once they bite. You have to kill them to get them off. He's like that. If he wants something, he gets it. If he loses something, he'll move heaven and earth to find it. If you're his friend he'll never betray you.'

Dr Wilde's own whereabouts at present are something of a mystery.

Jean Lamartine, *The Strange Life of Oberon Venn*

Summer showed no surprise on her pert pretty face, but Sarah knew the word Janus had hit home.

She said quickly, 'You remember him? The god who looks both forwards and back. The two-faced one.'

'I know of him.'

All at once, without a sign or a shiver, the Shee were there. They were sitting in the trees, on the garden chairs, on the grass, leaning in the crazily angled rooms . . . Their silver beauty was a mask; their eyes examined her incuriously. Sarah felt alone among them. Gideon, sprawled at Summer's feet, lay silent, gazing up at the featureless blue sky.

'Then you know how dangerous Janus is,' she said. 'Well he's here. At least a copy of him. A Replicant. Venn is missing and in danger. All of them are, if you don't help.'

Summer laughed. 'We don't *help*. We take, we give, we sing, we feast. What can you even offer me . . .'

'This.' Sarah put her hand in her pocket and brought out the diamond brooch. As she held it up it caught the sunlight and the flash of the gems was brilliant; all the bird-sharp eyes of the Shee fastened on it, and she felt their instant greed. In fact she was banking on it. They were lethal, but they were childish. Bright jewels, gold. What else would interest them?

Summer had not moved, but her gaze was on the brooch. 'You would give me that?'

Sarah shrugged. 'It's a great price. But you must . . .'

Summer stood. 'Don't tell me what I *must* do, human.'

Her eyes slanted to slyness. 'I don't want your trinket.'

'Then what? I'll give you anything . . .'

Gideon sat up, his whole lean body a warning.

'*Anything!* . . . What a foolish thing to offer.' Summer turned, a small graceful pirouette on the grass. 'What power you give me, Sarah! Think what I might demand.'

She was still with dismay. *Stupid*, she thought fiercely. *Stupid!*

'Don't worry! I won't ask for the world. I'll just have that.' Summer reached out and indicated the half-coin on its chain. 'Give me that, and I'll consider.' She held out a slender hand.

Sarah didn't move. She was still with alarm. 'Afterwards.'

'Are you mad? I can destroy you with one murmur.'

That was probably true. Sarah didn't let herself flinch. She closed her hand over the brooch and put it hastily away. 'Afterwards. After you've dealt with the Replicant . . .'

'Where is it?'

'In the Dwelling,' Gideon said. 'And a wolf.'

Summer looked annoyed. 'Too much work.'

'Venn will be grateful. Think of that.'

The woman shrugged. But the idea seemed to appeal, because suddenly she smiled archly and said, 'Very well. Call me, when you need me, and I'll come. If I'm not too busy.'

It would have to do, though Sarah knew full well that the promises of the Shee were worthless. But if she didn't get back soon she would be trapped here in this endless realm like Gideon. He was shaking his head at her; she looked back at him while she answered Summer. 'Keep your promise. I'll keep mine.'

And then, enjoying their complete astonishment, she made herself invisible.

Wharton stared at the empty scullery in utter dismay. Who on earth could have let her out? The boy from the Wood? But why?

He turned. Down the dark corridor an icy wind whispered. He had a sudden vision of wide-open doors and windows, the Abbey undefended, the enemy deep inside the house.

He had to use army tactics now. Get back to the Monk's Walk. Barricade themselves in. Ring of steel round the mirror. Without it Jake would never get back. And after all, he thought with wild hope, maybe Maskelyne had done it. Maybe Jake was back already, with Venn, even with David Wilde. Then he, Wharton, could go and spend a late Christmas in Shepton Mallet and pretend all this madness had never happened.

He walked warily to the hall, then ran up the stairs.

Halfway, on the wide landing, he turned.

Something clicked below in the hall. He lifted the shotgun.

'Sarah, is that you?'

Snow drifted. The cold was so intense he felt it was gnawing at him. He stepped up, backwards, keeping his gaze moving. Something was here. Something strange, and close. Then as if his eyes had focused, as if it had blurred out of deepest night, he saw the wolf.

It was slinking up the lower steps, against the bannister, a white, sinuous thing with no shape or outline, hard to see, except for its eyes, small glowing sapphires in the dark.

It gave a low, eerie growl.

He whipped up the gun with both hands, pointing it at the beast.

It came on, watching him.

'Get back. Get back or I shoot.' He stamped and threatened.

The wolf snarled, a terrible sound. Behind it, someone laughed.

Wharton backed. 'Who's down there? Control this animal or I'll be forced to! Do you hear me?'

No one answered but the ice-animal. It leaped three steps and streaked towards him.

Wharton gasped, missed his footing, fell backwards. And fired.

London, August 1848

Dear Jake,

I hope you finally get to read this in some archive of Symmes's papers, sometime, if it survives. I just want you to know that I'm OK, and I'm still trying to get back. I know Venn will be trying to find me, but I don't want – didn't want? – either of you taking stupid risks. When I found myself in 1840s London I knew Symmes was my only chance, but I'm honestly beginning to think this thing only works one way. I mean backwards. If I try again I may well just shunt myself back even further in time away from you. But I have to try. I don't have any choice.

Tell Venn I have calibrated to the second and the twelfth. I don't know if it's even enough.

Look, kid, have a good life, or if you're an old man now, I hope you had a good life. I hope you haven't/ didn't/won't waste it worrying about me. I hope you find a good woman and have kids and that somewhere, somewhen, I'm a grandfather.

I love you, Jake. Tell O to forget me and find Leah. Tell your mother I'm sorry.

Your lost, lonely, loving dad.
David Wilde.

Jake watched Venn fold the paper slowly, his face bleak. He said, 'Jake . . .'

'Don't talk to me about how sorry you are!' Jake's snarl was savage. 'You got him into this with your stupid, selfish obsessions! He would never have . . .'

'It was his idea.' Venn turned. 'He was as keen as I was.'

'Only because he couldn't stand to see your guilt! And you let him go! Don't fool yourself, *godfather* – you'd do anything, sacrifice anyone, to get her back. Me, Dad, anyone on earth.'

Venn's face was icy but before he could answer Symmes said calmly, 'Gentlemen. We are scientists and we must approach this problem in a scientific manner.'

He was back sitting by the fireside and had lit a small dark cigar. He seemed to have recovered from his shock; now he was self-possessed, smoking and thinking, one knee crossed casually over the other. 'I could never make the mirror operate fully before Dr Wilde came, but that was because I did not have the other device – the bracelet he wore on his wrist. He never removed it and when he left he was wearing it. You, I observe, have an identical one.'

Jake, still simmering, glanced at Moll. She grinned. 'Thanks to me he does, mister.'

'Yes . . .' Symmes inhaled deeply. 'So, with it, you may perhaps be able to re-enter the mirror and go home.'

'Without my father?'

'He is not here.'

'I need to know how the mirror was calibrated.' Venn came and stood over Symmes, looking down at him. 'I must see it. Now.'

In the silence the rattle of cab wheels was muted; the stench of the streets a faint tang.

Symmes tapped ash on a glass tray. Then he squashed the stub in and stood up. 'Very well. It's in the cellar.'

He tied the dressing-gown cord firmly and glanced with sudden distaste at Moll. 'Not the urchin though. Surely we have no further need of her.'

Jake muttered, 'She saved me, and the bracelet.'

'Nevertheless . . .' Symmes looked at Venn. 'I don't intend to give beggars a tour of my house and valuables.'

'I'm not a bleedin' beggar!' Moll snapped.

'We know you're not.' Venn searched in the pockets of the stolen clothes he wore and pulled out a heavy handful of florins and shillings and pennies. 'Here.' He dumped the lot carelessly in her hastily cupped hands. 'Take it. Go and get yourself some good food. And some shoes.'

Moll looked staggered. She had probably never seen so much money in her life. Jake wished he had something to give her too, but all he could do was wait until she had stashed the cash and take her small grubby hand and kiss it.

She giggled. 'Just like a lady.'

'You are a lady. Thank you, Moll. I hope we get to meet again, sometime.'

Symmes looked baffled, then amused. He rang the bell, and the butler came smoothly in. 'Show this . . . child out.'

The man went to put a hand on her, but she twisted away. She smiled at Jake – a wistful grimace. 'I hope you get back home. And find your pa.'

He said, 'Thanks, Moll.'

And then she was gone, the door closing firmly behind her small upright back, and Venn was turning impatiently. 'Right. Where is it?'

Symmes rose. He took a small key down from a hook on the wall and unlocked a door that was almost hidden in the panelling; it opened straight on to some wooden steps twisting down. 'Wait. We need light.'

As he crossed to a small oil lamp on the table Jake caught Venn's eye. But there was no time to speak; Symmes was back, and leading the way into a damp darkness redolent with the faint smells of spilt wine.

They hurried down. Behind him Jake heard Venn's boots scrape on the stone; both their shadows, huge and distorted, flickered over the brick walls. Symmes held the lamp higher. 'This was at one time my wine cellar, but I had it cleared and furnished as a laboratory, after the first attempt at burglary. By far the most secure location in the house.'

'Burglary?' Venn's voice echoed. 'By the scarred man, the one you stole the mirror from?'

'Maybe. But I did not steal it, Mr Venn, I rescued it. I shudder to think for what nefarious purposes it had been used.'

He had reached the bottom; there was a short corridor ending in a heavily barred door. 'Would you hold this, please?'

Handing Jake the lamp, Symmes tugged the rusty bolts. As he turned back, the lamplight flickered on the silver bracelet.

Symmes frowned. 'Strange. That is not the same.'

'What?'

'As the one your father wore. They are not the same.'

Venn pushed through. 'What are you talking about? They're a pair. Identical.'

'I assure you, no. Dr Wilde's was definitely not in the

form of . . . what is it, a snake? May I see?'

Reluctant, Jake unclipped the silver link and slid it off; he held it up and Symmes took out a pair of glasses, put them on and bent forward, examining it intently. 'The snake biting its own tail. An ancient symbol of eternity – originating perhaps with the ancient Egyptians. And yet . . . I'm sure it is different.' He took the arm-ring and turned it in the spilling light of the oil lamp.

A silver flicker cascaded down the walls.

And instantly Jake saw the man's hand flash out and felt a fierce shove that sent him flailing back against Venn. They crashed against the cellar door; it slammed open and they were tumbling inside, into a dark straw-scattered space of casks and cobwebs.

Venn was fast; he had rolled and scrambled up and thrown himself at the door but already Symmes had it slammed shut in his face; even as Venn beat his fists against it they heard the rusted bolts grate tight.

Venn roared, 'Symmes! You can't do this!'

The answer was mild and unapologetic. 'I wish I could say I was sorry, Mr Venn, but that would be a lie. You cannot possibly know how I have longed, these last months, to find another of these rings. How I have scoured the antique shops and fleamarkets of this city. And you have come in out of the night and put one into my hands!'

Venn closed his eyes. Jake, still kneeling in the straw, sank slowly down.

'I am not a criminal, however, not a thief. I simply intend to experiment – for a short while. Some days. Then I promise you, I will do all I can to help you return . . .'

'Symmes, listen to me.' Venn's hiss was savagely restrained. 'You'll break it. You'll wreck it. That is a device of such sophistication . . . For God's sake, you have no idea . . .'

'Hassan will make sure you're reasonably comfortable, given the circumstances. I'm so sorry, gentlemen. Perhaps you should both think of it just as a little *delay*.'

They heard his footsteps, in the soft slippers, go up the stairs.

The door at the top was noisily locked.

Venn turned, slid down with his back against the door and stared at Jake.

They were both silent with despair.

There was nothing left to say.

The recoil from the shotgun sent Wharton slamming back; in the confined space of the stairwell the report sounded like an explosion. The wolf took the full force; it went straight through the beast's chest and splintered the painted canvas forehead of a Venn of some distant century, thudding into the wood behind.

The wolf landed, astride Wharton. It was completely unharmed.

He gave a great yell, as much of astonishment as of terror. The creature's eyes were snow-sherds, its teeth dripped saliva, and its growl was so close he could smell the sickening cold stench of its breath.

He kept utterly still.

He could not even breathe, because if he did its teeth might snap, meet in his raw flesh. For a second of inhuman terror he did not even seem to be in his own body, as if he had shrivelled up somewhere dark, far inside.

Something rattled, down the stairs.

The white wolf looked up, behind him, over him.

Another rattle. The world came back with a crash of noise. Rebecca was shouting; he smelled the acrid flare of flame.

The wolf put its head back and howled, a sound so loud it made his whole body quiver with shock. Then it slid off him and turned, yelping and growling, twisting, and he saw a sudden rain of sparks was falling from somewhere above, on to the beast's fur, on his hands, the stairs.

Wharton gasped and wriggled back. Before he could realize it the wolf was gone, tumbling and yelping furiously down, and the darkness was back.

'Get up,' Rebecca's voice hissed in his ear. 'Quickly!'

She had him; she was heaving him up. He felt her stagger; then she had an arm round him and was half carrying, half dragging him away. He wanted to say, '*Stop, I can walk,*' but for some reason his voice had dried up in this throat, and all that emerged was a croak.

Up the stairs, back along the Long Gallery. 'What . . . ?' he gasped.

'Candles! All I had.'

They backed with reckless haste, but now Wharton could breathe; he gasped, 'I can manage,' but Rebecca muttered, 'It's back,' in nervous dread, and he saw the ears, and then the long muzzle of the wolf rose threateningly over the top stair, saw its moon-silver slink along the floor of the Gallery.

He scrambled backwards, raised the useless gun. 'Get that door open, Rebecca! Ready? *Now!*'

She had it wide; he turned, flung himself in, and as they slammed the door Wharton had one nightmare glimpse of the beast leaping, before its savage impact made the boards of the door crack and splinter.

Rebecca had the wooden bar; Wharton grabbed it and they forced it across, safe into the solid iron bracket.

The door shuddered again.

They stood back, breathless. Wharton felt as if he had been scraped from some collapsed building. Every inch of him ached.

'Are you hurt?' Maskelyne was running down the Monk's Walk; he grabbed Rebecca. 'Did it injure you?'

She shook her head, breathless.

Wharton was bent over, one hand on the wall. 'I shot it. I shot the bloody thing! And yet . . .'

'No weapon will kill it except mine,' Maskelyne said.

Wharton gasped, 'Well then I'll use it. Not you.'

'Shush.' Rebecca grabbed his arm. 'Quiet. Listen.'

Footsteps.

Not the wolf's, but the calm, measured tread of a man walking at his ease along the creaking boards of the Gallery, admiring perhaps the paintings, the glass cabinets of ancient books.

He came to the door of the Monk's Walk, and stopped.

Silent, they waited, and they knew the Replicant was waiting too. Until it said, 'I'm still here, Sarah. Master of all this house now. And you're the ones trapped in there. How long, do you think, might it take me to starve you out?'

Wharton growled, 'We have supplies.' It was a lie.

'Really?' A scrape, as if the Janus-image was drawing up a chair. Wharton imagined it sitting, propping its feet up on the locked door. 'Then you had better eat them quickly. I wish you a very Merry Christmas. You have until exactly midnight to crawl out of your bolthole and hand the mirror over to me. If you don't, on the stroke of twelve I will set fire to this ancient wooden house with all of you locked firmly inside it. And when the black mirror is the only thing left whole among the ruins and the ash, among the charred remains of your dreams, I will come and take it for myself.'

The time is out of joint;

O cursed spite

That ever I was born to set it right

CHAPTER TWENTY-ONE

I confess that my ruse pleased me exceedingly, and made me foolishly proud of myself. As I hurried to my study with the bracelet I chortled that a man like Venn, a man who had claimed to travel in time, could be tricked so easily.

I gave instructions to Hassan and secured the apartment. Then, with trembling fingers, I fastened the bracelet around my wrist. The metal was warm, and the eye of the snake seemed to shimmer and wink at me.

I was agitated with fear. But I switched on the apparatus.

Journal of John Harcourt Symmes

Jake was cold. Cold and hungry and tired.

He sat huddled up in a corner, his arms around his knees, trying not to shiver.

'Where's your watch?' Venn muttered.

'Stolen. As soon as I got to this god-forsaken place.' Jake didn't look up. 'They got the bracelet too. If it hadn't been for Moll they'd still have it.' Quickly, he outlined the events in the ruined theatre.

Venn listened without comment, his spare figure looking even leaner in the dark Victorian suit.

When Jake had finished he said, 'You did well. And now we've lost it again.'

In the bleak stillness they heard the rattle of cab wheels above them, the iron clang of horseshoes on the cobbles of the street. A tiny grid in the roof above Jake dripped rain.

'What about you?' he asked.

Venn shrugged. 'I think I must have arrived here about an hour or more after you. All I remember is grabbing your sleeve and then nothing. But we've discovered something – that it's possible for two people to *journey* together, and arrive at least close in time.'

'Were you in the alley?'

'No. A dilapidated garden behind a public house. A dog was barking – I was disorientated, dizzy, but I managed to scramble out. I turned a few corners and walked straight into a scene from Dickens. It was the Tottenham Court Road, I think, but with stalls, and a fish market . . . I just stared.'

'Where did you get the clothes?'

Venn looked uneasy. 'Well, obviously I had to go native. There was a . . . shall we say, very drunk gentleman trying to find a closed cab. I whistled one up and helped him into it. When I got down a few streets later I was wearing his clothes. I did leave him mine. In a neat pile.'

Jake couldn't help a grin.

Venn met his eyes. For a moment they were both laughing.

Then, abruptly, dismay rolled back. Venn said, 'Symmes could be doing anything up there.'

Jake glanced at him. His godfather's face was suddenly taut with anxiety – he stood and paced and kicked in convulsive rage at the door. 'A pompous, smug fool, and we let him do this to us. He could wreck everything – he could just vanish like David and leave us stuck here . . . We have to get out, Jake!'

'Don't waste your energy.' Jake uncurled and stood. 'That door is solid.'

Venn looked upwards. The damp bricks of the roof oozed lime-white secretions; mould blossomed in green velvet clumps. 'The pavement can't be far above us. If we had some sort of lever, some tools . . .'

'We don't.'

Venn swung round, his patience snapped. 'Can't you say anything useful? If you hadn't had the stupid idea of entering the mirror neither of us would be here.'

'I didn't want you to come. You could have stayed.'

'Are you mad? David would never have forgiven me if . . .'

'Don't talk about him as if he's dead!' Jake's frustration ripped out too. 'You don't care about Dad! All you care about is your guilt. Ending the way it makes you feel. Maybe you don't even care about Leah!'

It was said before he knew he'd said it and even in his cold fury he was appalled at himself. Venn stared stricken, disbelieving. For half a second the very darkness of the cellar seemed fractured, as if a stone had been thrown that had cracked the black glass of the world.

Then, in a whisper, the roof said, 'Jake! Can you hear me? It's me. Moll. Jake, where are you?'

He rushed to the corner where the grating was, stupidly grateful. 'We're here. How did you know?'

'Oh you really 'ave got no idea,' her voice said, acidly. He could almost see the pitying shake of her small tangled head. 'Did you think I'd just scarper with the dosh? No chance! I waited outside just to see if you'd come out. I didn't trust that cove Symmes. Too smarmy. Too cocksure.'

'Well, you were right. He's got the bracelet and we're locked in down here. Can you get us out, Moll?'

She laughed. 'Watch and learn, Jake. Remember?'

'Listen, don't get yourself hurt.' But she was already gone.

He turned.

Venn was leaning against the wall, watching him. As if Moll had not even spoken he said, 'Do you really believe that? That my selfishness could be so gross? Is that what you think of me, Jake?'

Jake frowned. 'I didn't . . .'

'You must have really hated me. Far off, in your comfortable school in Switzerland.'

'You had your obsession. I had mine. I thought you'd killed him.' He looked away. 'I had to blame someone. You were there. You were responsible. There was no one else.'

Venn nodded, slowly. He said, 'I see now that I failed you. I never really thought about you. I just wanted you out of the way, because I couldn't have interruptions. But you're wrong about Leah. Yes, it will ease my shame and guilt – and believe me, Jake, they are terrible. But I'll move hell and heaven to get her back, no matter who tries to stop me, or who gets hurt. Because Leah is a part of me. She's my soul, Jake. They say the Venns have no souls,

329

that they are half Shee, without remorse, ruthless. I was like that. Leah changed me. I'll force the whole world and time and fate to do it, but I'll get her back.'

His hubris was breathtaking. But for a moment Jake almost believed a man could do that.

Then, with a small scrape and rattle, the door was unlocked.

They spun round.

Moll stood there, hugely proud, hands on hips. 'Can't I leave you alone for a second, you poor sods?'

Jake grabbed her and swung her up. 'You're a wonder! What . . .'

A crash interrupted him. A vast, echoing crash, high in the house.

Venn leaped for the door. 'The mirror!'

Sarah ran through the Wood. Even in her invisibility its power snagged at her. In the corners of her eyes were fragments of places that could not be here; the edge of a ploughed field, the tilted plane of a city street. When she looked at them they were gone. She was in a kaleidoscope, a place of pieces, a broken universe, all in random order; she felt terrified that some great upheaval would rearrange everything in seconds. This was like that old story of the girl who had gone through the looking-glass into a world where cats grinned and eggs talked.

But going through the looking-glass was the one thing she hadn't managed to do.

Breathless, she stopped. As she bent over, gasping in air, she wondered why the Shee weren't following her, even trying to find her. Surely their curiosity would be intense.

Around her the Wood waited, silent.

And then, very faint and far away, she heard it; the sound that she had most dreaded. Even before she cried out in shock and clasped her hands tight to her ears she knew it was too late, that in that sharp, brilliant instant the damage had been done.

The music was piercingly sweet. A single note, high and enchanting.

She screamed, 'No!' and ran, hands crammed against her ears. If she stopped, if she listened, she was finished. It would haunt her for ever. She crashed through bushes and brambles, ducking under two leaning oaks, and suddenly there was no ground but only water, and she fell forward, headlong, into it.

Bubbling, airless dark.

She came up with a scream, coughing, weed plastered to her face. Between its strands she saw Gideon. He was standing on the bank, watching.

'Help me!' she screeched. Then she sank again, and there was no bottom. Long ribbons of weed tangled her; water slopped into her nose, down her throat; her cry was a gurgle of terror.

'*Gideon!*'

He stood on the brink. 'I can't! If I touch water . . . !'

'Help me!'

'I can't . . . Summer says . . .'

'*You're not Shee. You're human!*'

She grabbed a branch; it snapped. Crow-flowers snagged her clothes, daisies and nettles, long loosestrife, like dead men's fingers. She fought desperately to stay up, to swim, but they had never taught her that in the Lab, and every movement dragged her down to gulp and choke, and in the pain of no breath she saw herself in a nightmare mirror, lying dead in the flowers.

A hand.

It was close and tough. It grabbed her hair and hauled. She moaned, but the hand had her now, round shoulders, round waist.

Her foot stumbled on soil.

Then they were out, bursting into air, crawling up the bank, grabbing the hanging willow boughs to pull themselves up. Icy air stabbed into her lungs. Painfully she coughed and choked and vomited out water and weed.

When she could speak she said, 'You . . . did it . . .'

He sat, dragging his hands back through his streaming hair. Some of the green lichen had washed from his pale skin; he looked different. Less lost. Grabbing her arm, making her turn, he said, 'That's you and Jake. You both owe me a life now. The Shee never keep their word. So show me that humans are different. Get me away from her, Sarah.'

The intensity that broke through his usual languid carelessness made her nod, silent.

He dragged her up. 'Come on. Before you freeze.'

Between one step and another they raced into winter, a bitterly cold white-out of horizontal snow that stung her eyes to water.

The roar of the blizzard was ferocious. Sarah and Gideon stumbled through shoulder-high dead bracken and the crashed trunks of ancient elms, snow whitening their hair, their lips, the whole world a wall of snow coming straight at them, and as Sarah leapt aside into the path her ankle twisted; she fell sideways, hands down in the frozen drift.

Something gave a harsh cry, just above her.

A huge starling sat on a branch, huddled against

the blizzard. Its small beady eyes, tilted in curiosity, watched her.

Gideon stopped. 'They're here. You go on,' he yelled, his lips close to her ear. 'Don't forget me.'

She scrambled up and hobbled, shivering. Where was the Abbey? The wind was so ice-sharp through her wet clothes it was hard to catch breath. In seconds she was alone, not sure if she was even heading the right way. Maybe the Shee were enticing her back even now, towards that jagged place where the corners of worlds intruded.

She staggered out of the trees into the knee-deep snow of the drive.

And gasped.

Wintercombe Abbey was an arctic ruin in a wasteland.

For a moment she knew she had emerged from the Wood in the wrong time, centuries too late, because surely this was the ghost of a house, every roof and gable thick with snow, the very windows silted up, the door wide open and blocked with a great drift.

No lights burned, no chimneys smoked.

Maybe they were all dead, Venn, Piers, Jake. Maybe this was her own desolate winter, Janus's world of no hope and no colour . . .

Then, faint as the tiniest point of light in a dark eye, she saw the flame of a candle. It glimmered at a high window in the Long Gallery, then moved, as if carried past the panes. Someone was in there.

Sarah picked herself up and fought her way to the door. The steps up were thick with snow, but a trampled mix of deep prints led in.

She wiped her face and eyes, pushed back her soaking hair.

Then she forced her way through the snowdrift into the hall.

It was in darkness. The stairs were marked with wet prints. Very quietly she followed them up, running her hand along the thin snow-crust on the bannister. Reaching the first landing, she stopped.

A sound came from above her, in the high vault of the ceiling, a small creak, a tinkle. Dust fell on her. She saw that the chandelier up there was swinging, softly, as if the gale had set it in motion. A ripple of movement stirred the dark red hangings of the landing.

She turned, but the stairs behind her were dark and empty. Not even a cat.

Suddenly, panic rose up in her. She turned and ran, heedless, breathlessly up, because she had to get back, find the mirror, find Venn. She hurtled into the Long

Gallery, and almost crashed into the Replicant.

It was sitting with its feet on a chair, and it was so young! A slim soldier, hair tied back now, thin lips drawn in a delighted smile.

It was on its feet and had tight hold of her before she could twist away.

'How lovely to see you, Sarah,' it said.

The mirror stood in a fortified zone. Under Wharton's orders, Rebecca and Maskelyne had dragged the heaviest furniture against the door, then retreated to the labyrinth where the only weapon they had the shotgun was aimed at the entrance arch. Wharton kept it, and had the glass gun jammed in his belt.

'Because I don't trust you,' he snapped, when Maskelyne asked why.

Rebecca shook her head in disbelief. 'If that thing gets in here . . .'

'It wants the mirror. Not us.'

They sat, crouched in silence. Wharton breathed heavily.

Rebecca glanced at Maskelyne, a shadow in the darkness. She knew he was looking at the mirror. He had realized with sickening speed that there was nothing he could do without power. To be so close to it must be so tantalizing for him, she thought. A torment. She said, 'Can you feel it?'

'I can hear it.' His scarred face turned in the darkness. 'I hear it sing. A single high note, beyond sound. So strange and far off, like a voice from eternities distant. But I can hear it, Becky.'

From behind, Wharton said gruffly, 'I never got to hear how you two know each other.'

Rebecca was silent a moment. Maskelyne said, 'Tell him, if you want.'

Wharton heard her sigh. 'I don't know how to. It started so long ago. I was maybe six, seven, when I first saw him. In dreams . . . A man falling and falling through dark space, a rectangle of sky. He was calling out to me, but I couldn't understand what he was saying. I told my mum, but she laughed at me. Nightmares, she said.

'Slowly, he came to earth. I began to see him land, crashing in slow-mo. Between dreams a month apart he might only have moved a millimetre. I got used to it. I stopped telling people, because they thought I was strange. But I used to lay awake on rainy nights, worried, in case he would get wet.'

She grinned at him. 'Then one night, he was there, in my room. He was see-through, like a ghost. He sat on my window seat and whispered, "Don't be afraid. I'm a friend." No one else saw him. When my mum came in to wake me next day she walked straight through him. He wasn't there.'

Maskelyne said, 'It was a drastically delayed manifestation.'

'Talk English,' Wharton muttered.

'Time, stretched out like elastic. I was coming through the mirror, but it was taking years.'

'What?' Wharton stared, appalled. 'Might that happen to Jake?'

'Jake has the bracelet. I had nothing. I was lucky even to survive.'

Rebecca smiled. 'I didn't know any of that then. He was just my secret friend. He lived in my house and no one knew about him. Sometimes he was there and sometimes not, all over the farm, in the barns, in the fields, in the place down by the stream where I used to play.' She laughed, softly, in the dark. 'I wasn't scared of him. I liked him. Half beautiful and half ugly, like a man put together from pieces. He came out of my books; he was Heathcliff and Rochester and all those dark heroes. He was my shadow. I waited for him.'

'For me,' Maskelyne said quietly, 'her entire childhood was only a few frail moments. I was there, then gone, and when the world flickered back the girl who lived in it was a month, a year older, and it was summer, or a sudden autumn. I realized what must be happening, but what could I do? I was trapped.'

Rebecca said, 'Do you remember the day I was ten, and there was a party? I had all these kids round, and it was fun, but then suddenly Maskelyne was there, in the middle of them, sitting like a ghost at the feast, among balloons and music, and no one could see him but me. He looked so weary. I pretended to be sick and everyone got sent home. And then I made him go to sleep on the sofa.'

Wharton looked up. 'Listen!'

They froze. After a while he said, 'Sorry. Thought I heard something.' Still fascinated, he glanced at Maskelyne. 'How long before you . . . arrived fully?'

'In Becky's time, eight years. By the time she was fourteen I was here constantly, barely flickering. Then it got difficult – I took to living in an old mill house on the edge of her father's farm, up on the edge of the moor, because by then I needed food, warmth. Sleep. Slowly, I became a real person, not a ghost any more.' He was looking at her, smiling sadly.

She said, 'He told me about the mirror. So we started to research. We knew it must be close by. Then we realized Venn had it.'

Maskelyne said, 'I went to Switzerland and found Jake

and you on the point of leaving. I followed you on to the plane and phoned Rebecca from London. She got on the train. I think you know the rest.'

Wharton gave him a hard stare. 'So you want the mirror for yourself.'

Maskelyne glanced quickly at Rebecca. She said, 'It was his. It belongs to him. And when he goes, I go too.'

Astonished at the change in her face, Wharton looked away. She wasn't at all the ditsy girl that had nearly crashed that car. She was a young woman in love with a ghost.

Then Maskelyne said, 'There it is again.'

Wharton wriggled out of the labyrinth and inched his way to the door; now he was leaning against it, his ear to the ancient wood. He looked up. 'I can hear voices. Someone's out there, talking to him.'

He turned his head and listened again, and his face darkened. He said, 'I think . . . It is. It's Sarah.'

Then he took the glass weapon and held it out. Maskelyne's fingers closed around it.

'Thank you,' he said.

CHAPTER TWENTY-TWO

If a man be replicated, can his soul accompany him? Without a soul, is he even human?

And if he is not human, what evil may inhabit him without hindrance?

Does my blacke mirror open the world to vile spirits — is it a pathway for demons? And therefore should I shatter it or bury it deep in the earth?

Alas for my dremes then.

The Scrutiny of Secrets by Mortimer Dee

Sarah stood rigid. The Replicant's smile was charming. It held her arm in a tight grip. 'You're a little wet,' it said.

She threw a quick glance behind it. The door was locked — hopefully barricaded. But she was the one putting them all in danger. 'Let me go.'

'Both of us having come all this way?' It shook its head. 'I don't think so. I have to say, I'm surprised. I presumed you were locked safely in there with them – the worthy teacher, and Venn's clever genie.'

She looked stricken, but she thought fast. Venn and Jake weren't back. But she couldn't afford to wait for them.

'It would have been a shame to burn the place down.' It tipped its head sideways and smiled again.

'All this ancient timber . . .' It took its hand out of its pocket and she saw it had a small lighter; a tiny blue flame flickered.

'I mean, look . . .' The Replicant wandered away to the curtain that hung over the door. 'So much dust, so many old fabrics. What an inferno, Sarah.'

Carelessly it held the flame close to the curtain.

'Don't.'

As soon as she said it she knew it was a mistake. Janus's hand did not move. It said, 'You could ask them to open the door.'

'They won't. They know you're here.'

'Yes but now you are too.' It watched the edge of the curtain; with a shiver of fear she saw it had begun to smoulder. 'Tell them to open the door, Sarah.'

'Put that thing out first.'

Behind the spectacles its eyes flickered to her. 'Don't

defy me. Don't pit your will against mine. Tell them to open the door.'

Smoke was rising from the worn fibres of the curtain. In an instant it would whoosh into fire. She clenched her fists.

'Put the flame out. Then I'll talk to them.'

The Replicant did not blink. Its hand did not move. Red fire spurted in the damask folds.

Sarah ran. She snatched at the curtain and dragged it down, the worn cloth tearing as easily as tissue. Even as it fell it was already a mass of flame; small wisps scattered, scuttering down the bare wooden boards of the Gallery. She stamped and beat at it, gasping, jerking back, heat on her face. Sparks danced round her hair.

The Replicant watched her. As she dragged the singed cloth into a hasty heap she saw from the corner of her eye how it lounged, waiting. When the last spark was out, she whirled round. It was even faster; it had her arm and had dragged her close, hauling her over to the door, and she felt the small silver click of the lighter, jerked away in terror from the hot glow under her ear.

'Listen to me, in there,' it yelled. 'I have a friend of yours. Open the door.'

The flame was raised; she fought to pull away.

'Tell them.'

Gritting her teeth, she struggled, lashing out with her free arm, but it held the flame closer and the heat of it under her eyes made her gasp with terror.

Then, with a crack, the door unlocked.

'Let the girl go,' Wharton growled. 'Or I blow you to kingdom come.'

Venn and Jake thundered up the stairs.

At the landing the butler came out of a room carrying a silver tray; before he could jump back Venn had shoved him aside in a crash of china and raced past, Moll tight at his heels.

Jake glanced back. Hassan had dragged out a whistle; he blew it, three shrieking, terrified blasts.

Venn stormed down the corridor, flinging open doors, finding only bedrooms. The last door was firmly locked.

'That must be it!' Moll hissed.

Venn stood back. 'Jake.'

Together, they shouldered the door, and burst through.

'Get away from there!' Venn yelled.

Symmes turned. He was standing before a complicated assemblage of brass; a creation of springs and oscillating pendulums. Some ornate construction made of bands of metal had been fitted to encircle the mirror, like the meshed orbits of tiny planets. The glass itself was held steady in a frame ratcheted to the floor.

Jake saw at once that Symmes was wearing the bracelet. He leaped forward, but Symmes moved first. He caught a smooth lever that was set into the machinery and shoved it down.

'No!' Venn said.

'I have to.' Symmes was breathless. 'You know. You — an explorer. You know I have no choice.'

And he was gone, into emptiness, a great silent implosion that tore Moll and Jake into a rolling tumble of limbs, and made Venn cling to a chair as it was dragged across the floor.

The mirror rippled and closed behind him.

Venn swore. He scrambled up. 'Get that door closed!'

But Jake was too appalled to move. For a stricken moment his mind seemed as black as the glass, until Moll started dragging the chest of drawers across the door. 'Don't just stand there, Jake! Come on!'

He grabbed the furniture and hauled. Men were running up the stairs outside; a heavy fist pounded on the door. 'Mr Symmes! Sir?'

'Keep them out.' Venn stared at the mass of brass components in bewilderment. 'What in hell's name has he done to this?'

The door shuddered. The chest of drawers jerked,

even with Moll sitting on it. 'Come out of there! We are armed men, and if you resist, we'll shoot.'

'Do something,' Jake muttered, his back braced against the barricade.

Venn grabbed the lever. With one firm jerk he put it into reverse.

The mirror spat. For a moment the whole room seemed to turn. And then it opened, like a black hole in the world's heart.

The Replicant eased Sarah aside and walked towards Wharton, who pointed the shotgun with tense resolve.

Janus didn't pause. 'Even if you fire you'll find nothing happens to me. *I am not here.* How can you kill a reflection?' It stalked into the Monk's Walk and glanced down the dark stone corridor, then back, appraisingly, at Wharton. 'Look at you. A rational man, an educator of the young. And yet after less than a week in his company, what has Venn done to you? He has taken your mind and twisted it to believe impossible things.'

Wharton said, 'Sarah. Come over here.'

She stepped across to him. She couldn't see Piers – surely he must be staying close to the mirror. She said quietly, 'It's true. You can't hurt him. But he can hurt you . . .'

He glanced at her. She was staring at the Replicant with a bitter hatred.

The image of Janus smiled. It made to stride swiftly down the Monk's Walk, but Wharton did not move and they came face to face under the vaulted roof. Icy winds whipped snow through the open arches; far below Sarah heard the roar of the swollen river in its winter flood.

'You don't get past me,' Wharton growled.

The Replicant shook its head. 'You have no idea what I am. Or what she is. You're so out of your depth you've drowned and you don't know it. Get out of my way, *old* man.'

Wharton scowled. 'I've faced down bigger men than you in . . .'

He stopped, astonished. Janus had turned sideways and vanished.

He spun around. The dark figure of the Replicant was walking swiftly down the corridor. Snow gusted through the lean shape. It turned and laughed, and then whistled, and behind it the shadow of a wolf slunk at its heels . . .

Sarah grabbed Wharton. 'We have to protect the mirror.'

'I really fail to see how.'

She tugged the chain with the half-coin from her neck.

'If all else fails,' she said, 'with this.' She held it up. *'Summer! I call you. I need you. Now!'*

Maskelyne had only time to yell, 'Becky!' before the wolf raced in from the dark and leaped on his back. He fell and it was on him; he rolled and gasped to find its white teeth snapping at his throat. He gave a wild cry of terror, scrabbling for the dropped gun.

Rebecca froze. For a moment she could not even breathe. Then she dived for the glass weapon and whipped it round.

She raised it, double-handed, and pointed it straight at the wolf.

But there was a man in the way.

He was standing there, bewildered, a stout, perspiring moustachioed stranger in a red dressing-gown. He was staring blankly at the wolf, in a sort of horror, and he said something, but she didn't know what, because at the sound of the whisper the beast swivelled, its sapphire eyes glittering with instant new greed.

'Good . . . God!' Symmes backed.

'Fresher prey,' Maskelyne gasped. 'He's just *journeyed.*'

Rebecca swivelled the weapon. The wolf jumped. Symmes screamed, a sound that made Rebecca's fingers clutch and slip on the trigger.

Then he, and the wolf, were gone.

They burst back through the black mirror in a furious tangle of flailing limbs, the man and the white-furred beast a tight confusion of violence. Venn moved instantly. He grabbed the wolf and hauled it away, but it was a thing that twisted and dissolved through his fingers, it snarled and backed, its great muzzle snuffling, bewildered, towards Moll.

She screeched, ducking behind Jake.

But already they saw it was fading, its whiteness clotting. Whining, it squirmed round, biting at its own tail as if it would devour itself, but now they could see through it, and even as it died it tried to leap but Jake held Moll safe. With a shiver that struck deep into his heart he felt the thing fling itself over him, become nothing more than a jagged spark that briefly lit the keyhole.

And then nothing at all.

Outside, there was a brief silence.

Then the butler's voice. 'Mr Symmes! Sir!'

'He's fine,' Venn yelled quickly. 'Don't shoot. We're coming out.'

He already had the bracelet off Symmes's wrist. The man was in a state of complete collapse; he sat huddled on the rug, his eyes closed, his breathing a strangled gasp.

Venn went to the desk, swept papers aside, snatching up every notebook and journal he could find.

Jake picked himself up and helped Moll to stand. Even her composure was shattered; her eyes were wide and terrified under her tangled hair.

'Come on.' Venn grabbed Jake's elbow and hauled him towards the vacuum of the mirror.

'No! Wait!'

'That wolf must have been in the Abbey!'

'Yes I know, but what about Moll?' He dragged to a stop.

Venn clasped the snake tight on his own wrist. 'Not our problem. She'll be fine.'

'We take her with us.'

'Don't be ridiculous.'

Jake stared at her; she smiled back, wan. 'Don't worry, Jake. You can come back and see me any time, can't you?'

Numb, he nodded. He had a sudden understanding of her misery here; saw she would probably die young, in some stinking cholera-ridden slum. Her faith in him made him ashamed. He turned to Venn. 'Take her. Come back for me.'

For no more than a second Venn's ice-gaze flashed over her. Then, without a flicker of pity he said, 'No.'

'He's right.' Moll was moving backwards, to the door.

'I won't let you. I'll be out under the rozzers' arms and running, Jake. No worries.' Tears stood in her eyes.

'I can't,' he said.

'Course you can. Go on. Go now.'

'Come out of there!' the voice in the corridor thundered. With a great lurch, the chest of drawers was shunted away; the door shuddering its way inward.

Venn said, 'Goodbye, Moll,' and his cold clasp hauled Jake headlong into the mirror.

He looked back, but the room was already so incredibly distant she was tiny as a doll, her face lost in shadows. '*I'll come back*,' he breathed, but she was gone, and for a moment that had no measurement he was alone in a terrible, dimensionless space, alone and desolate, a small spark of light in an immense, whirling starfield.

Which was suddenly snow.

He gasped in the bitter cold.

He and Venn were standing knee-deep in drifts before Wintercombe, under a sky of breathtaking stars, and out of the Wood Gideon was walking, and he carried, high on a pole, the skull of the Grey Mare, its white jaw clacking in the howling gale.

Behind him, in a rustling, ramshackle flock, came the host of the Shee.

CHAPTER TWENTY-THREE

I will come when the wind is high she said,
I will come when the moon is bright.
I will come in the dark of Christmas Eve,
   When the beasts kneel in the night.

My faery troop I'll bring to you;
My magic songs and raiment,
And should I save your ancient House,
   Your heart shall be my payment.
      Ballad of Lord Winter and Lady Summer

The cats came into the Long Gallery. Seven in a line, their tails high, they padded and prowled down its silent length.

Outside, faint through the casements, the drums of the Shee pounded. Flame light rippled on the pargeted ceiling.

One by one the inky identical shadows climbed and dropped and searched. They leaped on chairs, under tables. They slid in through any open door. They sat and scratched on books, sprawled on the piled papers of desks.

One of them looked up at the jar.

It was blue and white and the cat's pupils widened as it jerked, very slightly. Once, then again.

Nearer the edge of the high shelf.

The cat climbed quickly up, padded along the tops of buckling books and crouched. It lay in a flat slant of fascination, its fur bunched, its tail fat. When the jar shuddered again it reached out, one swift, exploring paw.

The jar toppled. It slid and rolled. It crashed into porcelain slivers and the cat bolted to the safety of an armchair, green eyes wide.

Piers, dusty, hot and irritated, stood on the floor and spat out sherds of pot. Then he glared at the cats. 'What the hell took you so long?' he snarled.

Maskelyne picked himself up. Rebecca said anxiously, 'Are you hurt?' but he didn't answer her; he was gazing at something behind her. She turned, fast.

The Replicant smiled at her.

As Sarah and Wharton ran in they saw Rebecca whisk

the glass weapon quickly behind her back.

Sarah glanced round. Where in God's name was Piers?

Casually pushing through the broken remnants of the web, the Replicant walked right up to the obsidian mirror. It stood and looked at its reflection in it, the lank hair, the neat dark uniform, with a mild, humourless smile.

The mirror rippled. Wharton saw it clearly; a vibration that travelled within the glass, as if some unbearable tension had been set up.

Maskelyne must have seen it too. He stepped out, anxious. 'Don't stand so close. Keep away from it!'

Janus spared him a swift, interested stare. 'So there was an anomaly! It was you on the bridge last night. What sort of journeyman are you?'

Maskelyne said, 'Journeyman?'

'Don't play the innocent. Has ZEUS sent reinforcements?'

'No one sent me. I belong to no group. I travel alone.'

Behind the Replicant, Wharton edged sideways, towards Rebecca. From the corner of his eye he saw that Sarah was standing just inside the open doorway. She was listening intently.

The creature seemed intrigued. 'Alone! How?'

Maskelyne kept his eyes away from Rebecca. He seemed for a moment to be subtly altered, his dark hair longer, his face unmarked, but as he moved into the light the scar was back, the jagged violence of it ageing him.

'You wouldn't understand,' he said, quietly. And then, 'Step back. The mirror is troubled at your presence. It rejects you.'

'How do you know?'

'I know. I can feel it.'

The Replicant stepped forward, calmly. 'Can you? A wretched scarred thief from some lost stinking city? Don't tell me – you really think the mirror is yours. That it has some sort of loyalty to you. That's a common delusion for journeymen, did you know that? A slow, helpless fall into insanity. Unless, of course, you're different.' A glimmer of fascination lit its eyes behind the blue lenses. 'Are you different? Was it you who created the mirror?'

Maskelyne came forward too, so that they both stood before the glass.

'*Perhaps the mirror created me,*' he whispered.

And even as Wharton heard Sarah's indrawn breath he saw it too – all of them were reflected in that obsidian darkness – all except Maskelyne. Where his reflection should have been there was only the smooth image of the room.

The Replicant looked as astonished as any of them; there was a confused envy in its voice. 'Now that *is* interesting.' Suddenly it caught Wharton's stealthy movement and turned. Wharton froze, so near to Rebecca he might have touched her. Behind his back, he felt the cold grip of the glass weapon, as she slipped it into his hand.

Janus swung back to Maskelyne. 'In fact you're wrong about me. I have no intention of harming the Chronoptika. Quite the contrary. You see, I'm not the enemy. She is.' It pointed a bitten fingernail at Sarah, where she stood alone, in the shattered web.

'Me?' she said.

'Of course you.' The Janus-image shook its head, looking round at the others, its thin face tilted with false astonishment. 'Do you mean she really hasn't told you?'

Wharton was watching her. Sarah glanced at him. For a moment he knew she was afraid, in some silent plea to him, but he said it anyway. 'She's told us enough.'

The Replicant smiled. It took its glasses off and polished them on its sleeve. 'About her mission? Why they've sent her? She is part of a rebel organization that calls itself ZEUS . . .'

'We know about ZEUS,' Wharton snapped.

'Really?' It put the glasses back on and gazed at Wharton through them. 'And do you know that she's here to break your precious mirror into a thousand pieces?'

She looked at Wharton.

Appalled, he said, 'Sarah?'

Her face was pale, her lips pressed tight. And she was silent.

Jake said, 'What's happening?'

Venn didn't answer. He folded his arms and stood silent and grim on the steps of the house.

Behind Gideon the Shee were flocking from the Wood. They carried bells and chimes; many beat drums, and the deep, throbbing rhythm made starlings rise from the trees and call to each other across the sky. The snow had stopped falling; now it lay deep and still, and the clouds were clearing. High above, like a dust of diamonds on black velvet, the stars were coming out, sherds and slivers of brilliance, eerie over the frozen Wood and the blue-white hummocks of the lawns.

The Shee wore white and silver. Jake stared at them, astonished; they were a wild army of guisers, mummers, gaberlunzies, masked and costumed with the remnants of ancient Christmases. He saw a ragged St George, a black-clad Moor, a creature tailed and spined like a capering dragon, white fire flashing from its mouth. He saw morris men and caparisoned knights on skeletal horses. Tall beautiful beings like women walked out of the trees and turned their emerald eyes on him.

Behind, in the depths of the Wood, stealthier things moved; jewels and scales caught the starlight.

Shapes slunk like wolves.

He said, 'Where is she?'

Venn's voice was rough. 'There.'

Summer came sitting elegantly on a vehicle Jake's eyes could not quite focus on, a great glass sleigh, he thought, or maybe a crystal carriage, pulled by a huddle of her people, their hair bright, their eyes cold as the moon. But as they drew near the steps the carriage dwindled; it became a child's simple wooden sledge, painted in faded blue.

Summer stepped down and stood barefoot in the snow. She said, 'So you got back! Without your lovely wife.'

Venn snarled, 'This time.'

'Or the long-lost father.' She smiled narrowly at Jake. 'What a pity.'

'What are you doing here?' Venn glanced at the dark house, the snowdrift in the hall. 'What's happened?'

She ran lightly up the steps and peered in at the snow-covered hall. 'Your enemy is inside your defences, Oberon. And I've agreed to help.'

Venn snorted. 'For what price?'

She reached out and took his hand. 'A great treasure. And you can't stop me, because Sarah has invited me in.'

Jake shot a glance at Gideon. The changeling's green eyes were uneasy.

Venn was silent. He looked over the noisy, crazy army. Then he said, 'Summer, I may need your help now. But believe me, if things weren't desperate you'd be the last person I'd . . .'

'She was so clever!'

'Who?'

'Sarah. Did you know she can become invisible?'

He stared at her, as if nothing she said could be trusted. He said, 'I've spent years keeping you out.'

She touched his fingers. 'Then it's time things changed.'

Jake watched, not sure what was happening. Summer seriously scared him. Finally Venn said, 'All right. But just you. You don't need this rabble to deal with Janus.'

She laughed. 'So true. But they'll wait in a ring round your house. There'll be no way out for this Replicant.'

She made a signal to Gideon to stand aside. He didn't move. 'Let me come with you.'

She laughed. 'Why should I need you? Stay here.' She pulled the string and the Mare's jaw clacked. 'Stay and play, like the rest.'

She turned away, and swept past Jake, and he saw how Gideon looked after her, a look of pure hatred.

Venn led Summer into the Abbey. As she passed over the iron set into the threshold Jake saw how she shivered, but Venn held her white fingers tight, and then they were inside, hurrying through the ice-cold stillness of the empty rooms.

Jake looked back. 'Don't do anything stupid . . .'

Gideon turned the grey horse's skull to face him, and moved its jaw. 'I'm under a spell, Jake,' it clacked, in a sour, bony voice. 'There's nothing I can do.'

'But is it true?' Wharton snapped. 'What he says? You told us . . .'

Sarah shook her head. 'It's not that simple. He's trying to turn you against me . . .'

She glanced round, desperate. She was cold and shivering, despite Wharton's coat which he'd draped round her shoulders. Where was Jake when she needed him? Where was Piers?

'You've lied to us all along,' Rebecca said.

'You can talk! No! Listen to me! Janus is the future. A possible future. It all depends on what Venn does with the mirror.'

Maskelyne, standing between the glass and the Replicant, stared at her as if he no longer knew whom to trust.

'What do you mean?'

'What she means,' Janus said, smiling, 'is that if Venn succeeds in his plan to bring back his wife, it will have wider repercussions. The mirror will become a priceless artefact, and there will be no way he can keep it secret. In about a hundred years from now this faction, that calls itself ZEUS, tries to . . .'

'He's lying.' Sarah stepped up to Wharton. She shook her head, furious. 'He knows I can't tell you. I dare not tell you.'

Wharton said quietly, 'You have to. How can we understand otherwise?'

Sarah looked at Maskelyne, then at Rebecca. She felt suddenly so tired she just wanted to crumple somewhere and rest, but then in the black depths of the mirror something moved, and she caught a brief flicker in the corner of the room.

She stopped. Rebecca gave a gasp of delight.

Wharton turned.

Venn and Jake were standing in the doorway of the Monk's Walk. Just behind them was an astonishingly pretty young woman wearing a simple black dress and, Wharton noticed in surprise, no shoes.

'Jake! *Thank God!* What happened?'

Jake said, 'Too much to explain now.'

'And your father?' Wharton glanced at Venn, who shook his head.

The woman came in. She walked in a strangely delicate, girlish way, and her smile was so sweet Wharton felt oddly troubled by it.

She looked at Janus with open curiosity and Janus looked at her.

At once Sarah knew the Replicant was at a loss; that it had encountered something outside its knowledge.

'Who are you?' it snarled.

'Summer is one of my names.' She stared in fascination at the mirror. 'So this is it. Your obsession. Your gateway to bliss.' She was talking to Venn, but he had turned to Sarah.

He said, 'So what's the world like in your time, Sarah? Is it so terrible that you can't tell us about it? Do you want my mirror to change things, to make things better? Or is it so perfect that you don't want any chance of it being spoiled?'

His voice was raw with bitterness. Sarah stared back at him. Then she came up close to him and stood face to face, her blonde hair short and ragged.

She said, 'There is no world. In my time, the world is gone. All the people, the animals, the cities. Destroyed by a madman. And do you know what he used to destroy it? No meteor from space, no terrible plague, no nuclear explosion . . . *He used your mirror, Venn. Your mirror destroyed my world.'*

All the lights went on.

With a whine of power the web crackled.

The doors slammed. Every machine and piece of cable in the room seemed to flicker into sudden new strength.

From nowhere Piers's voice crackled from a speaker, making Wharton jump.

'The house is secure, Excellency. Welcome home.'

CHAPTER TWENTY-FOUR

The fate of humanity rests on our efforts. We are only a few against his power, but we have courage. We're the sacrifice. The avengers. If we succeed we'll never know it. Perhaps if there is a future we'll be looked back on as gods, or angels. Believe in your destiny. Let nothing: not hatred, not despair – not even love – stand in your way.

Illegal ZEUS transmission, Biography of Janus

December 1848
It has taken three days but finally they have found her. The men I employed brought her to the house this morning; a small, tousled, rather ill-smelling child wearing ragged clothes and boots that were too big for her. She was bruised and handcuffed. I fear my agents may have been a little too free with their fists.

She examined the room, stared at me, and altogether showed quite remarkable spirit. She said, 'Never thought I'd be in this gaff again.'

Her eyes fixed, as if drawn by fascination, on the mirror.

I have restored the order of the room. The rifled mess Venn had made of my desk is now neat again, and the gleaming brass machinery is silent. In the three days since he and the boy vanished I have not been able to obtain any sign of energy from the device at all.

'Release her,' I command.

'She's greased lightning, guv. She'll be gone before you blink, like last time, when we broke in. And she's a biter. Toby's got the marks of her all down his arm.'

I said, 'Then you will please stand outside and allow no one to leave. You, Toby, will be compensated for your . . . er . . . injuries.'

After they had gone, taking the cuffs with them, the urchin sat herself in a chair and looked at me with a fixity that made me uncomfortable.

'Cost you, didn't I?'

'More than you could guess.' I sat opposite. 'So, Moll . . . isn't it?'

'Might be.'

'Look here, Moll. I have a proposition to put before

you. *How would you like a warm, er . . . gaff, for a while? Plenty of food. New clothes.'*

She said, 'Here?'

'Yes. I . . .'

'I ain't no trull, mister.'

I blushed. I was appalled. For a child of . . . what, eleven? . . . her knowledge of the seedier aspects of the world was startling. 'My dear child, I assure you . . . Good heavens . . . No . . . Please, let me make myself clear. I need information. I simply need to know everything possible about Venn and the boy Jake Wilde. Everything! Where you fell in with them, what they might have told you. Did they speak about their future world? About flying machines? About travelling to the moon? About cures for diseases? About . . . investments?'

She eyed me, and I realized in my enthusiasm I had edged forwards and was perched on the edge of the chair, my voice hoarse with excitement.

I cleared my throat and drew back.

But I had already shown her what such knowledge was worth.

'Jake said a lot of things.' She shrugged, careless. 'Like, you was a pompous old git.'

'Did he?' I tried to smile.

'And other stuff.'

'Such as?'

She wriggled back in the chair and placed her muddy boots one by one deliberately on my velvet footstool. 'That depends. I suppose I wouldn't mind staying for a bit. Skimble's is too lairy these days. They know it was me what stole the bracelet; they've been through my stuff and if I go back there I'll get a lammering. Or worse.'

I had no idea what she was talking about but smiled brightly. And for a brief moment sensed the precariousness of her life. 'A hot meal. Some fresh clothes. And then you will begin to talk and I will take detailed notes. Because I must discover this bracelet of theirs, Moll. Do you see, it may also be here, in our time. And I must discover more about Maskelyne. Will you help me?'

She gazed at her feet. 'Wages, too?'

'We might consider a small stipend . . .'

She looked up. I saw the light of greed in her eye, and confess to a slight doubt as to who would be the shrewdest negotiator in this bargain.

With a great show of consideration she said, 'OK.'

'I beg your pardon?'

'OK. That's future talk. Code. It means I will. Jake

said it.' She glanced at the mirror among its gleaming, useless levers. 'He'll come back here for me, you know. Jake. He said so.'

That was also my most secret hope.

'Tea. Cake. Plenty of cake.' She sat back. 'And I'll tell you all the other secrets what I know.'

I was pleased, but I sighed as I touched the bell. This was going to be expensive. And it was not I who was in control here.

Moll grinned.

She really is quite an intelligent little thing.

She will run rings around me.

No one moved.

In the new harsh light Sarah saw they were all staring at her; it was with almost an effort that Wharton said, 'No world?'

'In July of 2097 a disaster destroyed . . . will destroy . . . the Earth.' She kept her voice calm. 'There will be no warning. Janus, his origin,' she pointed at the Replicant, 'is to blame. He built the Labyrinth, a government research establishment into heightened human abilities, deep under London. We – I mean ZEUS – knew he had some device of extraordinary power; every time it was used we detected power spikes of terrifying intensity.'

She shook her head. 'I was part of the group, I joined because . . . well, my parents were lecturers in the Academy . . . until they were arrested.' She frowned. 'I shouldn't talk about any of this . . .'

'Arrested?' Jake whispered.

She hurried on. 'We were just a small secret group – crazy kids with wild imaginations. They had given us strange abilities, so we used them. Those that survived. It got so that there were only a few of us left, and we were scared, because time was running out and no one – *no one* – was listening. So we made a plan. We would break into the heart of the Labyrinth and get evidence that the world couldn't ignore.'

Janus snorted. Jake saw Wharton took a stealthy step nearer the Replicant, holding something behind his back.

'Six of us got through the wolves, the razor-wire, the security. We found, linked to a network of computers, an ancient, black glass mirror.'

Venn came up to her, fascinated. 'It still existed?'

'Yes. But it was brittle, dangerous.' She glared at Janus. 'He had been using it, burning it out, replicating himself in vain journeys. Speculating, forestalling inventions, making himself rich. But there was a price. It was clear to us that the mirror wouldn't last much longer. It had begun to break down, and it was sucking matter and light into itself at a terrible rate. When it exploded – and that would be in hours, maybe only minutes – it would create a black hole that would engulf . . . who knows what? The world, the solar system, the universe? Because whatever the mirror is, it holds a terrible darkness at its heart.'

She looked at Jake. 'It was too late to destroy it then. Don't you see? We had to enter it, to go back. *To get some time*. Each of us made a vow that we'd enter the past, there and then, with no guidance, no safety, no bracelet, and wherever we found ourselves, in whatever time, we would seek out the Chronoptika and destroy it. So that there'd be no Replicants. No Janus. None of it would ever have happened.'

Venn said, 'You can't . . .'

She shook her head, fierce. 'They were my friends. My only friends. We shook hands, we kissed. I was the last to go. Alarms were ringing – the wolves were out. We only had seconds. I don't know if the others made it. But it's true, what that creature says. I'm sorry, but it's true. I'm here to destroy the mirror.'

Jake shook his head, struggling with the paradoxes. 'But if you do, in the future it won't exist, so how could you return . . .'

A small sharp laugh interrupted him. Summer sat on a stool, knees up. 'What fools you are with your reasons and your fears. So all-in-a-straight-line! We could tell you about time. Time is a circle, Jake. An eternal now. A drop of dew falling from the bracken. Time is only there if you say it is.'

Jake stared at her, then back at Sarah. He was so devastated he couldn't think. 'How do we know it's true?'

Sarah shrugged. 'You don't. But if it is, what's finding your father – or Leah, even – against the fate of billions, Jake? Think about that.'

He couldn't. He wouldn't.

The Replicant smiled, mild. 'Well. Perhaps we can make an arrangement here.' He took a step towards Venn. 'Let me deal with her. Take her off your hands. You . . .'

'Don't move another step,' Wharton said.

'If you think some crude shotgun can—' The Replicant turned, and saw the glass weapon. It stared, curious. 'What is that? Some sort of primitive Victorian firearm? Do you really think it can injure me?'

'I know it can.' It was Maskelyne that answered. He moved past Rebecca. 'Because it was designed just for that purpose. To kill Replicants. To obliterate reflections.'

Did Janus believe it? Possibly, Jake thought. He edged forward.

'You can't kill me, fool. I'm not even here. I'm three hundred years in your future, sitting in a steel-lined bunker under the ruins of Parliament.'

It moved, turned, grabbed Sarah and pulled her in front of it. She struggled, but the wiry strength of its hands held her tight.

'Fire it,' Maskelyne shouted.

Wharton stared. 'I can't. She . . .'

'It won't hurt her! Only him. Fire it, now!'

Wharton glanced at Venn. He raised the gun. His finger tightened on the frail trigger. Sarah stared at him, frozen in mid-fight, the weapon pointed straight at her heart.

His hand trembled. *I can't do this*, he thought.

Instantly, out of nowhere, a small dark object swung from the shattered webbing, snatched the glass gun and swung away with it, screeching with delight.

Wharton yelled. Jake stared up. 'Horatio!'

The marmoset leaped from cabinet to vault and down to the ropes of the web. It clung on with its tail, hung upside-down and with one long arm brought the weapon up and sniffed at it.

'Oh God,' Jake gasped. *'Don't!'*

The shot blasted out like a white laser. It cracked across the room and they all leapt aside; the beam hit the mirror and instantly with a great snap it was reflected everywhere, a vast spider of light that exploded across the room. The mirror leaped from its frame and fell, with a terrible crash, glass down.

Venn grabbed Rebecca and pulled her away; Wharton hit the floor chest first. When he looked up the room was clogged with bitter smoke; to his dismay Jake was clambering up, hand over hand, through the cables to the roof.

'Give it to me. Give it!'

Far from dropping the thing the monkey was fascinated by it. It transferred the glass gun to its back paw and climbed up a little further. Jake swore. Glancing down he saw that Janus was dragging Sarah to the door. Venn scrambled up, ran to the mirror and hauled it over. It was undamaged.

'Give me that!' Jake yelled.

Horatio chattered and jumped. He landed on the floor.

Summer said, 'Creature.'

The monkey stopped and stared at her. Then it did something that astonished Jake; it made a spitting, snapping sound he had never heard, all its fur standing up like a ruff of terror round its neck.

She held out her hand. Horatio flung the weapon down and screeched away, high into the roof.

Jake dropped.

Summer picked up the gun and turned, tossing it to Venn. 'Deal with him.'

Out in the Monk's Walk Sarah struggled in the Replicant's grip. 'They believe me.'

'Maybe.'

'And the mirror fell – you heard.'

It laughed. Its small eyes behind the glasses were close to hers. 'There is so much you don't know about the mirror, Sarah.'

Dragging her to the stairs, it stopped. 'What is that noise?'

She stood triumphant even in his tight grip. 'You can't get out. I've made sure of that.'

Venn raced after the Replicant, tearing through the house; Jake and Wharton followed, leaving Rebecca to help Maskelyne up, dazed by the ringing crack of the light.

'Where?'

Venn hurtled through into the Long Gallery. 'Downstairs.'

They raced down.

At the foot of the stairs Jake crashed into Venn's stillness.

The hall was a swirl of snow. The Replicant was a shadow in the drift, holding Sarah tight; she flashed a look at Jake and stood calm. Jake went to move, but Venn grabbed him.

There was no way out. In the snow the Shee waited, an ominous horde, their war drums a pounding beat. Some of them peered in, watching in calm curiosity, never crossing the threshold. Every window was clogged with their alien, inquisitive faces. The doorway darkened, and Gideon stood there, the horse's skull on its pole leaning beside him. His arms were folded; he smiled a slanting grin at Sarah. 'Don't fret. You're going nowhere. You owe me.'

Janus spun.

'Are you ready, Venn?' Summer was standing near the door; even though Jake knew she had not passed him. 'Look, my changeling's even guarding the threshold for you. Here are both your enemies. Why not destroy them together?'

Venn spared her a taut glance. 'I think my true enemy is you,' he breathed.

Summer nodded. 'I think so too,' she whispered.

Venn pointed the weapon straight at Sarah, as Janus held her.

'Let her go.'

'No. Clear the way for us. We escape into the night.' Janus was urgent. 'I take her. You keep the mirror. We both win.'

'The Shee . . .'

'Will do as you tell them . . .'

Venn hesitated. At once Sarah said, 'Don't listen to it. Shoot, Venn. Do it! Then smash the Chronoptika. That's what you have to do!' She looked up and saw Wharton watching, Maskelyne a shadow on the landing, Rebecca holding the monkey tight. 'All of you. Make him do it. You must!'

Jake glanced at his godfather. Venn's hand was steady. His grip did not tremble.

'What if it kills you?'

'I'm not even born yet. Do it, Venn. Save the world.'

Tears were blinding her. Through them she saw his eyes on hers. 'You don't know me well enough yet, Sarah. Before I save the world I'll save my wife.'

He fired.

She screamed. The white bolt of light drilled through her chest like a spear of pain; it passed right through her and struck the Replicant with full force, and for a moment, their faces so close, she saw the glasses vaporize, the ash-grey eyes widen in terror.

It was a weight against her, a hollow outline of brilliance against her retina, a clutch of long fingers.

Then it was gone.

CHAPTER TWENTY-FIVE

'Have you thought,' I once asked him, 'that before long there'll be nothing left for you or anyone else to explore?' We were sitting at a café terrace on the rue Saint-Honoré in Paris; it was three months before his wife's death. He said, 'The world is finite. Time isn't. Neither is the universe inside us.'

I thought he was joking.

But he never jokes.

Jean Lamartine, *The Strange Life of Oberon Venn*

Wharton put the match to the kindling and sat back, watching the small sticks slowly snap and crackle into almost invisible flame. Soon he felt heat against his chilled fingers; as the peats caught fragrant smoke spiralled into the chimney.

He scrambled up, dusting his hands.

Despite the return of the electricity, Jake had found some candles, and was lighting them obsessively round the kitchen, stabbing them into holders as if the heart of the house had to be made warm and safe again, the snowy night closed out.

Sarah sat by the table. She was staring into the crackling fire, one hand turning the small gold coin she wore at her neck.

Wharton sat opposite. 'How do you feel?'

She shrugged. She had no answer to that. How could she explain to him that the weird surge of light from the weapon had not hurt her, not like the angry despair in Jake's look, the way he lit one candle now from another and would not even meet her eyes. That was the wound. She wanted to destroy his father's way home. He probably hated her for it.

Wharton must have sensed it. He gave a quick glance at Jake and said, 'I'll just go and help Piers bring the food in.'

When he'd gone she got up and crossed the room. 'Jake. I'm sorry.'

She was standing close behind him. He kept hold of the last candle until the flame caught, then placed it deliberately in the iron candlestick. When there was nothing else to do, he turned.

She looked pale, and shaken, her eyes ice-blue. She had changed into warm clothes, but they were still someone else's, and for a moment he even wondered if Piers had found some of Leah's for her . . . But she was still defiant.

He said, 'Is it all true? About the black hole?'

'Yes.'

'You can't be sure. If you left before it happened . . .'

'It was inevitable. Otherwise I wouldn't be here.'

'And my father?'

'Like I said. He's just one person.'

Jake leaned against the table. 'To me he's everything.'

'You're so like Venn!' She shook her head, exasperated. 'You're both obsessed with your own needs. What about everyone else? What about the future?'

He shrugged. 'That's all too big for me. Too far off.'

'You're lucky, Jake. You haven't seen what the world will become.'

He wanted to ask her then, about how it was a hundred years from now, but he knew she wouldn't tell him, any more than he had told Symmes about cars and planes and computers. So he said, 'It's not up to me. Venn won't stop. You saw him. He fired that weapon even though he wasn't sure – not really – that it wouldn't kill you as well. He's ruthless. He'd sacrifice any future world to get Leah back.

And anyway, the mirror is unbreakable. Maskelyne says so.'

She didn't believe that. She wouldn't. 'If there is a way, that man knows it.'

She turned, as Summer said, 'I think so too.'

The Shee queen sat delicately on the bench in the inglenook; she swept her bare feet down and stood lightly. 'I've come for my treasure, Sarah. As you promised.'

Sarah glanced round. Slowly, she drew out the diamond brooch from her pocket.

Jake saw her reluctance. 'You promised her that?'

'She did.' Summer came and stood opposite Sarah; they were the same height, but the woman seemed oddly younger, with a peculiar, childish petulance. She said, 'But I told you, I don't want it. I want that.'

She reached out a small finger and touched the half-coin. Jake saw Sarah flinch.

'Why that?'

'A whim. No reason. *Anything*, you said.' Summer glanced round, smiling. 'Should I ask for him instead?' She pointed to Jake.

He went cold.

'No!' Sarah put her hands up and slipped the coin off, quickly. 'Have it. It has no value except that it once belonged to Symmes. My father gave it to me, but I doubt that means anything to you.'

'Nothing.' Summer eyed the shining thing; her sideways glance made Jake think of a bird's sharp, predatory greed. Then she walked calmly to the archway and through it, past Gideon. She touched his hair, lightly.

'Say goodbye to them, human child.'

When she was gone he leaned against the wall, his thin silky clothes still stained with snow. New swirls of green lichen obscured his skin; he seemed more Shee than they had ever seen him, defiantly alien. He smiled, cold. 'You should never give her what she asks for.'

'Come to the fire,' Jake said.

'What's the point?' Gideon glanced round at the racks of plates, the gleaming pans, the huge hearth with its hanging spits. He glared at Sarah, his resentment erupting into anger. 'You used me! You just wanted her help. You made me a promise you knew you could never keep.'

'I'm sorry,' she said.

'Are you?' He laughed, harsh. 'I thought I was the one trapped in a spell, but maybe yours is worse than mine. Maybe neither of us can ever go home.'

'It's not over.' Jake leaned on the table. 'I'm not going anywhere. And I make you a better promise. I'll get you free from Summer, if I have to give . . .'

Gideon jumped forward, alarmed. '*Don't!* Don't make stupid offers. It's not safe . . . Whatever you say, she'll hear it. Don't promise anything to her, because she'll take it. Your soul, your father, your life. One thing I've learned about the Shee, is that they don't give second chances.'

Wharton paused in the hall. The doors of the Abbey were shut and bolted, the windows locked, the cameras showing nothing, but there was a murmur of voices from the front entrance, and he went to the window and peered cautiously out. The hosts of the Shee were waiting, but as he watched Summer came out and stood in the deep snow, the moon casting a long shadow.

She said, 'Go home. It's all over.'

He hardly saw them change. They transformed before him, shrank, glittered, shimmered. Their clothes sprouted feathers, their beaked faces shrieked. Only their eyes, bird-sharp, attent, stayed the same. And then they were up and flying, a great swooping host of starlings, dark and furiously noisy against the starry sky, breaking and re-forming in sudden bizarre patterns, the whooshing of their wings loud as they poured and split.

He gazed, amazed, until the last formation fractured and broke.

And then they were gone, in long streamers of darkness over the sleeping Wood.

Summer watched, ankle-deep in snow.

Behind her, Wharton saw Venn.

'I could have dealt with the Replicant. Sarah had no right to come to you.'

'But she did. And here is my reward.'

She turned and held something up and it caught the moonlight as it hung on the gold chain. For a moment Wharton didn't recognize it. Then he saw it was the half-coin that Sarah had always worn.

'What use is that?' Venn asked, suspicious.

'No use.' Summer hung it carefully around her own neck. 'So. What will you do now, Venn? Go back to your useless experiments?'

He seemed to reach out for her. Wharton saw a sliver of moonlight; it lit Summer's cool smile as she stepped away.

'Let me use the Summerland,' he begged. 'Let me go through . . .'

'To save my rival? Never.'

He heard Venn say, 'You always hated Leah.'

'Did I? I don't need to. She means nothing. You belong to me. And one day, when you realize that, you'll come into the Wood and never leave it again.'

She raised her small lips to his, and Wharton felt a cold shiver travel up his spine as Venn stood still as a ghost and was kissed by her.

Far off and deep and sonorous he heard the bells of Wintercombe church, chiming for midnight.

The effect on Summer was instant. She drew back, like a snake. 'What is that?'

'You know,' Venn said quietly. 'It's Christmas Day.'

She shivered, and turned lightly in the snow. 'So it is . . . I'll be back, Venn. Now that I can get in, you'll never know what I might do.'

She took a step, and seemed to become in an instant nothing but an edge of the moonlight that fell across the blue-shadowed banks of snow.

Wharton swallowed his gasp and kept still.

So did Venn, for at least a minute, a tall, remote figure on the snowy steps, as he gazed out at the night. And then he said, so quietly Wharton barely heard the whisper, '*I love her more than you, my lady*.'

Gideon looked up, eyes sharp. 'Hear that?'

'What?'

'Bells. The church bells. I can't stay.'

'Of course you can.' Jake came and grabbed his sleeve. 'Don't go back to them! Stay here. They can't get at you . . .'

'Can't they?' Gideon laughed his practised bitter laugh. 'You have no idea.' He watched Piers come in, carrying a tray of hot spicy drinks. 'Enjoy it, Jake. Enjoy it while you can. The food, the warmth, the people. Do everything, taste everything. Enjoy your life because outside is only the cold and the dark.'

'We'll release you. I swear.'

'To be just dust and ashes?' Gideon shrugged. 'Maybe that would be better. Better than this.'

'I won't let you go,' Jake said, angry.

But even as he said it Gideon wasn't there; the frail green velvet faded from between his fingers, and he held only air.

He looked up to find Venn standing by the fire, watching. 'You can't hold them, Jake. It's like trying to hold the wind. She'll never let him go.'

Wharton came in behind. The teacher seemed a bigger man, somehow, than he had in the school, and his glance at Venn was oddly measuring. He said, 'The house is sealed now. The mirror is safe. Maskelyne and Rebecca are in the drawing-room, but we can't keep them here. Tomorrow, when it's light, you'll have to let her . . . them . . . go.'

Venn said to Piers, 'Get them.'

In the silence the fire crackled, smelling richly of

applewood. The room had grown warmer; Sarah went and stood by the flames. She felt as if the water of the lake had chilled her for ever, as if a splinter of cold had reached her heart and lodged there, like failure.

Wharton piled a plate with the sandwiches Piers had made. His hunger was suddenly an unbearable pain.

Maskelyne came in and stood by the table, Rebecca behind him. She looked at Sarah.

'Are you . . . OK?'

'Fine.'

'You and your secret friend are free to go,' Venn snapped. 'Don't let us keep you.'

'Surely,' Wharton muttered. 'Not in this weather.'

Rebecca looked at Maskelyne. 'Don't worry about us. The car is by the gates and if the snow is thick we'll walk. It's only a few miles.'

The scarred man stood dark and brooding in the red flamelight. He turned and looked at Venn, and Jake. 'First, I have something to say to both of you. In private. Please.'

He seemed agitated; he went out into the passageway and walked down it, waiting for them like a shadow under the coiled bells.

After a moment, Venn followed. Jake glanced at Wharton, and went after them.

Maskelyne waited until they were both close to him,

then gazed back at the lighted kitchen, where he could see both the girls and Piers, pouring out tea.

'What?' Venn said.

'Listen to me. Sarah wears a token round her neck. The right half of a coin.'

Jake, alarmed, said, 'But she gave it—'

'Shut up, Jake,' Venn said quickly. 'What about it? Was it the token Symmes had?'

'The one I sent him long ago.' Maskelyne leaned against the wall, his head back. He looked very tired. 'But you don't know its significance. I have no choice but to tell you, because you need the mirror safe now as much as I do. I have to trust you.'

It was as if he was arguing himself into it.

Venn said, 'The coin is a danger?'

'The mirror cannot be broken. Not by force or fire, by wind or water. There is only one way to destroy the mirror.' Maskelyne's haunted eyes flickered to Jake. 'The Zeus coin was forged in ancient times as a safeguard by the original creator, in case the power of the mirror should ever threaten the world. It contains enough energy to obliterate the Chronoptika, to destroy it utterly.'

Venn said, 'How do you know this . . . ?' but Maskelyne ignored him, talking in a low, rapid voice. 'It was cut in two, and the halves separated widely in time and space, so that they would never be brought together by accident. The left half is lost. It has been lost for centuries. But if it should be found . . . if they should ever join, and the crack be sealed . . .' his voice was a whisper now, his lips barely moving, 'a wave of terrible intensity would be generated. The coin holds the only power in the universe that could do this. Or so I believe.'

Jake stared, appalled. 'If Sarah knew . . .'

'She doesn't. She never must.' Maskelyne looked at them, his eyes dark. 'And you must somehow get that coin from her.'

He stopped, as if he was too weary to go on, as if everything he could say had been said.

Jake looked at Venn. There was nothing to say. Silent, the three of them watched Sarah talking to Rebecca, stirring sugar into her tea.

After Rebecca and Maskelyne had trudged away in the deep snow, warm in borrowed coats and boots, Wharton gave a great yawn and said, 'Sorry. I really need my bed.' He smiled at Jake. 'Maybe I might even get a few days at home, after all.'

'Before you go back,' Jake said.

Wharton's face fell. 'Great. The play's the thing . . . That bloody school.'

'Perhaps,' Piers said softly, 'Mr Venn's godson might need a personal tutor.'

Everyone looked at Venn. He shrugged. 'What do I care? Do what you want.' He stood up, then turned on the small man abruptly. 'And you! Where were you when all this was going on? You're supposed to be guarding the place and you just vanish . . .'

Piers shrugged. 'Busy busy. Janus scuppered every power source we have. Cue heroic efforts by yours truly.'

One of the black cats, washing its face on a chair by the fire, stopped and stared at him. He glared back at it, hard.

Venn said, 'Stay if you want,' and went out, towards the study.

'Let me think about it.' Wharton turned. 'Merry Christmas to you all.'

To his surprise Sarah came and kissed him on the cheek. 'Merry Christmas, George,' she said.

Jake ran upstairs to check on the monkey. He found Horatio curled in tight sleep on the pillow of his bed, and just for a moment lay next to him and rubbed the smooth dark fur.

The marmoset snuggled under his arm.

They had failed. But they could try again. Dad was out

there somewhere, and they had time, all the time in the universe, to find him again. And Moll. Maybe even Moll . . .

He woke with a start.

The room was dark. Someone had put the lights off and pulled the quilt over him; he shrugged it away and sat up, then slid off the side of the bed and hurried to the door, opening it and listening.

Something was wrong.

Wintercombe Abbey was utterly silent in its deep frost. But there was one sound, very faint, and it was coming from below. He raced down, filled with an unreasoning dread, fleet and fast below the moon-striped faces of the portraits, hurtling along the corridor to the kitchen, but it was empty, the teapot cold, the fire almost out.

Cursing himself, he ran back. Outside Venn's study he stopped, hearing her voice, and then Venn's, low and ominous.

He went in.

Venn was lounging in his armchair, one arm hanging over the sides, a whisky glass in his hand. The bottle, half empty, stood on the littered desk.

Sarah, by the window, turned.

They both looked at Jake.

'What's going on?'

She shrugged. 'It's time for me to go.'

'No . . .' He stepped forward, barring the door. 'No way!'

'Why stay? I can't do what I came for, and you see me as a danger, rightly. I have a duty to ZEUS – I have to find my own way, sort out my ideas, do research, work out what to do next.'

Venn laughed, slurred and bitter. 'And if you find out how to save the future, you'll come back and tell us how?'

'Yes,' she said.

Jake took a step forward. 'Sarah . . .'

'Goodbye, Jake.' She was at the window.

He said, 'You know this house in the future.'

She was still. 'I know its ruins,' she whispered. Then, abruptly, she turned to Venn. 'Don't give up on the mirror. You will succeed.'

He shrugged. 'Words. Meaningless.'

His moroseness annoyed her. 'I know. In my past Leah *does* come back . . .'

He sat up, slowly. His ice-blue eyes caught the moonlight. Shadows of branches moved down walls and ceiling.

'Prove it.'

She came over and pushed something into his hands.

It was a small diamond brooch in the shape of a starburst. He stared at it with open, vivid astonishment. 'Sarah . . . !'

She smiled. 'Till next time.' She turned away.

And wasn't there.

Jake gasped, dived after her.

The window latch was lifting, the casement swinging wide. He heard a scrape, a breath of effort, but Venn had leaped up, shoved him away, was grabbing at the swinging casement, hauling himself on to the windowsill, yelling at the empty snowfield. '*Sarah!*'

Her whisper came so close it tickled his skin. 'You and Leah had no children.'

Her breath warmed his cheek. Close behind, Jake barely heard his answer. 'No.'

'But you will have,' she said.

A crunched landing in the snow outside. Her voice, calm and clear in the frost.

'I'm your great-granddaughter, Venn. Yours and Leah's. *That's how I know.*'

Then there was nothing but the creak of the window against the frame, and a soft shower of dislodged frost.

Jake said, 'She might be lying.' His voice was quiet.

Venn spun, slid down with his back against the bars.

He stared at the brooch in astonishment. 'This was Leah's, Jake. I buried it with her. *In her coffin.*' He looked up, and out at the snow, then flung the window wide and yelled, 'Sarah!'

No one answered . . .

A single set of footprints led away, through the snow, into the dark.